Altered Childhood

by
P.B. Alden

Cover design by Patricia Branigan
Fonts and cover art images courtesy of Adobe Stock. All images and fonts are licensed for commercial use.

First edition 2024
ISBN 978-1-7361636-8-9
Copyright TXu 2-424-654

For engaging book club discussion questions, visit
butterybraniganbooks.com

Email butterybraniganbooks@gmail.com
with questions, thoughts, and comments.
We love to hear from our readers.

This book is dedicated to Henry

and to every extraordinary child who has weathered the storms of the foster care system. Although the Henry depicted in these pages merely mirrors your smile and hair color, this dedication is a tribute to your strength and determination.

chapter one

Drew and I wear our plastic grins like masks, ready for the show. Inside the trunk of my car is an assortment of items: a box brimming with romance novels, my trusted Xanax supply, Drew's prized collection of whiskey, and a display of modern art nudes. Our family room now boasts a sign bearing the inscription "Bless This House," complemented by magnificent paintings that would surely earn Bob Ross's admiration.

I spent hours preparing, ensuring every little detail was just right. The emerald classic wrap dress I chose brings out the green in my hazel eyes and complements my tan skin. I curled my chestnut brown hair and let it cascade around my shoulders like a protective shield.

Drew looks handsome in the new khakis and white button-down we bought for the occasion. His dusty blond hair is neatly trimmed, with a bit of gel to style the longer strands on top, adding a youthful energy to his appearance. His well-kept mustache and beard complement his rugged charm, framing his features.

Despite days of preparations, the doorbell sends a jolt through my body. Helen looms on our front porch, her face etched with a deep frown. She seems to carry an ancient grudge, radiating an air of disdain. Her navy blazer and crisp white shirt give off an aura of authority and professionalism. Her hair is in a sleek, flawless bun, without a single strand daring to stray from its designated place. Her intense demeanor makes me doubt my appearance and the effort I put into making our home perfect. Sensing my anxiety, Drew reaches for my hand, giving it a gentle squeeze.

I welcome Helen inside, offering to take her coat and bag. She declines, saying she's a bit chilly. She moves through the living room with measured steps. I watch her face, curious about her reaction. As her eyes land on our sofa, she scrunches her nose. It's a subtle gesture but hints at her disapproval, and we're only just getting started.

With a clear goal in mind, she marches into the kitchen. I can sense her growing disappointment as she proceeds to yank open drawer after drawer before inspecting the food choices in the fridge. She checks the expiration dates on the almond milk and yogurt.

"You only have two days left on that one," Helen says, pointing to a large container of mixed-berry yogurt.

"Thanks for noticing. We hate to waste food. It's yogurt for breakfast and lunch tomorrow," I force a laugh to inject some humor into the situation, immediately regretting my decision.

"You don't keep much food in the house." The judgment in Helen's voice hangs heavy as she scribbles on the stack of papers clutched in her hand.

I muster the courage to defend myself. "I... I take pride in my culinary skills, and we prioritize healthy eating." Seeking validation, I gesture towards a colossal bowl on the countertop arranged with an assortment of carefully chosen fruit. Drew told me she wouldn't know it was organic, but I assured him she would. Mainly because I left all the organic produce stickers on.

Sensing my anxiety, Drew steps in. "Charlotte is an incredible cook. She ensures I'm always well-fed." A broad smile reminiscent of the Cheshire Cat crosses his face as he rubs his fit stomach.

"We do keep some snacks in the house," I assure her, opening the cupboard next to the pantry where we have an array of pretzels, granola bars, and Drew's favorite Little Debbie Snack Cakes. She resumes her note-taking frenzy as if she stumbled upon a meth lab rather than a simple stash of Nutty Buddy bars.

"What a fancy coffee maker." Helen eyes the unit on the counter.

"It was last year's Christmas bonus. Apparently, you don't have to pay taxes on gifts. It makes a mean cup of joe. My boss said it fell off a truck, if you know what I mean," I joke in an Italian accent. She doesn't laugh and once again scribbles something in her damning notes. Why am I talking so much? I remind myself to shut the hell up.

She heads to the hall bathroom, swinging open the medicine cabinet.

Holding up a prescription bottle, Helen squints to read the label. "You take Wellbutrin."

I'm unsure if it's a statement or an inquiry. "Yes, I do. It's for minor depression."

Her attention shifts to my migraine medication. She picks up the bottle, studying it. "And what do we have here?"

"That's for migraines."

"Your paperwork doesn't mention migraines."

"I don't get them often. I must have forgotten to write it down." I regret not stowing away every medication in the house within the safety of my car's trunk.

"You know you have to turn the caps on these bottles upside down to make them childproof." Her demeanor suggests that we rank among the most ignorant individuals she has ever encountered.

"Of course, I will do that right now." As she leaves the bathroom, I stay behind to fix the bottles, fully aware things aren't going well. Facing the mirror, I lock eyes with my reflection and take a moment to gather my swirling thoughts. Placing my hands on my hips in my favorite power pose, I reassure myself, "You've got this."

I spot Drew, his tall, slender frame leaning against our bedroom doorframe, sporting a mischievous schoolboy grin. Catching his eye roll as I enter, I can't help but stifle a giggle. Times like these make me appreciate Drew's ability to lighten the mood no matter what's going on. His constant support reminds me I'm never alone.

Helen is in the back of my closet, looking at the tags of the XXL flannels. "Is there another man who lives here?"

"No. Those belonged to my dad. I wear them when I want to feel close to him." I wish I had one on now, but I resist the urge. As Helen examines Drew's limited clothing options, I glance upwards and silently mouth the word "help" to my dad.

Looking into the ensuite bathroom, Helen pursues her lips. "You certainly have a lot of beauty supplies."

"I like to look my best." My cheeks feel warm, and I'm frustrated because she's making me self-conscious. There's nothing wrong with wanting to look good.

The next stop is the room across the hall. The paint is a cheery yellow, and Winnie the Pooh, Piglet, and Tigger prints adorn the walls. A teddy bear perches on the twin bed. The rocking chair quietly waits for its next occupant in the corner. I glance at it, and a wave of sadness overwhelms me as I gently rub my stomach.

Helen opens one of the dresser drawers. "Not many clothes."

"We wanted to wait for Henry so we could take him shopping to buy the things he likes. Do you think we should have more on hand?" I ask, the knot in my stomach tightening.

"Children can be overwhelmed when they first arrive at a new home. It is best not to plan big outings right away."

Her eyes fixate on the toys lining the bookshelf—a Duplo block set, a firetruck, a doll, and Drew's childhood Lincoln Logs.

"You have a doll for your son," Helen says, leaving me again uncertain whether she's looking for a response.

Drew takes charge. "We don't believe toys have gender specificity; we believe children should be free to play with any toy they want." He winks at me as Helen writes in her notes that we are amazing, accepting parents or idiots.

We proceed to the next destination on the home tour, the spare bedroom that doubles as my office. "This room is nice," she comments upon observing the uninspired beige room.

Helen ventures into the basement, diligently inspecting the furnace, water heater, and electric fuse box. I inquire if she might have been a home inspector in a previous life, but my attempt at

9

humor falls flat as she doesn't laugh. Once again, I berate myself for trying to lighten the mood.

Pointing out the carbon dioxide and smoke detectors, I emphasize our commitment to prioritizing safety. I go on a tangent, rambling about how we've already taken CPR and first aid training classes. I talk about my experience as a lifeguard during my teen years, unable to resist the urge to fill the silence with random chatter.

She opens a few bins containing Christmas decorations. I am relieved that the one with unused baby items is buried at the bottom, so I won't have to explain why I can't bring myself to part with them.

Helen makes her way back upstairs and looks in the backyard. "I don't see any play equipment."

I glance out the window, realizing how boring our backyard looks. "We're considering purchasing a swing set or a trampoline. We want Henry's help in deciding."

Helen's eyebrows furrow. "Trampolines can cause serious injury."

Drew wraps his arm around my waist. "In that case, let's go with a swing set."

Helen makes herself at home at our kitchen table and rummages through her bag. She pulls out a stack of clipped papers that I recognize as our application. When we had filled it out, I felt like we were undergoing a CIA job interview and an IRS audit.

"Would you care for a water, coffee, or shot of whiskey?" I nervously giggle. "I'm joking. We don't even have whiskey. We are not drinkers. I will have a glass of wine if there is a celebration, and sometimes Drew will have a beer if we eat out, but we don't drink and drive or get drunk," the words tumble out of my mouth. Drew reaches for my hand and gives it a reassuring squeeze, reminding me everything will be alright.

Helen meticulously reads every word, leaving me unsure if she's searching for a reaction to gauge our honesty. I stare at her, realizing that most of my words are true. However, I may have portrayed ourselves as more organized and healthier than we are. We didn't mention Drew's addiction to snack cakes in the paperwork.

Helen examines the next paper closely before glancing up with a puzzled expression. "According to this, you don't practice a formal religion but consider yourselves spiritual."

I respond, "Yes, that's correct. However, if Henry chooses a specific religion, we will respect his choice."

With disbelief, Helen asks, "So you're going to let a three-year-old dictate your family's religion?"

"Of course not," Drew says. "But if he has already been following a certain religious practice, we will support his choice."

Helen shakes her head and writes a note, asking why we chose to adopt a preschooler instead of a baby.

Drew takes the lead in sharing our journey. He recounts our heartbreaking struggle to conceive, only to be told by a specialist that my uterus was a hostile environment, leading to a devastating miscarriage at sixteen weeks. I'm grateful he can narrate the story, as I find it difficult to tell without breaking down. Drew concludes by sharing how we stumbled upon Henry's profile on the children's home website. He describes how his adorable face instantly captivated us and appeared to resemble ours. He believed it was a sign from the universe that we were meant to become his forever family. Drew assures Helen that we possess the qualities and dedication to provide the little guy with a loving home and a wonderful life.

Helen reads the letters of recommendation aloud. She begins with one from Drew's captain, who affirms his exceptional skills as a firefighter and his significant role within the community. Then, she moves on to a letter from my boss, highlighting my competence as an employee during my eight years with the company. Drew's sister's letter emphasizes our caring nature towards her young son and daughter.

My mother did not participate, saying she didn't want a "used grandchild." Her response hurt, but I can't say her reaction shocked me. My mother and I have never been close. She never wanted a child and was jealous of my bond with my dad. He would have written me a glowing recommendation if he were still alive.

Helen peruses our financial statement. "It looks like you have the means to support a child."

"Yes. We do. And since I work from home, I can be flexible with evening and weekend hours so Drew can take care of Henry while I work. We're committed to giving Henry everything he needs." I can't help but grin. I'm finally happy with my response.

Helen gathers the papers and taps them on the table, securing them back in place with a clip. "I have all the necessary information I need today, Mr. and Mrs. King. Unless there are surprises in your background checks, I don't see any reason you can't become Henry's parents." For the first time, a smile graces her face. "Henry is a remarkable little boy who has faced many challenges. I assure you he will thrive in a home like yours. However, helping him adjust to living in a house with loving parents will demand significant effort, considering he's not used to that situation."

Drew clears his throat. "We understand the responsibility ahead and are ready for it."

"I hope you are. But please do not let a three-year-old determine your family's religion. That would be crazy." She smiles and chuckles before gathering her belongings. We passed the test.

As soon as the door closes, I collapse into Drew's arms. He kisses my head and whispers, "I told you she would see how much love we have to offer."

"That was a close call. I thought it was all over when I revealed your Little Debbie addiction." I let out a sigh of relief.

Drew's eyes light up with excitement as he exclaims, "I've got something special for us!" He slips on his shoes, runs to the car, and returns with a bottle of champagne. "I knew things would go well, but I didn't want to tempt fate by keeping this in the house. Let's celebrate, Mama."

I kiss him and then retrieve the monogrammed glasses from our wedding, which I had stowed away at the back of a cupboard.

"Here's to becoming a family," Drew cheers, raising his glass.

We enjoy the champagne, cuddled up in bed, our bodies intertwined. Sleep eludes me as I spend hours imagining Henry playing with his toys, sleeping in the room next to ours, and calling me "Mommy."

chapter two

I have constantly daydreamed about our time together since meeting Henry at Horizons of Hope Children's Home two weeks ago. Those brief moments of connection reinforced my belief that adopting him was the right choice.

On the day of our visit, four of the seven children receiving care at the facility had scheduled family visits. The remaining three included a four-year-old girl, her younger brother, and Henry. The home's social worker, Hailey, instructed us not to disclose the specific child we were there to see. Instead, she encouraged us to connect with all the children.

As the five of us settled on the floor next to a large bin filled with Duplo blocks, Drew wasted no time constructing an impressive tower, skillfully piecing the bricks together.

The little girl, Macy, snuggled close to me, her wispy blonde hair and green eyes capturing my affection. In a quiet voice, she asked, "Are you going to be my mommy?"

"We're just visiting today." I forced a smile despite the ache in my heart.

When we started looking to adopt a child, we considered

Macy's brother, Markus, a possibility. I had imagined adopting a boy first for some reason. My therapist thought it might be because of the grief from losing our daughter and adopting a girl might feel like trying to replace her. However, the state preferred to keep Macy and Markus together, and I wasn't ready to be a mother to a toddler and a preschooler all at once. I hope they find a loving family for them soon.

Henry kept himself apart from the rest of the group, his body language showing his hesitation as he sat with his back pressed against the wall. His petite size gave the impression he was younger than his three and a half years. Henry's dusty blond hair and deep brown eyes mirrored Drew's—like they already had an unspoken bond.

Hailey had forewarned us that it might take some time for Henry to feel comfortable, and his cautiousness was not necessarily a negative trait. She stressed the importance of patience and allowing him to set the pace.

Drew shared his occupation as a fireman with the children, sparking their interest. Macy, wide-eyed with curiosity, asked if he had ever saved anyone. Seizing the opportunity to impress the kids, Drew pulled out his phone to show them a picture of a golden retriever—his most recent rescue.

A staff member approached and reminded him of the no-cell phone policy. Drew returned it to his pocket, shifting his focus to his captive audience. With enthusiasm, he told the thrilling tale of rescuing the dog by venturing onto a partially frozen lake. Despite the piercing cold, he didn't give up, knowing he was the dog's only hope for survival.

The kids listened intently, growing more excited with each

detail. Henry slowly inched closer to Drew as the story neared its end.

Macy exclaimed, "You're a hero!"

A satisfied smile spreads across Drew's face. "All in a day's work."

Henry ran toward a nearby bookshelf and returned, holding a book featuring a firetruck on the cover. He handed it to Drew and sat beside him. Drew read that book and three others.

Next, it was time for arts and crafts. We gathered around a table with overflowing bins of weathered crayons, dried-up markers, and worn pencils. Each of us started with a blank piece of construction paper. Drew focused on sketching a fire truck using squares while I stuck to what I knew best: drawing a cartoon cat.

"Do you have a cat?" Macy asked.

"Not yet," I said. "But I hope to have one someday. Or maybe a dog? What about all of you? What's your favorite animal?"

Markus eagerly shared, shouting, "Dogs!"

Macy declared her love for colorful polka-dotted fish.

Turning to Henry, I asked, "And what about you?"

Silence hung in the air momentarily before Drew asked, "Do you like animals, Henry?"

In a soft voice, he said, "Zebras."

"Why zebras?" I asked.

"I like stripes." My heart melted. Henry spoke to me instead of Drew.

As the clock struck noon, a chime echoed through the room. A young staff member announced it was lunchtime. We had brought a surprise for the children—unicorn cupcakes from

16

The Salted Carmel Bakery. Handing over the treats, the staff greeted them with hesitant smiles. But when Macy saw the colorful cakes, her entire face lit up. She ran toward me, reaching out her arms. I hugged her, enjoying the connection.

"It was wonderful to meet you," I whispered.

Henry approached Drew and me cautiously. I asked if I could hug him. With a quiet "Okay," he came closer, allowing me to embrace him. I held back my tears, not wanting to frighten him. As I stood up, I noticed Drew wipe away a tear with his shirt sleeve.

"Oh, look who's getting emotional," I joked, nudging him with my elbow.

A faint smile tugged at the corners of his mouth as he tried to dismiss the evidence. "Allergies."

Nodding, I played along, "Ah, yes. We both suffer from those dreadful eye allergies."

As we followed Hailey to a small office to review Henry's file, Drew whispered, "I love him so much already."

"Me too."

Once settled, Hailey asked what we thought about Henry.

"We are in love!" I replied, a wide grin spreading across my face.

"I knew you would be. Henry is adorable," Hailey said. "However, I need to caution you that his file might be difficult to read. We want to make sure you're aware of his history so you can adequately address his physical and mental health needs. Henry came to our facility after spending two weeks in the hospital. He was dehydrated and had a severe rash, open wounds, and a respiratory infection. Henry was discovered in a residence where his mother had died of an overdose. According to the police report, he had been alone with his deceased mother for three days. We're unsure if his biological father is still in the picture. Locating him has proven to be difficult, leaving us to consider the possibility that he might be deceased, intentionally avoiding us, or unaware that he has a son."

I cover my mouth in disbelief. Tears form in my eyes, blurring my vision. I wipe them away—afraid if I start crying, I won't be able to stop.

"When Henry first came to our facility twelve weeks ago, he was very withdrawn and had trouble interacting with staff and the other children. But in that short time, he's made incredible progress. Although his cognitive abilities are behind for his age, the doctor and I believe he has the potential for a full recovery. We can only imagine how much better he'll do in a loving home where he can receive consistent one-on-one care."

"Here's his file." Hailey handed Drew a thick binder. "Take the time you need. We want to be transparent. But I must warn you, reading everything this little guy has been through is difficult. I'll check back in an hour to answer any questions."

I looked at Drew and confessed, "I'm not sure if I'm ready for this."

"It will be hard, but we know being parents will have challenges. We'll do it together, amore."

We opened the binder. On the first page was a photo of Henry taken when he arrived at Horizons of Hope. The picture showed a small, sad figure with a tiny blue cast on his arm, making him appear even more vulnerable. Underneath the image was a short list of Henry's belongings—a shirt, a pair of pants, and a well-worn blue blanket.

The next page contained images of Henry in the hospital. The extent of his condition was worse than I had imagined. His eyes seemed to sink into his petite face, and his hair was matted to his head.

The report provided a detailed account of Henry's injuries. Due to the delayed treatment of his broken arm, he had to have surgery to re-break and properly set it. The enormity of his trauma hit me, and tears rolled down my cheeks as I thought about the journey Henry had been through already. How long had his arm been broken? And then, he had to undergo surgery all alone. I quickly turned the page—unable to read more.

Detailed daily records from the staff documented Henry's activities at Horizons of Hope. Seeing him paired with a "big brother" named Tom was encouraging. Several photos showed Henry and Tom reading books and playing games together. Henry's bright smile, matched by Tom's, revealed their strong bond, indicating they had formed a connection.

Several incident reports detailed times Henry acted out. Things like throwing toys at other kids. One report mentioned him hitting a girl in the head with a Lincoln Log. The staff first gave him a yellow light warning, but when he continued misbehaving, he was put on a red light, causing him to lose some privileges. What was striking was how he reacted to this system. His behavior improved over time. The records showed he was willing to learn from the consequences and change his actions, showing he could grow within a structured environment.

A disturbing entry from just over a week ago was among the reports. It described how Henry refused to go to bed and ended up assaulting a female employee by hitting, kicking, and biting her. The report outlined how she held Henry to keep him safe, but he kept shaking his head violently, accidentally hitting her face and making her lip bleed. Two more staff members had to help restrain him until he calmed down.

Drew shook his head. "That's excessive, considering how small he is."

"I was thinking the same thing. The poor little guy must have been terrified."

The subsequent reports from the child psychologist documented Henry's journey. The psychologist noted that Henry experienced severe suffering, suggesting a possible diagnosis of a trauma disorder. She mentioned that he often acted out the scene where he couldn't wake up his mom, which supported her assessment. She suspected he used dissociation to cope with the traumatic events in his life, also mentioning the difficulty in calming him for sleep and his nightmares.

While the psychologist considered the possibility of Henry having Oppositional Defiant Disorder (ODD) or Reactive Attachment Disorder (RAD), she couldn't provide a definitive prognosis at the time due to his age and the bond he had formed with Tom. She recommended ongoing monitoring of Henry's behavior. The report concluded on a good note, highlighting his significant improvements. The psychologist had confidence that with consistent therapy and a supportive home environment, Henry would experience both physical and mental growth.

Drew exhaled deeply. "That's quite a journey. Given everything he's been through, seeing how far he's come in this setting is impressive. I can only imagine how much he'll thrive with us."

"I agree. Henry just needs stability and a lot of love."

Hailey came back into the room, wondering if we had any questions.

"When can we take him home?" Drew and I asked in unison.

She chuckled and answered, "I admire parents who aren't afraid of reports like that."

I nodded, acknowledging her comment, before asking, "What's the plan for Henry's treatment? What do we need to do next?"

"I would recommend finding a child psychologist specializing in trauma, preferably a male," Hailey said. "I also suggest establishing clear boundaries and consequences for Henry in your home. He has responded well to our red, yellow, and green light system, which helps him understand expectations and the rewards of following the rules.

"It's important to note that we don't use time-outs or corporal punishment. We practice gentle parenting, seeking to discern the child's motivations behind their behavior and explaining why certain actions are unsafe for themselves and others. We've found that children who have experienced trauma respond well to this approach.

"Try not to make him feel ashamed or guilty when he acts out. Instead, reassure him that he's not a bad kid; everyone makes mistakes sometimes. Remember that Henry will love both of you; it will just take some time. You've scheduled your home visit and completed all the required classes, so if things go well, the adoption could be finalized by next month."

We thanked Hailey for her helpful advice and snuck one last peek at Henry before we left. He sat on the floor with Markus and Macy, watching *The Lion King*.

I couldn't wait to bring him home and give him the love he needed and deserved.

chapter three

The total amount of our Target run exceeds three hundred dollars. We fill our cart with everything I think Henry will need: ten outfits, five pairs of pajamas, underwear with superhero designs, and so many books. I couldn't resist adding a stuffed zebra to the pile, confident Henry would love it.

As Drew loads the bags into the back of the car, I ask, "Can you think of anything we missed?"

"The store will still be here after we bring him home," Drew says.

"I just want him to know he's loved."

"I know, amore. He will."

I can't believe Henry will be here in two days. The first several weeks will be a trial period, but if everything goes well, we'll become his parents. Drew and I have decided to take the next week off from work to focus on giving Henry all the love and attention he needs as he adjusts.

The important people in our lives know that Henry will join our family soon. Drew's fellow firefighters bought new toys for Henry and planned Drew's favorite meal at the firehouse. I, on the other hand, am not close to my co-workers. Working from home is perfect in all areas except building social connections, but I prefer to keep to myself anyway. When I lost the baby, I was grateful I could adjust the lighting, cake on makeup, and still attend the online meetings without anyone knowing my struggles.

Drew's sister Emily and her husband Ryan live near Detroit with their children, Amelia, who is six, and Mason, who is four. When Drew and I began dating, he mentioned that he and Emily fought like cats and dogs during childhood—she followed the rules, whereas Drew was a free spirit. However, in early adulthood, they discovered some common ground, and now they enjoy hanging out when they can.

Emily couldn't have been happier when we told her about the adoption. We all decided to go on a vacation to Florida together to tell Drew's parents in person. The grandparents-to-be were overjoyed when we informed them Henry would soon join the family.

Being an only child, I didn't have anyone I wanted to share our exciting news with. I wasn't about to tell my mother we had been approved to care for her "used" grandchild. She was busy in New York, pretending to be an actor. In my younger years, my mother chased her dreams by moving us from LA to Europe and everywhere in between. She refused to acknowledge that her lack of talent, not our location, was why she didn't become a superstar.

Our nomadic lifestyle brought my dad and me closer. Despite not having much money, he always found ways to show me fun places. It never showed if my dad was exhausted from working all night as a cab driver. We spent our days eating day-old bagels and exploring free museums. Thanks to the special bond I shared with my dad, I didn't feel the need for other friends.

My only attempt to develop a friend group was in third grade when I received an invitation to a sleepover with some girls from my class. Laughter filled the air as we tried on the host mom's party dresses, strutting through the living room like runway models in Milan.

Next up was the beauty shop. The kitchen table overflowed with colorful makeup palettes and brushes in every shape and size. We voted to determine the lucky winner who would be the first customer. I held my breath as each person cast their vote for me.

I perched on the dining room chair while one girl applied my eyeshadow, adding a burst of color to my face. The others took turns with scissors. It dawned on me too late that they weren't pretending to cut my hair. I looked down at the floor in shock, horrified to see my once beautiful, long locks lying in clumps around my makeshift throne.

As I lay inside my sleeping bag that night, pretending to be asleep, I heard their whispers—ridiculing my thrift shop clothes and cheap tennis shoes. They said I should go back to the dumpster they imagined I crawled out of. I buried my head in my pillow so they wouldn't hear me cry.

The next day, my dad took me to get a proper haircut. He hugged me, saying those horrible girls were jealous of my beauty. He explained that some people lack inner beauty while assuring me I was beautiful inside and out. The experience taught me an unforgettable lesson—you can't trust people. From then on, it was me and Dad against the world.

A massive heart attack took him from me six months before my high school graduation, leaving me overwhelmed with grief and feeling totally alone. Consumed by my pain, my only comfort came from the happy memories we shared.

On my most challenging days, I clung to a particular memory of when I was ten years old. My mother had a inconsequential role in a local theater production in a charming Michigan town. We spent the entire summer living in a cozy cabin near Lake Michigan. It was a magical time filled with playing on the dunes, fishing with my dad for hours, and swimming in the vast lake.

When I went to college, I wanted to remain close to my dad's memory, and being by the water seemed like the perfect way to achieve that. I knew I belonged there when I received my Grand Valley State University acceptance letter. The campus had a serene atmosphere and was less than an hour from Lake Michigan.

I earned scholarships covering almost all of my tuition expenses. As always, I couldn't rely on my mother, but I worked my butt off and graduated in three years. My statistics degree starkly contrasted with my mother's dreams of becoming an actress. Because of my difficult upbringing, I found comfort in seeking concrete facts and analyzing data. But even my choices regarding education drove a wedge between my mother and me.

"I can't fathom why you'd want to stare at numbers all day. Where's the enjoyment in that?" she asked during one of our rare phone calls while I was still in school.

"Numbers are a constant; they don't compel you to wander the country in pursuit of elusive dreams," my response came out sharper than intended.

"Best of luck to you," Mother said theatrically before abruptly ending the call.

Throughout my time on campus, I kept to myself and pushed through, hoping to magically find a group of friends in the next phase of my life. I envisioned a scenario like Robin on "How I Met Your Mother," spotting my people from across the bar at the local hangout. They would welcome me into their established circle, appreciating me for my intelligence, sweetness, and wit. That never happened.

After college, I had no desire to leave West Michigan. I loved the lakes and the four distinct seasons. Unfortunately, the only place I could afford was in a neighborhood where drug deals and drive-by shootings were common occurrences. Police lights would dance along my walls several times a month as law enforcement struggled to contain the crime. Most evenings, I stayed in, reluctant to venture out into the city alone. The isolation left me incredibly lonely.

However, everything changed one fateful night when I set my kitchen on fire. The incident unfolded just like one of those cliché Hallmark movies my mother used to make me watch.

Lost in my thoughts, I stood away from the chaos and failed to notice a firefighter approaching. I screamed when he greeted me. Surprise crossed his face, and he apologized for scaring me.

I drew a sharp breath, taking in the gorgeous man before me. He towered over me, his dark brown eyes staring into mine as if searching my soul. His sweaty, tousled, dusty blond hair added to his rugged charm. He asked if I was okay, and I stuttered a response, unable to form any coherent words.

"Trying to extinguish a fire by throwing a towel on it isn't a good idea." His tone dripped with sarcasm.

"In the movies, plenty of people throw a wet blanket over a person on fire," I countered.

"Key words—wet blanket on a person, not a dry hand towel on a burner. And I'm positive you're supposed to turn off the burner first." He smiled, revealing his perfectly straight teeth. "I think I should go to the station, get cleaned up, and take you to dinner to teach you the art of fire extinguishing. My name is Drew, by the way."

"So, Drew, is this your usual approach to women who set their kitchens on fire?" I asked, surprised by my willingness to continue the conversation. Typically, I avoid talking to strangers, even if they happen to be attractive firefighters.

"No, you would be the first. Considering your lack of safety skills, my commitment to keeping the community safe, and the fact that you won't be able to cook in your kitchen again, it's my civic duty to offer you this personalized training."

"Is that so?" I couldn't help but let a smile slip past my attempt to keep a straight face.

"Is there a boyfriend we should include in this training?"

"Nope."

"A girlfriend?"

"There's not a single anyone."

"Alright. Can I pick you up in an hour?" Drew asked.

"I guess so. If it's a matter of community safety."

His eyes met mine. "I'll need your name for your certificate of completion and complimentary badge."

I grin. "It's Charlotte."

Our whirlwind romance started that night at dinner. I picked out a flowing red dress and paired it with stunning high-heeled shoes reserved for special occasions. My hair cascaded down my back, and I spent extra time on my makeup. I completed the look by applying deep red lipstick—wondering if it might be too much. However, when I met Drew outside the quaint Italian restaurant, he greeted me with a mischievous grin. He leaned in close and whispered, "You look beautiful," reassuring me that I had made the right decision.

The candle-lit dining room cast an enchanting glow around us. Our server, Leo, introduced himself as a first-generation Italian immigrant and kindly informed us about the specials. A delicious bottle of Chianti complemented our homemade ravioli and bruschetta. Our conversation flowed effortlessly, and I felt comfortable enough to confide in Drew. I shared details about my life, something I don't do. I struggled to hold back tears as I talked about my dad and our nomadic lifestyle. Drew held my hand across the table, his eyes filled with empathy and understanding.

On the way out, I thanked Leo for the wonderful evening.

"You're very welcome, mi amore," he said, kissing both of my cheeks.

In the parking lot, Drew wrapped me in a farewell hug. "See you soon, amore," he whispered into my ear.

My phone chimed as I arrived at my soon-to-be-condemned apartment—a message from Drew saying I had completed my safety training. Another message followed with an invitation to join him and his friends at the bowling alley the next day. From that moment forward, we became inseparable.

Searching for a new place to live proved to be a bigger headache than expected, and I was thankful Drew joined me. The last apartment on my list was my breaking point. As Drew and I stood in the cramped living room with blood-red, warped walls, my stress skyrocketed as I contemplated my next step. I screamed while squashing a cockroach, realizing this place only guaranteed one outcome—the fear of being murdered in my sleep.

We stopped for lunch at Yesterdog to gather our thoughts. I had no idea how I'd find an affordable apartment that didn't resemble a horror movie set. As we ate hot dogs with all the fixings, Drew reached across the table, took my hand, and expressed his love for me. He admitted he couldn't imagine a future without me and handed me a key to his apartment. That evening, we collected the few things I had left to my name, and I moved in with him.

Six months later, we married in a small ceremony in Drew's sister's backyard. The only thing that could have made the day more perfect is if my dad had been there to walk me down the aisle.

Drew and I were unbelievably happy until the struggles to expand our family started. After years of trying, it was evident that having children wouldn't be easy. I withdrew and became more isolated, while Drew coped by spending more time drinking with his friends after work. The loss of our baby girl was the tipping point, and I wasn't confident that our relationship would survive.

When I came across Henry's online profile, I felt a glimmer of hope, and we decided to adopt. The strain in our marriage started to ease, and we began to be our old selves again as we planned for our future and embraced the excitement of our journey into parenthood.

chapter four

The drive to Horizons of Hope feels endless. We left early, allowing for a couple of bathroom breaks. My stomach was in knots, so I couldn't drink my usual cup of coffee this morning, leaving me with a pounding headache. I can't believe today is the beginning of my journey as a mom—I just might throw up.

We pull into the parking lot with thirty minutes to spare. Drew picks a spot overlooking a field. The sunlight dances through the trees, making the dewy grass sparkle. Drew turns to me and takes my hand, intertwining his fingers with mine. His touch always calms me.

"Are you ready for this?" he asks.

"I've been ready for a long time. Are you nervous?"

"Nope. We are going to be excellent parents. I'm excited to get Henry home and show him his room. Maybe I can take him to the station next week to let the guys meet him."

"Hailey said not to overwhelm him," I remind him.

"You're right. It's probably best to wait a while."

"Let's give him options and see what he wants to do," I suggest, knowing how eager Drew is to introduce Henry to his friends and family. "Are you disappointed that I couldn't have a baby?"

"I have never been, and will never be, disappointed in you. What matters to me is that we become parents. It's love that creates a family, not a uterus." He kisses me. "Henry is meant to be with us. People have babies every day, but it takes a special person to fix the wrongs of others. We will give Henry the life he deserves."

Drew holds my hand as we sit in silence, lost in our thoughts about what parenthood will be like.

At 9:00 a.m., we stand at the front door of Horizons of Hope. Our lives are about to change forever. Drew presses the buzzer, and the door swings open just as I'm about to push it again. Hailey greets us with a faint smile, her messy hair and flushed cheeks betraying her usually composed demeanor. She steps aside, allowing us to enter.

"Henry is having a difficult morning," Hailey informs us. "He displayed disruptive behavior yesterday and needed to be restrained. He thinks he's leaving because of his actions. We've been trying to tell him he's going to a new home with his own family, but he doesn't understand. I'm sure he'll be fine once he gets used to you and sees his home."

We walk into the rec room, where all the kids are watching a movie. Henry holds onto Tom's arm like a lifebuoy in the middle of the ocean.

"Some special people are here to see you." Tom pries Henry's hand from his arm so he can stand up. Tom walks over to us, and Henry scrambles after him. We introduce ourselves and thank him for the care he has given Henry.

"It was my pleasure." Tom smiles. "He is an amazing kid. I

have never seen anyone grow and change more in such a short amount of time." Henry stands behind Tom, peeking out from between his legs.

Bending down, I talk to Henry in a soft voice. "We are so happy you are coming to live with us."

He wraps his arms around Tom's leg. Tom gently removes Henry's grasp and kneels.

"You get a new home, buddy. With a mommy and a daddy." Tom gestures toward us. "And I bet you have a room with toys in it."

Drew kneels, too. "There are so many toys. We have books, legos, stuffed animals, and a firetruck waiting just for you."

Henry stares at the ground. Tom tries a different tactic. "You can write me letters, and I will write back. Okay?"

"No go," Henry cries. All I want to do is comfort and assure him everything will be alright.

The rest of the kids notice the commotion and assemble near us. "I'll go with them!" an older boy shouts.

Hailey takes charge, guiding us into a small conference room. She starts the conversation by talking to Henry and asking him how he's feeling about going to his new home. It's obvious how he feels.

"Stay here." Henry points to Tom.

Hailey steps in. "Henry, I know you love Tom. He has been an awesome big brother to you. How about if Charlotte takes a picture of you and Tom? Then you can see him whenever you want."

Pulling out my phone, I snap a photo. Tom smiles, but Henry is sobbing, tears streaming down his face as he clings to

Tom.

"Let's take a photo of everyone together," Hailey suggests.

Drew and I position ourselves on opposite sides of Tom and Henry, but Henry continues to cry.

Witnessing Henry's distress at leaving Tom behind, I question our decision to remove him from the only support he's ever known. I realize that providing him with a home and two loving parents is better than keeping him in foster care, but my heart is breaking for Henry.

Drew pulls a Matchbox firetruck out of his pocket and shows it to Henry. He eyes it uncertainly, but at least he stops crying.

"Wow, that's cool, don't you think, Henry?" Tom asks.

Drew hands the truck to Henry, who examines it.

"Drew is a firefighter," Tom says. "Maybe you can visit the station and sit in a real firetruck!"

"Absolutely. All my buddies can't wait to meet you. They have a firefighter uniform for you."

Henry's face reveals a subtle smile, and Hailey takes advantage of the moment, snapping a photo.

"Guess what stuffed animal we have for you?" I ask, despite my mixed feelings about resorting to bribery.

Henry looks at me quizzically.

"It's your favorite," I drop a hint.

"Zebra."

"Yes! And he is waiting just for you in the car."

Tom takes Henry's hand. "Let's go and see, buddy."

They walk down the hallway toward the front door.

"Should he say goodbye to the other children?" I whisper to

Hailey.

"No, they had a going away breakfast, and all the kids gave him letters. They're in his bag." She hands me a tiny backpack with dinosaurs on it.

Hailey stops at the door, kneels, and hugs Henry, telling him she is proud of him. She uses her ID tag to open the door. Henry glances back, holding Tom's hand for dear life, then turns around and walks toward our car.

"The car is blue, your favorite color." Tom continues trying to elicit some excitement, but Henry remains stoic.

As Drew opens the door, I grab the stuffed zebra, thankful I decided to bring it along. To my relief, a faint smile appears on Henry's face when I hand it to him.

"Wow, buddy. What a great-looking zebra." Tom's efforts to get Henry excited finally work, and Henry smiles as he hugs the stuffed animal. Tom hugs Henry and whispers, "I am so happy for you, buddy. You're going to have a family and an amazing life." His voice breaks with emotion.

With reluctance, Henry gets into the backseat of the car and allows Tom to buckle him into his car seat. Drew extends his hand to shake Tom's.

In an impulsive moment, I hug Tom. "Thank you for everything you've done for Henry."

"You're welcome." Tom wipes his eyes before leaning into the car to talk to Henry one last time. "I will write to you, and you write back, okay?" Tom closes Henry's door and walks back toward the building, not looking back.

The ride home goes smoothly. We make a pit stop at a gas station for a bathroom break and let Henry pick out a treat. He wants Goldfish crackers and a sharable-size bag of M&Ms. We guide him towards the smaller bag, and the compromise works better than I thought. Henry happily eats his snack and then falls asleep with chocolate smeared across his face, but he looks adorable.

"You're home," I whisper, unbuckling Henry's car seat.

Henry steps into the house cautiously. "You can either take off your shoes and coat or leave them on. It's your choice." The books I read about adoption stressed the importance of giving the child a chance to feel in control.

Henry decides to keep his shoes on but take his coat off. I point out the designated hook reserved just for him. Drew and I show Henry the kitchen, living room, bathroom, and bedrooms. He grins when he sees the toys lining the shelves in his room. We sit on the rug as he explores his new surroundings.

"Mine?" Henry asks, standing by the toy shelf.

"Yup, all for you, buddy," Drew reassures him.

chapter five

We let Henry make all the decisions for the rest of the day. He picked pepperoni pizza for dinner and ice cream for dessert. We watched Toy Story, not once but twice. When he fell asleep at 10:00 p.m., he still didn't have his pajamas on.

As I climbed under the covers, Drew was already sleeping, his breathing deep and steady. The day's events wore us out. Even though I am exhausted, my mind continues to race, preventing me from falling asleep for another hour. I finally drifted into a light sleep, only to be startled awake shortly after—my eyes snapping open and my heart racing.

"Are you alright?" I whisper, realizing Henry is standing beside my bed.

"Accident," Henry murmurs.

I'm momentarily confused, but I realize Henry wet the bed as the urine scent hits my nose.

"That's okay, sweetheart."

I guide him back to his room to assess the situation and discover his sheets are soaked. We need to rethink letting him refill his water bottle three times in one evening. I remove the bedding and throw it into the hallway. Henry stands motionless, his eyes locked on the wall.

"Don't worry, Henry. Accidents happen." I kneel to his level. "Let's get you out of these wet clothes. Do you want to rinse off in the shower or bath?"

Henry remains silent but follows me into the bathroom. Considering his size, I decide a bath will be more manageable. I help him remove his shirt as the tub fills with warm water. I'm stunned when I see circular marks covering his back and arms, resembling cigarette burns. It's shocking how many there are.

"Your first bath in your new home. How exciting." I muster up as much excitement as I can.

Removing his pants, I see more scars that make me inhale sharply. I steady myself, determined to maintain my cheerful façade. I lift him into the tub, pour shampoo on a washcloth, and hand it to him. He holds it but remains still. I add more shampoo to the cloth, lathering it up to create a cascade of bubbles. To my amazement, Henry smiles, so I blow on it, sending bubbles floating into the air. Henry's eyes light up, and he lets out a little giggle. It's music to my ears.

Drew enters the bathroom, rubbing his eyes. "Hey, why wasn't I invited to the bubble party?" he says mid-yawn.

As his eyes adjust, they widen in surprise at the scars on Henry's body. Drew glances at me, and I broaden my smile, attempting to reassure him. He mirrors my expression, forming an even more animated grin to conceal his shock.

"Henry had a little accident. Would you mind throwing his clothes and sheets in the washer and remaking his bed while we finish here?"

Drew gathers the clothes; moments later, the washer hums

to life. I help Henry rinse off the soap and wrap him in a fluffy towel. We return to his room, where Drew is making the bed. Henry picks out the pajamas with tigers on them.

"Don't worry. We'll keep the lights on in the hallway and the bathroom," I say. "That should make it easier to find your way if you need to go."

Henry nods.

I lean down and kiss his forehead. "Good night, Henry. I am so glad you're here."

"Goodnight, buddy," Drew says from the doorway.

Back in our bed, Drew turns toward me. "I can't believe how bad his scars are," he whispers.

"It's so sad. I don't remember anything about scars mentioned in the binder."

"Maybe we overlooked it. That binder is thick."

"I wonder what else we missed," I reflect aloud.

"Are you having second thoughts?"

Without hesitation, I say, "Not at all. I'm grateful we can provide Henry a safe home and make up for everything he's been through."

Drew kisses me, and I nestle closer to him, needing comfort. As I doze off again, I remind myself to call the psychologist Hailey recommended first thing tomorrow morning.

chapter six

In the morning, Drew and I review Henry's entire file while he watches *Paw Patrol*. The documents paint a disturbing picture of the abuse he went through. The hospital reports note burns from cigarettes, angry welts on his back, and a severe diaper rash in addition to his broken arm. The doctor thought Henry likely didn't get enough food from birth, which might have caused more delays in his cognitive development. However, since Henry's mother passed away and he couldn't explain what happened, the true extent of his suffering remains unclear.

Child protective services added a report from the neighbors outlining months of overlooked signs. Several neighbors complained of noise from the apartment, and another recounted numerous men frequenting the residence at all hours of the day and night.

"I can't believe no one did anything." I wipe away the tears streaming down my cheeks. "It's heartbreaking that no one stepped in."

"I am so glad Henry is ours, and we can help him heal." Drew gets up and kisses me on the forehead. He grabs a bag of fruit snacks and sits with Henry on the couch while I put the binder on a high shelf.

THREE DAYS later, we're sitting in the waiting area of Dr. Wilson's office. The space is calming, with soft colors on the walls and comfy chairs. Sunlight floods through the windows, making the room warm and cozy. One wall has shelves filled with bins of toys and an extensive collection of picture books. On the opposite side, there's a mirror painted with an intricate border of flowers, butterflies, and birds.

Despite the serene setting, I'm on edge. I grab a Slinky from the side table and fidget with it, moving it back and forth between my hands while my knee bounces up and down. Drew's gentle touch on my thigh reminds me to relax. It helps, but before long, my leg starts shaking again.

Drew points to a sign on the wall with the simple instructions, "Just Breathe." I follow the advice, taking deep breaths to calm myself as I prepare for Dr. Wilson to evaluate Henry's needs and discuss our family's future.

Finally, the door opens, and Dr. Wilson walks out with Henry. "Can you play with the toys while I meet with Mommy and Daddy?" Henry furrows his eyebrows but nods his head yes.

As we enter Dr. Wilson's office, I mention Henry doesn't call us Mommy and Daddy yet. We are holding off until he's more comfortable with us being his parents. I look at Henry through the office's window, only now realizing that the mirror in the waiting area is two-way glass.

"I get where you're coming from." Dr. Wilson gestures toward the couch, inviting us to sit. "However, it's crucial to present yourselves as Mom and Dad to Henry. He needs to realize that you're not a caretaker but his permanent family. This approach will help strengthen the bond between all of you."

I glance around his office. The room is warm and pleasant, with colorful paintings on the walls and soft music playing in the background. Dr. Wilson appears to be in his thirties, and his gentle and kind demeanor enhances his striking handsomeness.

He starts the conversation. "I've reviewed Henry's chart and worked with his therapist at Horizons of Hope Children's Home to coordinate his care. They were making progress in helping him cope with his trauma. It's challenging because he's young and doesn't fully grasp what's happening. What might be distressing to us was normal for Henry. Someone most likely burned him with cigarettes as punishment for things like being hungry or wetting himself."

My hand covers my mouth in shock. "That's awful. Will the abuse have a long-term effect on him?"

"I anticipate some issues as he adjusts to the dynamics of a loving family. My role with Henry will involve assisting him in understanding his emotions. I'll work on helping him realize that he's in a safe environment and receiving the support and care he requires.

"I suggest setting clear and consistent rules and expectations for him. Encouraging him when he behaves well and acknowledging his efforts when he faces challenges can help his growth. Avoid using any physical punishment at all costs. It also might be helpful to create a space where he can go whenever he needs to sort through his feelings."

"Do you think enrolling him in preschool is a good idea?" Drew asks.

"It would bring some structure into his daily routine. Consider exploring a Montessori program where Henry can have more freedom to choose activities he enjoys."

"Do you have any other suggestions to help him settle into our home?" I ask, hopeful for more insight.

"I recommend including Henry in decision-making by giving him a few options when possible. For instance, let him decide whether to sit in the cart or walk beside you at the grocery store. If he chooses to walk, be sure to stress the importance of staying close without using words that might remind him of his past trauma, like being scared or hurt. Keeping things positive is crucial."

Drew and I both nod in agreement. It's reassuring that the advice I've received from the books I've read matches Dr. Wilson's suggestions.

"And one last thing to consider is joining a support group with other parents who have adopted children with traumatic pasts. They would provide valuable insights and strategies for guiding and parenting Henry. It's important to connect with others who have been through similar situations. Traditional resources might not be the best fit for Henry's needs, as they cater to children with standard behavior and expectations."

We thank Dr. Wilson for his time and guidance. I schedule weekly sessions for the upcoming months, confident we are moving in the right direction toward creating a happy family.

chapter seven

The week we spent together before Drew returned to work was magical. One of the highlights was our visit to the zoo. Henry looked so happy and laughed as a baby sheep nibbled his hand while he fed it.

Drew became an enthusiastic guide at the local museum, leading us from room to room. He shared the history behind each object that caught Henry's interest. I cherished every moment, thankful for the time we spent as a family and the memories we were making.

Our trip to the library for story time was just as memorable. Henry sat with the other children and listened to the stories. Afterward, the kids colored pictures. Henry handed me his picture of Clifford the Big Red Dog, whom he had transformed into a rainbow of colors. I praised his talent and later hung his masterpiece on the fridge. Seeing my child's artwork on display was a dream come true, a tangible reminder that I am a mom.

We made a cozy corner in Henry's room by putting a beanbag chair under a canopy with twinkling lights. I was ecstatic when I discovered him cozied up in his bean bag, absorbed in his books.

During the week, we visited a Montessori school. The students appeared happy, and the teachers reassured us that we were making a good decision to start Henry in preschool, where he could socialize with other children.

To help with his nighttime accidents, we bought pull-ups and limited his beverages after dinner. Our bedtime traditions became my favorite; Henry climbed into his bed smelling of baby shampoo and lavender body wash. He would snuggle between us as we read story after story.

The night Drew selected *Where the Wild Things Are,* my heart swelled with emotion. As a child, my dad read it to me every night. I always hoped to have the same close connection with my children as I did with my dad, and it felt like I was well on my way.

We joined an online support group for parents of kids who have been in the foster care system. As I scrolled through discussions about children misbehaving and parents feeling overwhelmed, I couldn't help but feel thankful for how well Henry was adjusting with us. I struggled to connect with the other parents when we attended one of the virtual meetings. The atmosphere was negative, mostly spent airing grievances about their kids. I told Drew I didn't think the group was the right fit for us.

Henry received a letter from Tom, and I was torn about whether I should give it to him. I didn't want to bring up memories that might upset him, but I didn't want to hide the message from his friend. In the end, I decided to share it with him. Henry seemed happy at first, but as I read it to him, he stared at the wall blankly.

After Henry's second appointment, Dr. Wilson gave us positive feedback, assuring us we were on the right track with Henry. He also cautioned that we might face challenges once the initial excitement wore off and we returned to our regular schedules and routines.

On our way home, Drew and I discussed Dr. Wilson's assessment. Drew was optimistic, believing Henry was thriving and would adapt well to the upcoming changes. His upbeat attitude was contagious, and I shared his confidence in our parenting abilities.

chapter eight

When I woke up on Monday morning, Drew had already left for work. I must have been exhausted because I didn't even hear his alarm. As I sat up in bed, I saw Henry standing in the doorway, staring at me.

"Drew," Henry says.

"He had to go to work, sweetheart," I remind him as I get out of bed and slip on my robe. "Remember, we talked about it yesterday. Drew will be at work when you wake up, but he'll be home for dinner unless there's a...?"

"Fire."

"Yes. You have an excellent memory. How about I make you some breakfast? Would you like eggs, pancakes, or cereal?"

"Cookies."

"Cookies taste yummy, but there are better options for breakfast. Let's choose something healthy for now."

"Cookies!" Henry screams.

Kneeling to his level, I say, "It's hard when we want something we can't have right away. How about this: You eat something healthy first, and then we'll make some cookies. You can have one as soon as they're cool."

He walks off, likely returning to his room—my compromise a success. I get dressed, tidy up the bed, and brush my teeth before going to Henry's room. He's not there. I call out for him, but the house remains silent.

Continuing to shout his name, I make my way towards the kitchen. My voice trails off when I see the chaos. Milk spills from an overturned carton on the floor. The tiles are covered in shattered eggshells, flour, and cereal, creating a sticky disaster. Henry sits on the couch in the nearby family room with a book, oblivious to the mess he has caused. His feet are coated with the gooey mixture, leaving tiny footprints across the carpet.

"Henry, what happened?" I say louder than I intend, immediately regretting my tone.

"Drew did it," he says without looking up from his book.

I take a deep breath before responding, "Please don't lie to me."

He meets my gaze. "Not lying."

Losing my patience, I reach for my cell phone. "I guess I'll call Drew to ask him why he did that," I say, pretending to dial.

"No!" Henry shouts.

Feeling silly for having a standoff with a three-year-old, I slip the phone into my back pocket and try a different approach. "You made some poor choices this morning, so now you need to help me clean up. Otherwise, you'll be on a red light." I'm hopeful the mention of the behavior system will give me some leverage.

"No!" Henry sprints to his bedroom, slamming the door shut.

I walk to his room, taking deep breaths along the way. He is curled up in his bed, hidden under the blankets. Sitting on the edge of his bed, I reflect on Dr. Wilson's advice.

"I'm guessing you're upset because you wanted cookies for breakfast, and that's why you made this mess. How about we make a deal? If you help me, you won't be on a red light. After cleaning up, we can go to the store and buy the ingredients to make cookies since most of them are on the floor."

Henry gets off his bed, leaving a sticky trail behind—adding another task to my to-do list. He follows me to the kitchen, where I demonstrate how to use a spatula to scrape up the goo and put it in a trash bag, trying to make it into a game. He helps for less than a minute before saying he's hungry.

"Me too, but we need to finish our work first," I say. Henry looks at me blankly as if my words haven't registered.

I explain the importance of working together to solve problems, but Henry just stares at the wall. With a heavy sigh, I start cleaning up by myself.

As I clean, I discover the picture Henry colored for me at the library ripped into pieces. Overwhelmed by the morning's chaos and the loss of my first memento of motherhood, I sink onto the floor, defeated.

"Why did you tear up my picture?" I ask, struggling to hold back tears.

"Drew did," he says, avoiding eye contact.

"This makes me very sad. That picture was my favorite, and now it's destroyed." I pick up the shreds and toss them in the trash, wiping tears from my cheeks.

I fill a bucket with warm water and grab two towels. "Would you like to help me mop?" I ask in the kindest voice I can muster.

Henry remains quiet while I scrub the floor. Once I finish, I propose that we wash his feet in the sink, thinking it could be more fun for him. But when I pick him up, he screams, slips out of my hands, and runs down the hallway.

Henry is in his room, hiding under the blankets on his bed again.

"How about a bath? I'll make lots of bubbles." He doesn't budge. "Do you want me to carry you to the bathtub, or would you prefer to walk?"

With no answer, I lift the blanket, and the distinct scent of urine fills my nose.

"Why didn't you use the toilet?" I ask, my tone sharper than I intended. I take a few deep breaths to calm down before speaking again. "Let's clean up so we can have breakfast." I attempt to lift him.

He kicks and screams, flailing his body. The back of his head hits my face, and I scream in pain. I release my grip, letting him fall back onto the bed. My hand instinctively touches my lip as I taste the metallic tang of blood in my mouth.

"We both need a time out," I say through clenched teeth, retreating to the bathroom. Tears spill down my cheeks as I look at myself in the mirror. Today is my first day as a mom, and I am already failing. Overwhelmed by my emotions, I call Drew, my sobs getting louder when he answers.

"Amore, are you alright?" Drew's voice is filled with concern, causing my tears to flow even more. I attempt to explain what happened.

"Henry is probably confused because he didn't realize I wouldn't be there when he woke up," Drew reassures me. "I'll explain things more clearly to him when I get home tonight. You're doing great. Take a deep breath." His calmness begins to ease my racing thoughts.

"You're an incredible mom. Henry will figure that out soon. Just wait until he starts creating tons of pictures to cover our fridge. His amazing artwork will decorate every wall, and whenever we have guests, we'll show off each masterpiece, bragging about how incredible our son is."

His voice radiates happiness, and I can't help but smile at the amusing scenario Drew described.

"Thank you. I messed up and overreacted," I admit, feeling disappointed in myself.

"You didn't mess up, amore. You're doing your best, and that's all anyone can ask. Your efforts are far better than those of the adults previously in his life."

He tells me he loves me, and I feel better as we end the call. With Drew by my side, I know I can handle the challenges of parenthood.

Deciding on a different approach, I tempt Henry with toys to make bath time more fun. It works. My attempt to engage him by making his plastic fish sing nursery rhymes in silly voices doesn't work, and he remains quiet and unresponsive. I guess it's better than him being upset.

Henry chooses his outfit for the day, and I suggest he eat in his room while reading some books so I can finish cleaning up the house. He sits still in the middle of the floor, lost in thought. I quickly grab his food and bring it to him.

"Here you go, sweetheart." I hand him a granola bar and a sippy cup with milk. Then, I carry over a stack of books and place them next to him.

I linger in the doorway, watching until he takes a bite of his bar. Despite the difficulties we may have faced this morning, seeing Henry in a moment of contentment reassures me. I know I can be the mom he needs.

Returning to the kitchen, I fill a bucket with warm water mixed with a cleaning solution to scrub the carpet in the hallway. Sounds of Henry talking and laughing drift from his room. His mood has improved, perhaps because he was simply hungry.

When I detect the unmistakable sound of him jumping on his bed, I call out, "Everything alright in there?"

Silence.

I stop scrubbing to check on him, pushing his bedroom door open. Henry is standing on his bed, naked. A brown substance covers his hands; at first, I think it's the leftovers of his granola bar. But then, the stench hits me. The room begins to spin as I realize the marks on his freshly painted yellow walls are shit. I feel like I'm about to pass out, and for a moment, I can't speak.

Finding my voice, I scream, "What have you done?"

A mischievous smile spreads across his face as he laughs at me. The disgusting smell overwhelms me, making me gag and hurry to the bathroom.

I rinse my mouth out and splash cold water on my face. Rushing down the hallway, I grab a trash can, two containers of Clorox wipes, and my bucket. Hurrying back to Henry's room, I wrap him in the towel from earlier, set him on the rocking chair, and order him not to move—my voice filled with panic. Fueled by adrenaline, I start cleaning as fast as I can.

"I can't believe what you've done! You've ruined your room!"

I shout, my anger boiling over.

His eyes widen, but he remains silent. I use a whole container of Clorox wipes to wash the walls, scrubbing every inch. Then, with my spray cleaner and a roll of paper towels, I wipe down the surfaces I just cleaned.

Holding Henry at arm's length, I bring him to the bathroom and command him to stand still while I get the baby wipes. Unwrapping him from the towel, I come face to face with the angry red scars covering his tiny body—reminding me why he's acting out.

Kneeling beside him, I apologize, "I'm sorry for getting so mad. I shouldn't have yelled at you."

"Bad boy," he whispers. "Make new picture."

"You're not a bad boy. You just made a mistake, sweetheart." I do my best to comfort him, scolding myself for losing it.

First, I use baby wipes to remove all visible traces of feces. Holding his hand, I help him climb into the tub. After rinsing him off with the handheld shower head, I fill the bathtub with fresh, warm water and add lots of bubbles. Henry rewards my efforts with a tiny smile as I sing "One Little Blue Fish" while popping the bubbles. When I'm confident he's completely clean, I lift him out of the tub and wrap him in a towel.

"Can we put some lotion on your skin?" I ask.

He doesn't answer but lets me apply a small amount of cream to each scar on his back, arms, and legs. Afterward, I wrap him in the towel and hug him. Although he stays stiff in my embrace, he doesn't push me away. I feel his breathing slow down, which brings me some comfort. I carry him back to his room and let him choose his clothes.

"What a morning we're having," I chirp as I help him get dressed.

"Hungry."

"Me too. How about cereal?" I propose, wanting to keep it simple.

He sits at the kitchen table while I show him two options. He chooses Fruity Rings, eats every last bite, and promptly asks for cookies. I tell him we are not going to have cookies today. When he accepts my answer without throwing a fit, I exhale the breath I've been holding, feeling the tension leave my body.

I let him watch cartoons so I can finish cleaning. I keep him in sight while scrubbing the living room carpet. I've learned from my mistake and won't let it happen again.

Glancing at the kitchen clock, I see it's not even noon, and I'm already exhausted. Drew won't be home for another seven hours, and my plan to work while Henry plays will not be happening. I decide to text my supervisor, explaining that I have a family emergency and will be available to work tonight instead.

Sitting on the couch, I put my feet on the coffee table— finally able to relax for the first time today.

"Park?" Henry asks.

I sigh. "Sure, fresh air and sunshine sounds wonderful."

He jumps up and rushes to put his shoes on.

"Take it easy, sweetheart; the park isn't going anywhere." I gather some energy to pull myself off the couch.

Henry dashes to the car, and I jog to catch up. "Time to get in your seat," I say, opening his door.

"No. For babies," he protests, shaking his head.

"We can't go to the park if you don't sit in your car seat."

"No, no, no!"

"Well, you must not want to go."

He stands beside me, arms folded across his chest, his gaze fixed on the ground. I do my best to muster up all my patience while waiting for him to sit in his seat. Time slows as the minutes drag by. Sensing that Henry is determined not to use the car seat, I inform him that we won't be going to the park today, but we can give it another shot tomorrow.

I take his hand, trying to lead him back inside the house. As we reach the door, he pulls away and races down the driveway. Chasing him, I scream for him to stay off the street. At the last moment, he detours onto the grass, sprinting across several lawns. I eventually catch up, but as I lift him, he kicks and screams in protest.

"Is everything okay out there?" an elderly neighbor asks from her front door.

"Yup. Someone didn't want to sit in his car seat. But I've got it handled," I assure her, hoping she'll take the hint and give us some privacy. She shakes her head in disapproval before shutting her door.

Carrying Henry back to our house, I struggle with his kicking and screaming the entire way. Utterly embarrassed, I'm convinced I'll never be able to show my face in the neighborhood again. After taking him to his room and placing him on his bed, I step out, closing the door behind me. Leaning against the hallway wall, I slowly sink to the floor.

Needing to vent, I call Drew again to tell him about the latest fiasco. "Oh, amore. I'm so sorry. That sounds awful," he sympathizes.

"It was. I feel so lost," I admit. My throat tightens as I try to hold back tears. "I'm already screwing everything up, and it's only the first day."

"It will be okay. We just need to set firm rules and use the green, yellow, and red light system he's used to. We will figure this out."

"I'm not sure I can handle this. Henry is so strong-willed."

"You are stronger than you think. I'll be home soon to help," Drew promises.

chapter nine

Henry is sitting on the couch with his worn-out baby blanket wrapped around his shoulders. He's eating a large bag of fruit snacks while watching cartoons. I'm seated across from him, laptop open, trying to find parenting advice for abused children. It's a quiet moment, but my mind is racing as I type in search terms and scroll through articles, blog posts, and forum threads. I make mental notes of relevant suggestions and click on promising links, hoping that somewhere in this virtual maze, there's wisdom that can help guide me.

I'm surprised when Drew walks into the living room, realizing it's already 6:30 p.m. Closing my laptop, I rise to give him a hug. He wraps his arms around my waist and kisses me.

Next, he goes to Henry, who's completely engrossed in watching the dancing bear on the screen. Drew ruffles his hair. In response, Henry jumps up from the couch, spilling the rest of his fruit snacks, and hugs Drew, calling him Daddy. They both have huge smiles, leaving me to wonder why it's so difficult for me to connect with Henry.

"Heard you had a rough day, buddy," Drew says.

"Good boy," Henry responds.

With Drew's gentle coaxing, Henry promises not to make messes and agrees to help when asked. Drew points out the spilled fruit snacks, and Henry eagerly picks them up. Drew suggests I take a relaxing bath while they prepare dinner. I gladly accept his offer.

Relaxed after a long soak, I climb into bed to close my eyes for a few minutes. My head is pounding. I hear the bedroom door creak, and I open my eyes to see Drew standing there with a mischievous grin on his face.

"Dinner is served, amore." He's wearing a "Kiss the Cook" apron and has a dish towel draped over his shoulder.

After we eat, Drew reveals a creative solution he and Henry created. He's set up a whiteboard displaying house rules using the green, yellow, and red light system. Paper figures represent Mom, Dad, and Henry and are attached with magnets. They stand as a united front on the green light.

I am grateful for Drew's help. We should have established clear boundaries when we first brought Henry home. Still, even with a plan in place, I'm unsure if I can handle another day like today, let alone manage it for a lifetime. We might have underestimated the extent of Henry's needs, but I keep my worries to myself. Drew is thriving in his role caring for Henry, and I can't take that away from him now.

Drew embraces me and whispers that he's taken tomorrow off. He encourages me to unwind for the rest of the evening while he helps Henry get ready for bed. With a cup of chamomile tea in hand, I withdraw to the coziness of our bedroom.

chapter ten

The sound of laughter wakes me from an unsettling dream of Henry smearing shit all over my white duvet. The scent of coffee gradually melts away my tension, and I can't help but smile as I remember Drew's decision to take the day off. We devised a plan last night. Drew will spend quality time with Henry and accompany him to his appointment with Dr. Wilson while I use the time to catch up on work.

The kitchen is messy, with flour and eggshells scattered across the countertop. Henry and Drew are eating their way through a towering stack of pancakes, their smiles stretching across their faces.

"Morning," I greet Drew with a kiss, tasting the sweetness of syrup on his lips. I hug Henry, but his whole body tenses at my touch.

"We made you pancakes, Mommy." Drew slides a plate my way. "Don't worry. Henry and I will clean up this big mess," Drew says, spreading his arms wide.

I grab my coffee and a dry pancake, return to my home office, and begin working. The sounds of Drew and Henry laughing make me smile. Maybe Drew was right, and yesterday was just an off day. I resolve to be more patient and better at explaining things to Henry.

When they leave to do the errands, the house is blissfully quiet, allowing me to focus on my work as the morning slips away.

That afternoon, I receive an email from Dr. Wilson.

Charlotte,

In today's session, I noticed that Henry was withdrawn and hesitant to discuss his challenges from yesterday. I attempted to engage him in role-playing using a dollhouse and dolls, but he resisted letting the mom doll interact with the rest of the family. When I inquired about his reasoning, he mentioned she was "bad." When I asked if he thought his mom was bad, he disassociated and refrained from answering.

While I cannot diagnose at this point, further assessment will help us understand Henry's emotions and behavior, enabling us to develop an appropriate solution.

The fact that he seems emotionally connected to Drew is encouraging. Continue to shower him with love, explaining things as if he were closer to two years old. I'm confident he will catch up to children his age with time and support.

Please know you are not alone in this journey.
Best regards,
Dr. Wilson

I am relieved knowing Dr. Wilson is on our team and can help guide us in the right direction.

The rest of the day flies by as I dive into my work. Drew prepares his signature dish for dinner, a plate of noodles smothered in Prego sauce. Drew and Henry laugh as they slurp up the spaghetti, competing to see who can eat them the fastest. Their laughter is contagious, and I have a renewed sense of hope.

After dinner, we discuss tomorrow's plans with Henry. We remind him that Drew will be at the fire station when he wakes up but will be home in time to put Henry to bed. I suggest some activities to keep us occupied during the day, and Henry chooses a few.

Following Henry's bedtime routine, I collapse into bed. Today went well; I caught up on work, and I'm hopeful tomorrow will be a fun day.

I JOLT awake—my heart pounding. Henry is standing next to my bed, staring at me. I pause to catch my breath, not wanting to startle him or wake Drew.

"What's going on, sweetheart?"

Henry remains silent, so I slip on my robe and lead him to his room, only to discover his sheets are soaked.

"Weren't you wearing a pull-up?" I wonder if Drew forgot to make sure he had one on.

Henry doesn't say a word. I help him remove his damp pajamas and replace them with a dry pull-up and fresh jammies before removing his soiled bedding.

"You have to keep your pull-up on," I say as I put the clean sheets on his mattress.

Glancing beneath his bed to look for the missing pull-up, I discover a pile of unexpected items: an apple, a bag of chips, a yogurt container, and a cereal box.

"Why is all this food hidden under here?" I ask.

Henry looks right through me.

Attempting to connect with him, I sit on the floor. "Are you worried about not having enough food? You can have something to eat whenever you're hungry, sweetheart. But things like yogurt will go bad if they're not in the refrigerator, and I'm sure you wouldn't want your room to smell like stinky feet, would you?" I scrunch my nose and stick out my tongue. Henry doesn't react.

"Are you hungry right now?"

He stands still, staring at the ground.

"Alright, I'll take this stuff back to the kitchen. We'll set up a box of safe snacks you can keep in your room. I can put them in a container with a lid to keep the bugs away. How does that sound?"

Henry gives a slight nod but doesn't speak. He gets into his freshly made bed, and I bend to hug him, feeling him tense at my touch.

"I love you, sweetheart." I switch off his light and go to toss the sheets in the washer before finally returning to bed, completely exhausted.

chapter eleven

Drew wakes me with a kiss on the cheek, "Henry's up."

Dragging myself out of bed, I shuffle into the kitchen, desperate for a strong cup of coffee. We both wave goodbye to Drew, wishing him a good workday. The exhaustion is already setting in.

"You're up bright and early. Do you want to color a picture while I make us something to eat?" I grab a brand-new sketch pad and a box of crayons. Henry chooses the red one to fill the page.

"Is red your favorite color?" I ask.

He doesn't respond.

"What do you want for breakfast?" Henry stops coloring and stares at his paper. "How about you choose between eggs or cereal?"

"Pancakes."

Unprepared for an argument, I whip up a batch and add my own twist. One looks like a broken heart, another vaguely resembles a car, and the third—well, it's a bit of a stretch to see a little boy, but I gave it my best shot.

I set the plate of pancakes in front of Henry. "Can you guess what shapes they are?"

He looks at them and, to my surprise, answers, "Heart."

"That's right! What about the others?"

"Truck. Monster."

"It's supposed to be a car and a Henry-shaped pancake. But it does resemble a monster. Maybe I should consider taking a pancake-making class."

He requests some syrup. I grab the large container of pure maple syrup from the farmer's market (a bulk purchase Drew insisted was a cost-effective choice) and pour some into a small cup, handing it to Henry.

Just as I'm about to sit down, my work phone rings in the spare bedroom. "Eat your breakfast. I'll be right back."

It turns out to be a demanding client, and it takes me ten minutes to calm him down. I promise to resolve his issue by tomorrow.

Henry's sweet laughter makes me smile as I return to the kitchen. However, my mood changes when I see the mess he created. He has emptied the syrup from the bottle onto his plate, creating a brown river stretching across the table and dripping to the floor.

"Oh my God! What the hell happened?" I slap my hand over my mouth, regretting my word choice.

"You yell. Yellow light," Henry says, his face lighting up with a mischievous grin.

"Alright, I'll move my clip while you explain," I say, sliding my paper figure into the yellow square.

"It spilled."

Taking a deep breath, I try to slow my heart rate, telling

myself he just wanted more syrup. Because of its size, no wonder it spilled.

I grab the garbage can and bring it closer to the table, using the drawing pad as a makeshift scoop to slide the sticky liquid into the trash. I fill the sink with soapy water and throw the crayons in.

"The paper is beyond saving, sweetheart. But I will get you a new one. We can rescue the crayons, though. Do you want to help me wash them?" I'm pleased with myself for keeping my cool.

I pull a chair to the sink and help Henry stand on it, singing, "Both you and the crayons are feeling quite sticky; let's tidy you up so you're not so icky."

Henry looks puzzled, and I sense he might not appreciate my musical talent. He splashes around, causing water to spill onto the floor.

"Let's try to be a little more careful, sweetheart. We want to keep the water in the sink," I say casually, not wanting to upset him.

He grabs my mug off the counter. My attempt to snatch it back is too late—he hurls it down. Coffee and ceramic pieces scatter in every direction.

"Why on earth would you do that?"

"You yell. Red light." Henry folds his arms across his chest, scrunching up his face like a little old man.

His adorable expression eases the tension, and I struggle not to laugh. The last thing I need is for him to think this is funny.

I try again, recalling the tips from the parenting audiobook I listened to yesterday. "Were you upset because I corrected how you cleaned the crayons? Is that why you threw my coffee mug on the floor?"

Henry gazes at me as if a dense fog separates us, and he's straining to see past it. Breathing in deeply, I begin cleaning up the pieces.

Henry starts to climb down, and I panic, shouting, "No! Stay there!"

He ignores me and continues his descent from the chair. As I grab him and put him on the countertop, a piece of the broken mug stabs my foot.

"Damn it!" I scream in pain and frustration.

"Red light," he taunts in response.

Ignoring him, I snag the roll of paper towels and lower myself to the floor. I wrap several around my bleeding foot and return to cleaning, grumbling under my breath. Suddenly, there's another loud crash, and glass pieces scatter across the floor. Confused, I glance at Henry to ensure he's alright. His face contorts into a sinister grin as he grabs another glass, ready to drop it.

"No!" I shout, reaching out to snatch it from his hand, but an intense pain shoots through my big toe, causing me to fall to the floor. More pieces of glass scatter nearby.

With no other choice, I get up and pull Henry from the counter. I maneuver through the minefield, wincing as the shards crunch beneath my feet. I hobble to his bedroom, place him on his bed, and instruct him not to move.

Following the trail of blood down the hallway to the bathroom, I sit on the edge of the bathtub and carefully extract the glass from my throbbing toe. I put antibacterial cream on both cuts and wrap them with bandages, hoping they won't require stitches.

I limp to my room to slip on my flip-flops and then back to the kitchen to sweep up all the bits of glass. While running the vacuum over the space to ensure every piece is collected, I rationalize that Henry must have been frustrated, and this is how he chose to show it. The parenting book I've been listening to mentioned that kids often act out more with people they feel comfortable with.

Returning to Henry's room, ready to discuss what happened, I'm momentarily confused when I push open his bedroom door. Henry is sitting in the middle of a paper blizzard. It gradually sinks in that the origin of this paperstorm is his collection of books. They've all been pulled from the shelves. The torn pages turned into confetti covering his floor. My eyes sweep through the room, revealing the wreckage of his cozy corner—the starlight canopy lies in a heap. White fluff is everywhere, confusing me until the horrifying realization hits—all of his stuffed animals have been decapitated. A paring knife sits next to his zebra, the only one spared from the beheading.

My patience is gone, replaced with anger. "Henry! Why? You've wrecked all your books! We won't be able to read them to you anymore, and your stuffed animals are going in the garbage." Grabbing the knife, I head towards the kitchen for a trash bag— my foot protesting the entire way.

Returning to Henry's room, I push the door so forcefully that it slams into the wall, making a loud bang. "Help me clean this up and consider yourself on a red light. That means no privileges for the rest of the day. Drew won't be happy with your behavior."

"You on red light. Drew not happy with you."

I ignore him and continue tossing the pieces of his book collection into the trash bag until Henry suddenly punches me.

"No! You may not hit me." He winds up for another strike, but I intercept his hand mid-swing. "No, Henry!"

He kicks my face, causing me to scream more out of shock than pain. Still dazed, he sinks his teeth into my arm, drawing blood.

"Oh my god, look what you did!" I shout, releasing him.

I retreat from his room, slamming the door behind me. In the bathroom, my reflection in the mirror reveals my flushed cheeks and hair tangled in syrup, making me look like a mad woman. He's probably terrified of me. I splash cold water on my face and frantically try to pull my unruly hair into a ponytail, but it's useless. I'm on the verge of a nervous breakdown.

Upon reentering Henry's room, an overpowering stench fills the air, leaving no room for doubt that he has shit his pants. Again. He's just about to put his hands down his pants.

"No!!!" I scream, startling him. Our eyes lock, and an unsettling grin creeps across his face.

He shoves his hand in. Panicked, I scoop him up, rush into the bathroom, and hold his clenched fist over the toilet, demanding he release it. I apply pressure to his wrist until he opens his hand, letting the unsightly lump fall into the bowl. Before I can reach for a wipe, Henry smears his shit-covered hand on my shirt. The sight and smell make my stomach churn, and I turn away, gagging into the toilet.

chapter twelve

Henry's behavior has been night and day for the last two weeks. He acts like an angel with Drew but is a devil for me. This situation has pushed me to the edge, leaving me nervous and anxious. My hands shake, my heart races and my hair is falling out at an alarming rate. It's like Henry is purposely torturing me.

Due to Henry's unpredictable actions, we packed away most of the breakable items in the kitchen and secured all the sharp knives. As a result, our cupboards now resemble a Target store's well-stocked plastic products aisle.

Once a tranquil haven, our house has gone through a troubling transformation. The cozy and inviting atmosphere now feels gloomy. Random scribbles of graffiti cover the walls. The carpets are worn with stains, evidence of numerous "accidents." Colorful toys have invaded and are scattered everywhere. I used to take pride in keeping my space clean and organized, but now I've given in to the constant chaos—too exhausted to care anymore.

Work is daunting. I'm so far behind I can't even see the finish line. Deadlines are coming up fast, and my once-effective task management skills are failing me.

Helen drops by to check in on us. Henry behaves well with Drew at home, and she is pleased with his progress. I wrote down some of the issues I've been facing with Henry and hand her the paper, mentioning we've had a few challenges. Helen glances over it, acknowledging that some problems are inevitable. She remains relaxed and unconcerned, smiling as she watches Henry and Drew build a Lego tower.

DREW TOOK the day off from work so we could both take Henry to his first day of preschool.

When we arrive at the school, Henry grabs Drew's hand, and they race to the front door together. I call out, "Just one picture!" They turn back with big smiles, and I quickly snap a photo capturing their excitement.

Once inside, we walk Henry to his classroom, where Miss Luna, his teacher, greets him with a warm smile. We linger uncertainly until Miss Luna reassures us it's okay to leave. We step out of the room, and I glance back to see Henry playing with the train track, his face lit up with joy. Relief washes over me, and I know we made the right decision.

Back at home, Drew and I shower together, something we haven't done since Henry became a part of our family. Afterward, we make love, enjoying the closeness. We cuddle in bed, and I reluctantly remind Drew I'm supposed to be working.

"Just five more minutes, amore." He holds me close, and I melt back into his arms.

My phone rings, and my first instinct is to ignore it. Whoever's calling can wait. But then Drew's phone begins to ring, too. He picks up. Miss Luna is on the other end, her voice so loud I can hear the conversation. She requests that we come to the school immediately to pick Henry up. Drew attempts to ask about the situation, but she refuses to go into detail. She only says that Henry is okay but to please hurry.

On the way, my mind races, conjuring up different scenarios about what went wrong. The possibilities are endless, and my imagination runs wild.

At the school, a staff member shows us the room where they have Henry. My heart drops when I look through the window. Henry sits on the floor, repeatedly hitting his head against a wall covered in exercise mats. He assures us they are using the padded room for Henry's safety as he leads us down the hallway to a door labeled "Principal Jones." Heading to the principal's office on the first day of school isn't entirely surprising, but still, my heart hammers in my chest.

"Hello, Mr. and Mrs. King. Please take a seat," Principal Jones warmly greets us, pointing to the chairs across from her desk. "We had an incident today. Henry and another student were playing with the train set. When the child wouldn't share, Henry grabbed the track from her hand and hit her with it, causing a cut on her cheek. Miss Luna attempted to de-escalate the situation, and Henry bit her on the arm."

My cheeks burn with embarrassment. "Oh my god, I'm so sorry."

Principal Jones delivers the next piece of news in a heavy tone: "We've decided to suspend Henry for two weeks in light of the violent incident. Our school maintains a strict zero-tolerance policy for such behavior." The words hit me like a punch to the gut. I glance at Drew, who mouths, "two weeks," with a questioning look.

Drew brings Henry to his classroom to pick up his stuff, and I head outside to call Dr. Wilson. Dr. Wilson agrees to meet with Henry during his afternoon lunch break. As Drew and Henry leave the building, Henry smiles, holding Drew's hand in the parking lot.

"What happened today?" Drew asks while securing Henry into his car seat.

"Nothing," Henry says.

"I heard you hit a friend with a toy," I chime in.

Silence.

"Go to park?" Henry asks Drew.

"Sorry, buddy. Mommy needs to go home and work. Before we go to Dr. Wilson's office, you and I are going to the library to read some books."

"Okay." Of course, Henry complies with Drew.

Later that afternoon, Dr. Wilson calls and puts me on speakerphone to join the conversation with Drew.

"I wanted to touch base with you both," Dr. Wilson says. "We've discussed Henry's behavior at school. While it's not unexpected for a child with Henry's past to act out, the lengthy suspension is unfortunate. Today, he learned that if he misbehaves, Drew will come and pick him up, and they will spend the day together. It's not much punishment for Henry, considering his dad is his favorite person.

"In light of Henry's continued problematic behavior, I would like you to consult a pediatric psychiatrist for a second opinion. I hope you don't mind, but I contacted a respected colleague. She has an available slot this Friday to evaluate Henry," Dr. Wilson shares. "Dr. Laura Shepard is recognized worldwide for her research on early childhood trauma and cognitive development. She is the founder of Radiant Minds Center of Psychology. We are fortunate to have her state-of-the-art facility in this area. Families have traveled great distances to meet with her.

"And one final suggestion," Dr. Wilson continues. "Installing a video monitoring system in your home to record Henry's disruptive behavior would be beneficial for Dr. Laura and her team. It can be challenging for children to express their true selves in a clinical setting. Capturing Henry's reactions to various situations through cameras in his home will facilitate a more genuine evaluation of his responses."

The constant knot in my stomach starts to loosen as hope for Henry's future emerges. Despite all the issues we've faced, I'm not ready to give up. I still believe Henry can have a fulfilling life with Drew and me as his parents. I have confidence in Dr. Wilson's advice, as he has been an invaluable source of support for our family.

DREW AND Henry return with high-tech camera equipment. Henry sticks close to Drew as he installs the cameras: one in each bedroom, one in the kitchen, one in the hallway, two in the living room, and one in the backyard. Once Henry is in bed for the night, we download the corresponding app and link it to our smartphones.

"Maybe we should try out the cameras." Drew gives me a suggestive wink.

I offer him a weak smile. "Not tonight. Let me work on my acting skills before my debut."

Exhausted, I lean in to give Drew a quick kiss on the cheek before wrapping the blankets around me. The only thing I want right now is a night of uninterrupted sleep.

chapter thirteen

The following morning, I abruptly sit up in bed, my heart pounding like a drum. It takes me a moment to understand why. Henry is standing in my room, wearing a creepy grin. He holds Drew's old fishing knife in his small hand.

Suddenly, I'm more awake than ever. I slip out of bed slowly, not wanting to alarm him. Henry turns around and bolts out of the room, his manic laughter reverberating down the hallway. Chasing him into the living room, I trip over an unexpected obstacle—Drew's old tackle box. Hooks and lures scatter, turning the floor into a minefield.

Ignoring the pain in my knee, I scramble to my feet. "Henry, you've got to give me the knife! It's not safe!"

He runs around the sofa, jabbing at the cushions, leaving significant holes in the fabric. His amusement intensifies, seemingly fueled by the havoc he's creating. In a desperate attempt, I threaten to call Drew, but Henry ignores me. He heads toward the recliner and cuts through its back, a surprised expression crossing his face as he realizes the extent of the damage he's causing.

Panic begins to overwhelm me when Drew bursts through

the door, shouting, "Give me the knife!" A flicker of fear flashes across Henry's face as he drops it and runs.

"How did you know?" My voice trembles.

"I was showing the guys at the station our video system, and one of them said, 'Isn't that your kid with a knife?' I couldn't believe it and rushed home. I didn't think about stowing my tackle box where Henry couldn't reach it. I'm sorry, Charlotte," he says, pulling me into a hug.

Drew leads me to our bedroom, assuring me he will take care of everything. Over the next hour, he goes through our house, removing anything that could be used as a weapon. As I watch him locking items into the safe in his closet, I reflect on how my life has changed. My mind fills with doubt, making me wonder if I'll ever be a good mom. Perhaps I'm more like my mother than I realize.

Our circumstances feel like a mistake, and living like this indefinitely is unimaginable. But it's difficult to justify being selfish enough to consider sending Henry away, which would only add to the list of people who have disappointed him. Drew's love for Henry is undeniable, and it's clear Henry loves Drew. I hope Henry grows closer to me soon because I'm not sure how much more I can handle.

THE NEXT day, while Drew is at work, Henry smears shit on his bedroom walls. As I clean the mess, he knocks over all my potted plants, scattering soil and leaves everywhere. Overwhelmed, I kneel on the floor, tears streaming down my cheeks as I try to scoop up the dirt with shaky hands. I wipe my tears, spreading a mud mask across my face. Seeing my distress, Henry laughs.

I flip the television to Henry's favorite show, fully aware that rewarding his misbehavior isn't the best way to handle things. I just don't have the energy to engage in another power struggle.

When I finish cleaning, I plop beside Henry on the couch, but he moves further away. I look over at him. He looks so tiny in the oversized *Paw Patrol* t-shirt Drew's parents sent. He has been through a lot in his short life; perhaps, with time, he'll find a way to trust me.

Since Drew has to work late tonight, I make Henry's favorite meal and let him eat in front of the TV in hopes of a peaceful evening. I sit at the opposite end of the couch, staring into the distance.

In just three days, we've recorded hours of video capturing Henry's erratic behavior. The distressing footage includes scenes of Henry holding the knife, moments of him banging his head against the floor, instances of him hitting and kicking me, and the disturbing image of him smearing shit on the walls. Drew watches it in horror, and I think he finally understands the challenging reality of my daily life when he's away at work.

chapter fourteen

We drive to the Radiant Minds Center of Psychology early Friday morning to meet with Dr. Laura. A young man, Josh, greets us at the entrance of the building. He welcomes Henry with a high-five, eliciting a slight smile.

Josh guides us through several hallways until we reach a spacious playroom. He suggests Henry take a look around. Henry hesitates, staring into the open space, which is vibrant and welcoming. The walls are painted with whimsical murals of playful animals and landscapes. Various toys fill the area: soft, oversized blocks, a miniature playhouse with bright curtains, a large racetrack, and a rainbow-colored tunnel.

Drew leads Henry to the track, knowing it will be his top choice. The strategy pays off, and Henry gradually relaxes, joining a research student in racing the cars. Drew asks Henry if he can play for a bit so the grown-ups can chat. He agrees with a slight nod.

Josh leads us to a room next to the main area. As we enter, Dr. Laura welcomes us. She's a middle-aged woman with salt-and-pepper, curly hair framing her face. She's wearing an open white lab coat, showing off a tailored pantsuit underneath. Glasses, held by a sparkling chain, rest on her chest. While she radiates professionalism, her overall demeanor is warm and friendly.

Accompanying her are several young adults whom she introduces as her research students. One holds a notebook, observing Henry through a two-way mirror, jotting down everything he does. The others stand close by, enthusiastic and eagerly awaiting Dr. Laura's guidance.

"It's so nice to meet you." Dr. Laura reaches out her hand to shake mine and Drew's.

"Dr. Wilson spoke highly of the work you've been doing," I say.

"That's wonderful. I'm thrilled you're here. Please take a seat." She motions towards some chairs by the window overlooking the play area. "I've devoted my life to the study of human behavior. Through my extensive research, I've unearthed a solution offering families with vulnerable children newfound hope. My revolutionary study centers on a participant pool of children who've undergone profound traumas in the initial three years of their lives. Giving a child like Henry the opportunity to participate in this innovative program will transform his life and the lives of many others facing similar struggles."

The room goes quiet as we all take a moment to watch Henry through the two-way mirror. He appears tiny and adorable, darting from one activity to the next with barely a moment's pause to consider the toys and games available. A pleasant-looking young woman sits in the center of the space, trying to chat with him. Henry doesn't respond or acknowledge her.

"Today, our first step is to observe Henry during playtime." Dr. Laura breaks the silence, her voice authoritative yet reassuring.

"For the initial hour, he can do as he pleases, allowing us valuable insights into how his brain functions. Our team will document all of Henry's actions for thorough analysis.

"After the free-play session, I will introduce specific tasks for him to complete. Then, I'll present a challenge. One of my students will restrict Henry from engaging with something he desires. We will monitor his reactions throughout the process to gain a deeper understanding of the functionality of his brain.

"You have the freedom to come and go as you wish. Your day pass will allow you access to the building. I suggest taking breaks during the day, as certain aspects will be challenging to witness," Dr. Laura cautions. "From the videos you've shared, it's evident that Henry is prone to episodes of rage. There may be a need to restrain Henry for his safety but rest assured, I don't take such measures lightly and strive to avoid them whenever possible. Do you have any questions before we begin?"

"After today, will you know how to help him?" Drew's voice is filled with hope.

"Yes, I'm confident that we can formulate a treatment plan following today's observations. We will reconvene later, and I'll provide you with my recommendations."

Dr. Laura touches my arm, meeting my eyes. "I understand what you've been dealing with has been incredibly challenging, perhaps even feeling insurmountable. You are here now because I can offer the assistance your family requires. Please don't worry. Why don't you take a break and grab a snack? I'll take it from here." She stands and exits the room.

Drew holds his hand out to help me up. He wraps me in a hug as a rush of emotions overwhelms me. It is a relief to have someone with her expertise acknowledge my experiences with Henry.

"It's going to be alright, amore," Drew says, rubbing my back.

"What if it doesn't work?" I mumble into his chest. "Our adoption date is coming up, and I can't imagine not adopting him, but I also can't keep living the way we have been. I'm at my breaking point." The words pour out of me, spoken aloud for the first time.

"We can help him, Charlotte." Drew releases his embrace, holding me by the shoulders to look into my eyes. "We have the leading team in the world for kids like Henry helping him right now. After you went to bed last night, I spent hours researching Dr. Laura; her work is remarkable. I found quotes from parents whose children she treated. Those kids are leading happy, fulfilling lives. I know there's hope for Henry." He pulls me into another hug and suggests we get some fresh air.

We walk downtown and end up at MadCap Coffee. We bring our drinks to one of the outdoor tables, soaking up the perfect weather while people-watching. After two hours, we decide to head back to check on Henry.

Drew uses our key card to enter the building and leads me down the hallway. He opens what we think is the observation room door, but we quickly realize our mistake. This room is well-lit, with a green screen dominating the back wall. There's a room resembling a nursery, a cozy living room, and a kitchen.

"This is weird. What do you think this space is used for?" I ask.

"Maybe a film class?" Drew says, and it sounds more like a

question than a statement.

Exiting, we wander in the maze of hallways for several minutes before finding the door to the observation room. As soon as we step inside, Henry's blood-curdling screams greet us. Looking through the two-way mirror, we witness a scene of chaos.

Henry is hurling objects at a research student, who skillfully dodges each one. The room echoes with Henry's deep growls, sounding like the cries of a wild animal. The student stays calm and attempts to talk to him, but he continues throwing blocks at her. Henry eventually falls to the floor, thrashing, kicking, and banging his head against the ground. While I've witnessed similar behavior from him at home, I will never get used to seeing him like this.

A muscular man enters the room. In a matter of seconds, he skillfully restrains Henry. Despite his imposing size, he handles Henry with care. Speaking to Henry in a steady voice, he explains the need for restraint. At first, Henry resists, but the man continues holding him, unfazed.

As time passes, Henry regains control over his emotions, his chaotic outbursts subside, and he becomes calmer. It's then that I notice Henry has wet his pants. The man remains unruffled and offers Henry the choice to change into dry clothes, but Henry is silent. Releasing his grip, he allows Henry to sit on the floor. As the man leaves the room, a female student enters to take charge.

She asks Henry to get the yellow ball from the ball pit, trying to tempt him with the promise of a small package of fruit snacks. Henry turns down her offer and chucks various balls at her head instead. A male student walks into the room and asks

Henry to join him in coloring until lunchtime. Henry agrees, choosing a red crayon from the bin. The student tries to engage in light conversation, but Henry does not speak. His sole focus is on filling his paper with angry red scribbles.

I glance over at Drew. He's sitting in a chair, his face buried in his palms—silent tears escape between his fingers. I rush to him, placing my hands on his shoulders.

He looks up and meets my gaze, his eyes filled with grief. "I saw how he acted in the camera footage, but I didn't fully accept it," he says, wiping the tears from his eyes. "What are we going to do?"

"We will do whatever it takes to help Henry." It feels good to be the one providing support this time. I feel a weight lifting off my shoulders as Drew witnesses firsthand just how troubled Henry is.

A different male student enters with Henry's lunch and convinces him to change into dry clothes. While Henry eats, Drew and I decide to take a break. We find a cozy restaurant, hoping that a change of scenery will provide some relief from the intensity of the situation we've just experienced.

The sound of clinking silverware and the soft murmurs of other diners create a background for our shared contemplation. I can't help but replay Henry's erratic behavior in my mind. Every now and then, I look at Drew. He hasn't touched his meal, lost in his own worries and thoughts.

chapter fifteen

Upon our return, Dr. Laura is waiting in the observation room. She invites us to have a seat. "I won't mince words. Based on my evaluation, I suspect Henry's condition falls under Reactive Attachment Disorder, or RAD for short. Although the DSM-5 doesn't specify severity levels, my assessment suggests that Henry's case is on the severe end of the spectrum."

"What do you mean?" Drew asks, his eyebrows knit together.

Dr. Laura responds with warmth in her eyes, saying, "The DSM-5 is the current manual of mental health disorders. RAD occurs in children who don't develop connections with their caregivers during their first three years. When a baby is neglected, abused, or separated from their primary caregivers, it can lead to problems in how they behave, regulate emotions, and relate to others as they grow up.

"I've carefully considered this diagnosis after thoroughly examining Henry's history notes and reviewing the surveillance videos. When a child has severe RAD, their social relationships are, for the most part, impossible. They exhibit mannerisms differing from age-appropriate norms. Things like acts of violence towards themselves and others, resistance to close interactions, and an inability to form friendships. Children with RAD at Henry's level often persist in unpleasant behaviors well into their adolescence, such as smearing fecal matter and destroying objects. In many cases, parents put locks on their doors to ensure their own sleep," she says gravely.

I twist my hands in my lap, tears filling my eyes. The articles I read about RAD while researching how to help Henry haunt my thoughts.

"Can he be cured?" Drew's voice still carries hope.

"Children showing mild RAD symptoms can improve, but in my two decades of working with cases as intense as Henry's, I've never seen them go on to live a normal life. Being a functioning adult involves having compassion and forming connections with family, community, and friends. People who struggle to create these attachments and express empathy engage in unregulated, negative behavior. Most children who experienced early trauma as severe as Henry land in the criminal justice system by the time they are teenagers."

I'm reluctant to accept Dr. Laura's assessment. "What about Henry's attachment to Drew? That proves he can form a bond with someone."

"I don't perceive that as a healthy attachment. Children with RAD often manipulate one family member, using charm to gain control. This is a common symptom, and it can create chaos in the household when one caregiver is treated very differently from the other. This video will help clarify my observations regarding his connection to Drew." Dr. Laura taps a link on her iPad. Henry is eating animal crackers with Josh.

Josh asks, "Do you like your snack?"

"Yes," Henry replies.

"What else do you like?"

"Cookies."

"Anything else?"

"Ice cream and *Paw Patrol*."

"Those are nice things. What about people? Are there people you like?"

"No."

"What about your Dad?"

Henry gazes into space and remains silent.

Josh asks, "What if your dad fell and got hurt?"

Henry's eyes narrow, his lips curling into a sinister grin. "It funny."

Dr. Laura stops the video. "This clip offers a glimpse into Henry's true feelings about Drew."

One look at Drew tells me he's devastated. My heart aches for him because I know how much he loves Henry. "What can we do?" I ask.

"I am so glad you asked. I have created a method to heal Henry's mind, enabling him to connect with both of you and others," Dr. Laura shares enthusiastically. This treatment approach resembles EMDR, which facilitates the processing of traumatic experiences within a secure and nurturing setting.

"Essentially, it's rewriting how the brain and body experienced past trauma," she explains after seeing our confused expressions. "My extensive research has shown that we can apply a similar method of reframing traumatic events with children who have endured severe abuse in their formative years. Currently, Henry's brain lacks the pathway that forms a healthy attachment. Typically, someone comes to their aid whenever a baby cries, addressing the issue and offering comfort and love. The baby becomes attached to their caregiver, developing empathy for them.

"In 1975, Edward Tronick conducted the 'Still Face Experiment.' This fascinating study involved mothers and their babies. When the mothers were happy, the babies also showed signs of happiness. When the mothers displayed sadness, the babies made repeated efforts to cheer her up. Initially, the baby would smile, but if the mother remained unresponsive, the baby gave up, becoming sad and often crying. It's important to note that the babies were well-fed, not tired, and surrounded by things they enjoyed, like a bouncy chair and pleasant music. Despite these comforts, they still cried when their mother appeared unhappy. This experiment highlights that babies start to understand and share the feelings of others from a very young age.

"Henry's brain did not develop the typical pathways due to the abuse he endured. He never felt love, which means he cannot express love. This is one of the most devastating diagnoses a person can receive, suggesting a life filled with emptiness. However, I have dedicated countless hours to developing a revolutionary cure for children like Henry. This goes beyond treating the symptoms. I will reprogram his mind, making him believe he was loved and cared for as a baby."

"How?" Drew asks, his voice carries a mixture of hope and disbelief.

"Allow me to start by posing a question," Dr. Laura says, her eyes brightening. "Are you aware that each time you recall a memory, it is altered?"

"What do you mean?" Drew asks.

"Suppose you visited a theme park with your dad as a child and later wrote about the experience. You would describe the events as they happened. Now, let's imagine that ten years down the road, you discovered your dad had been having an affair, and he had brought his mistress to the park with you that day. With this knowledge, remembering that day would alter your initial memory. This effect would be even more pronounced if you had witnessed your mom suffering as a result of your dad's infidelity. So, despite the actual events of an enjoyable day with your dad, your perspective as you've grown older has led to a different recollection of the event. Every time you go back to a memory, you modify it."

I have to admit her explanation is logical.

Dr. Laura continues, "My goal is to reshape Henry's formative years by incorporating your caring and loving parenting from birth. I will create a scenario where you've always been his parents, ensuring his physical well-being and surrounding him with the unconditional love he should have received from the beginning."

One look at Drew, and I can tell his wheels are turning. "How do you plan to do that?" I ask, reluctant to get ahead of ourselves.

"The process involves multiple steps and will require dedication. The effort invested at this stage will be crucial in ensuring Henry leads a gratifying and productive life. Our primary goal is to recreate situations involving both of you that should have naturally occurred in Henry's early life. We will seamlessly integrate Henry into your home videos and photographs, reenacting the scenes as needed. As he watches the movies, you'll emphasize that it's you and Henry in those special moments and how meaningful those days were to you. His mind won't distinguish that these events did not happen. He'll begin to develop the belief he was nurtured and loved. It's remarkable how the brain can adapt and evolve, forging the right neural pathways for Henry to establish genuine connections, develop empathy, and have the capacity to experience and express love," Dr. Laura concludes, her eyes reflecting confidence.

Her proposal catches me off guard. She frames it as the only way for Henry to lead a normal life. While I understand the importance of helping him, this strikes me as morally questionable. I shift my focus to Drew, who looks spellbound, soaking up every word.

"So you're saying he'll forget about his mother and the abuse he suffered?" Drew asks, his voice filled with eagerness.

"In a sense, yes, that is precisely what I am saying. Positive memories will replace the traumatic ones, causing them to be deeply buried. If any negative memories resurface, you can attribute them to something Henry saw on TV. He will accept it, given that his childhood has been centered around the love you both have offered, and he will have numerous new cherished memories to draw upon."

"Is it ethical to change someone's memories?" I am uneasy about altering Henry's life story so significantly.

"To be honest, this is a complex issue. In the past, a number of psychological experiments were considered unethical. Still, we gained valuable insights from those studies and the individuals willing to participate. Some people question the morality of EMDR, as it involves altering how individuals process traumatic events. However, it's rewriting those events that make them less distressing.

"So, I ask you, was it morally justified for Henry to undergo abuse, neglect, and a lack of love? Henry had no say in those circumstances, and now he confronts a life burdened with suffering. When we reflect on what matters, it's not our jobs or homes but our connections with people. Without this intervention, Henry will be deprived of such experiences—he won't encounter genuine love or meaningful friendships."

I must admit, she's very persuasive, and judging by Drew's expression, it looks like he's already on board with this plan. However, I'm still undecided. "Has this worked in the past?" I ask, needing more clarity.

"Henry would be our fifth child. Three have surpassed our expectations, while one child's outcome was inconclusive due to the parents' inability to complete the work. This leads me to clarify that this process will involve certain challenges. You will need to move to a different location and explore new job opportunities. Also, the cooperation of your entire family and close friends is essential. It won't be successful if even one person is unwilling to participate, so you may have to consider letting some people in your life go. Allow me to show you some remarkable results through a video," Dr. Laura says, not waiting for a response as she presses a button on her iPad.

A young boy who looks a lot like Henry appears on the screen. He's furious, hitting and kicking a woman in one scene. Another clip shows him smearing feces on the walls and screaming—mirroring Henry's behavior. The video transitions, showing a scene six months later. In this new footage, the boy is cozied up with the woman, reading a book together. He kisses her cheek sweetly and says, "I love you, Mommy."

Emotion washes over me, tears welling up in my eyes. I would do anything to have Henry act like that toward me. Dr. Laura's words linger in my mind—who gets to decide what's morally right or wrong? If this experiment can give Henry a happy, successful life, isn't it worth facing any challenges on the journey?

"This is a lot to process. Please, take the time you need to consider it," Dr. Laura says.

"What about the cost?" I ask.

"We've obtained a grant, so our services won't impose any financial burden on you, except for relocation expenses. I believe enabling Henry to have the life he deserves is priceless." Dr. Laura smiles before changing the subject. "We will initiate the process of crafting videos, scrapbooks, and photos for you to share with Henry after his adoption. According to your records, you expect to finalize the adoption in less than a month. Is that accurate?"

"Yes," Drew and I say in unison.

Another question pops into my mind. "What about Henry's scars? Won't they be a constant reminder of his past abuse?"

"I am so glad you asked about that. I had the team create this for you for today." Dr. Laura hands me a photo of Henry covered in calamine lotion. In the image, he is being held and rocked by someone with their head turned, but it could easily be me.

"In Henry's modified memories, he endured a severe case of chickenpox," Dr. Laura says solemnly. "This photo shows you providing care and affection while he dealt with this common childhood ailment."

I stare at the picture; its realness almost makes me believe that I cared for Henry during his illness.

"As I mentioned, this is quite a lot to process," Dr. Laura interrupts my thoughts. "Please take the time to research. I also recommend reading some books on the subject of RAD. I suggest starting with *but, he spit in my coffee,* by Keri Williams." She jots the title down and passes me the slip of paper.

"Take the time to process with one another and reach out to your family members who will play a role in Henry's life to gauge their willingness to support the treatment plan. Your decision should not be taken lightly. It will entail a significant shift in your life, and the initial phase might be challenging. Henry could resist these implanted memories before fully accepting them as the truth. However, once the new memories are established in Henry's mind, his strong-willed nature will lead him to believe in their authenticity."

"Can I talk to a family who has undergone the treatment?" I ask. I want to trust this could work for us, but my gut still tells me otherwise.

"Certainly, I will arrange the necessary permissions for you to speak with one of our participating families. I don't want to rush you; however, we must act quickly to help Henry. Each day he recalls his past suffering is another day we'll need to rework. This treatment becomes impossible once he reaches the age of four. If we want the best possible outcome for Henry, we must begin now. I'll need your decision within a week to start the process. Here is some reading material to assist you in deciding," she concludes, handing me a folder.

Drew reaches out to shake Dr. Laura's hand. "Thank you so much for everything you have done to help us today."

Josh and Henry meet us in the hallway. Drew bends to Henry's level and asks, "How did it go, buddy?"

"Good."

"You're wearing different pants. What happened?" I ask.

Without missing a beat, Henry says, "I spilled my milk."

The ride home is silent, each of us absorbed in our own thoughts. The unspoken tension hangs heavy in the air.

chapter sixteen

I'm glad Drew doesn't have to work this weekend, so we can catch up on chores and keep researching. After an early dinner, Drew takes Henry out for errands and to play at the park to wear him out. He falls asleep quickly when Drew puts him to bed. With Henry settled, we sit at the kitchen table with the information Dr. Laura gave us and our laptops, ready to begin our research.

I start the conversation, "I'm uncomfortable altering Henry's memories."

"Me too, but his memories are terrible. If someone could erase all your awful experiences, wouldn't you want them to?"

"You have a point. But wouldn't all the good memories disappear with the bad?"

Drew sighs. "Henry doesn't have good memories."

"He had Tom."

"Tom was paid to be kind to Henry."

"I doubt Tom's pay rate included kind acts. He genuinely cared for Henry, and I'm certain Henry loved him back."

"Instead of remembering a man just doing his job, we can give Henry memories of a loving family," Drew says, trying to convince me.

"Yeah, you're right," I agree, making Drew grin.

"Can I get that in writing?" He refers to a joke from our earlier days before kissing the top of my head and heading to the fridge. "I believe working with Dr. Laura is the best decision, and we're lucky to have her right here in our city. It's a sign from the universe, amore." He hands me a glass of wine.

Drew suggests learning more about reactive attachment disorder. While he pours himself some of his favorite whiskey, I find a YouTube video where parents share their experiences with children affected by RAD.

Thirty minutes in, Drew presses the pause button and goes to refill both of our glasses. "Maybe this wasn't the best place to start. Each story is worse than the last."

I take a long sip before showing Drew the comments section. Scrolling through, we read messages from other families about their heartbreaking situations and their sadness about being unable to help their children. Some recount disturbing details of their child harming pets or threatening to hurt other family members. Many talk about the harsh truth that older kids with RAD often end up in institutional care. We also find comments from individuals living with the disorder. They share their struggles to build meaningful connections or nurturing relationships as adults.

"This is worse than I thought it would be. I can't imagine this being Henry's life or ours," Drew says, pouring us another drink.

"We should read the book Dr. Laura recommended. It might help us better understand what we're dealing with."

We bring our drinks to bed, and I purchase the e-book. Cozy and with a slight alcohol-induced brain fog, Drew dozes off before I finish reading him the first chapter. His breathing becomes steady, his face softens, and he appears years younger. I tuck the covers around him and continue reading.

The child in the book reminds me of Henry. He's well-behaved with his dad but a terror for his mom. She repeatedly tries to enlist her husband's help, but it doesn't work. Their son's aggression goes from bad to downright terrifying. The boy is institutionalized multiple times, but he never gets better and is unable to lead a normal life. All of the information makes my head throb. I lay awake for another hour, seriously considering the treatment Dr. Laura has recommended for Henry. Eventually, I fall asleep, only to dream of Henry trying to kill me.

I JOLT awake just before I hit the ground below—a tiny shadowed figure pushed me from the thirteenth floor of an abandoned hotel. Laying still, I take several deep breaths to bring myself back to reality—it was just a nightmare.

The familiar sound of the washing machine tells me Henry had another accident. Drew and Henry are busy building massive Lego towers in the living room. I go to the kitchen for coffee and stop at the hall closet for fresh sheets.

While making Henry's bed, I lift the mattress and see Drew's pocket knife on the boxspring with the blade open. Even though the knife is small, finding it under Henry's mattress sends an unsettling chill through my body. I call out to Drew, urgently asking him to come to Henry's room.

"Are you okay?" Henry is right beside him, curiosity on his

face.

I discreetly show the knife to Drew. "I thought you took care of everything."

Drew runs his hand through his hair. "I'm sorry. I thought I did." His regret is unmistakable.

Drew turns his attention to Henry, crouching to meet him at eye level. "Why is my pocket knife under your mattress?"

"Kill the monster."

"What monster?"

"Mommy."

Horrified, I ask, "You want to kill me?"

Henry points at me. "You bad."

"Henry, Mommy is not bad. Why would you think that?"

"No cookies."

Drew doesn't hide his surprise. "You want to hurt Mommy just because she won't give you cookies?"

"Yes."

"Mommy is nice. She loves you. You don't really want to kill mommy, do you?" Desperation creeps into Drew's voice.

Henry's lips curl upward into a devious grin. "No, Daddy. Won't hurt Mommy," he says before darting out of the room.

Drew hugs me and apologizes once more before going to check on Henry.

I return to the kitchen, double-checking for any sharp objects we might have missed when we thought we hid all the knives. I collect the corkscrew, letter opener, and several other things Henry might use as weapons and lock them into the safe.

I text Drew, " I need a break. I'm going to get some fresh air. I'll be back later." He texts back a thumbs up and a heart emoji.

Returning from my walk, I find a note from Drew on the counter, saying he and Henry are running errands and will pick up something for dinner. He included a heart with our initials inside. I pour myself a glass of wine and relax on the couch with my feet up, attempting to watch an episode of *House Hunters*. But my mind refuses to focus on the show. All I can think about is how much my life has changed in the past month. Instead of enjoying a cozy evening with Drew, sharing a bowl of popcorn, and watching the latest movie, I'm alone, contemplating how we ended up here.

Drew and Henry return with our favorite pizza for dinner. Henry smiles when I propose watching *Paw Patrol: The Movie* while we eat—his eyes never leave the screen. Drew takes care of putting Henry to bed, and I continue researching. Once Henry is asleep, Drew joins me at the kitchen table to discuss our next steps.

In a quiet voice, I share my fear with Drew, telling him I'm scared of Henry.

He places his hand over mine. "I think we should discuss this with our families to get everyone on the same page. We need to consider Dr. Laura's offer for help because I don't see any other option."

I have another option, but I don't say anything, knowing how much Drew wants things to work out with Henry.

The first call we make is to Drew's sister, Emily. We lay out all the challenges we've been dealing with and Henry's diagnosis. Drew shares that the only way for Henry to lead a normal life is through participating in a potentially controversial treatment. Emily responds with all the right words, showing her readiness to support us. She offers to send family videos from the past few years and mentions explaining the plan to her husband, Ryan. Since their kids, Amelia and Mason, are still so young, we're hopeful they'll easily buy into our story.

Next, we contact Drew's parents, who reassure us that they support our decision.

The final call I need to make is to my mother, and I dread it.

"I told you a used child would be no good," she says in a tight voice.

"Henry has been through a lot of abuse. Don't you think he deserves a chance to have a happy life?" I'm already frustrated.

"It's just like you, Charlotte, always trying to save every little broken thing. How many birds and butterflies did you try to nurse back to health?" Her tone is one of disapproval. She knows how to push my buttons.

"Dad taught me that because you were never around." I can't resist a jab.

"I had to work to support us," she counters. "Your dad was a deadbeat."

"Mother, I don't want to argue about the merits of the dead. Can you please help us with Henry? All I'm asking is for you to pretend that I gave birth to him. You've always been a fantastic actor, so this should be easy," I say, trying to hide my annoyance as I glance at Drew and roll my eyes. "I just need a few photos of you so they can add Henry as a baby. I would appreciate it if you could email or text them to me."

Though she hesitates, she eventually agrees. After hanging up, I reach for a bottle of wine.

Our next topic is moving. Dr. Laura clarified that it is a

crucial step to ensure Henry's new memories become firmly established. With no friends and on leave from work due to Henry's behavior issues, the move allows me to start fresh in a house untouched by an unruly three-year-old.

Drew discovers a job opening at a fire department in Traverse City, a couple of hours north of us. It's a beautiful resort town along the shores of Grand Traverse Bay, with gorgeous summers, harsh winters, and more snow than I'd like. However, it's a decent-sized town with plenty of resources for Henry. As we look into schooling options, we find a promising Montessori.

"How about this: if I get this job, it's a sign from the universe to go ahead with our plan. If I don't, we can look into other treatment options for Henry," Drew suggests. "Some families have tried intensive therapy, and their kids turned out okay-ish."

"Remember the video of the boy who had been in therapy for years, only for them to find out he was abusing the neighbor girl?" I remind him.

Drew grimaces, nodding his head. "If this job doesn't pan out, I'll explore other options."

"Do you think we should tell the agency that it might not work for him to stay with us?" The words slip out of my mouth before I can stop them. I blame the wine. Drew's expression immediately turns distressed, and I regret bringing it up.

Drew holds my hands in his, locking eyes with me. "Henry has already lost so much; he needs us. We can be the ones to save him. I know this process has been harder on you, but we can't turn our backs on him."

I know he's right. Tomorrow, we'll meet a family who participated in Dr. Laura's study. They live in Grand Ledge, and we've decided to meet halfway at a wild animal park. I'm feeling a mix of excitement and nervousness.

chapter seventeen

We meet Shelly Watkins at the park entrance. She is a petite woman with vibrant orange, curly hair. Her face lights up with a smile as she announces, "I'm a hugger," and embraces me.

She acts like we've been friends for years instead of just meeting. While we wander around the wild animal exhibits, Henry gets along well with her sons, Trevor and Cody. Shelly talks incessantly about her kids and the challenges of handling a hectic family life.

I am relieved when the boys beg to ride the children's train, hoping for a chance to ask more direct questions about Shelly's involvement with Dr. Laura. When the boys are securely on the train, we stand by the fence to supervise, and I ask how the treatment is working for them.

Shelly sighs but gives an encouraging smile before saying, "At first, I doubted it would make a difference. A month in, Trevor's behavior was still out of control. It felt like being trapped in a nightmare. He continued to do terrible things, mostly directed at his little brother. It got so bad that we had to move Cody's crib into our bedroom to keep Trevor from harming him at night.

The exhaustion took over, and I struggled to piece together any coherent thoughts."

Shelly waves to the kids as they pass by on the train before continuing, "Our situation was unique because we adopted both boys. Cody became part of our family when he was just one week old, while Trevor was already three. Their birth mother was an addict, living in poverty, and had untreated health issues. She died giving birth to Cody. Since he was with us from the start, there's only one video related to him. It shows me pregnant, with Trevor rubbing my belly. All the other materials focus on Trevor.

"We packed away everything from his past and replaced it with the things in the new pictures and videos. Initially, Trevor resisted watching the videos, but they continued to run on a loop morning to night. A breakthrough came with the baby book. Trevor had a preference for my husband, Eric, so he would sit and go through the book with him every night.

"After two months, the raging stopped, and Trevor stopped trying to harm his brother. Shortly after that, he snuggled with me and started calling me mommy. We enrolled him in school, and he did even better than we could have hoped. Trevor is a kind and caring boy, completely different from the troubled child he used to be." Shelly finishes her story with a warm smile, observing Trevor as he helps his younger brother climb off the train.

Drew suggests checking out the petting zoo, and the boys excitedly lead the way. While we walk, I ask Shelly if it was difficult to convince their families to participate in the study.

"My brother and sister had doubts, but their mindset changed when they saw Trevor's behavior on a family vacation.

After that, they were open to exploring any possible solutions. Eric's and my parents are supportive and help out a lot. My social media accounts are gone, and I've distanced myself from acquaintances. Luckily, I still have a couple of close friends I can rely on," Shelly says, mentioning that none of their new friends know the boys are adopted.

The kids enjoy petting the goats with the help of a young zoo volunteer, and I am happy to see Henry behaving so well.

"Did you guys move and find different jobs?" Drew asks.

"Eric got a new job, so we moved from Ohio to Michigan. I decided to leave mine to stay home with the boys."

From the corner of my eye, I notice Henry picking up a stick and swinging it at Cody. Drew rushes over, grabbing the stick away before Henry can take another swing.

"I'm sorry, but we should go," I say, observing Henry screaming and kicking Drew. "Thank you so much for taking the time to meet us; it means a lot."

"It was my pleasure. Feel free to reach out if you need anything or have more questions. It's been wonderful to talk with someone who truly understands."

Henry's screams echo the whole way to the car. I follow behind Drew, keeping my head down to avoid the stares from others. My face burns with embarrassment.

chapter eighteen

Drew's phone interview with the Traverse City fire station is successful, and they request to meet him in person. We turn the opportunity into a family day trip to check out the city.

The drive to Traverse is lovely, with Henry watching *Paw Patrol* episodes on his iPad the entire way. Drew leaves us at a park by the bay while he goes for his interview. The area is gorgeous, and being close to the water relaxes me. However, Henry plays for less than ten minutes before saying he's hungry.

I'm glad I brought snacks in my purse. I offer a few options, but Henry insists on cookies. I search my bag again and find Scooby Graham crackers, his favorite. However, when I show him the package, he screams, "NO!"

My attempts to reason with him prove futile, and he runs across the grass. I chase after him, almost catching up when I stumble on a dip in the lawn. As I fall, I hear a disturbing pop as my ankle twists. Collapsing in pain, I call out to Henry, but he ignores me and continues running. Stranded on the ground, unable to move, I burst into tears.

I'm startled by a deep voice asking if I'm okay. Looking up, I see an older gentleman in jogging gear. I express my concern for my son, gesturing towards Henry. Without hesitation, the man sprints across the field and soon returns, struggling to contain a screaming and kicking Henry in his arms.

He guides me to a picnic table, and I reassure him that my husband will be back any minute, so he doesn't need to wait around. The last thing I want is to have an awkward conversation with a stranger. After texting Drew to inform him of the situation, I let Henry watch videos on my phone, and it does the trick to calm him.

I don't think I've ever been happier to see Drew as he walks across the grass with his medical bag. My own personal fireman to the rescue. While he checks my ankle, I ask how the interview went. He tells me he's confident he will receive an offer and informs me that our next destination is the hospital.

I'm relieved to have only sprained my ankle. The doctor wraps it up, hands Drew an ice pack and gives me a pair of crutches. Drew suggests returning to Grand Rapids so I can rest at home, but I insist on looking around from the car, not wanting to waste the trip.

We grab burgers from a drive-thru and eat in the car while Drew takes us on a tour. Traverse City blends the warmth of a small town with stunning landscapes. The downtown area is welcoming and filled with local boutiques and cozy cafés. Neighborhoods differ; some have large, beautifully preserved historic homes or lakeside houses, which I'm sure are beyond our budget. However, the residential areas feature well-maintained, smaller homes and yards, giving me confidence that we can find a home that fits our needs and is affordable.

As we drive through the hills, passing gorgeous vineyards, I reach over to hold Drew's hand. Whether it's the breathtaking lake views, the quaint neighborhoods, or the effect of the pain pill, a sense of calm comes over me. I smile, bringing Drew's hand to my lips for a kiss. At this moment, I feel the start of a beautiful new chapter for our family.

chapter nineteen

The next day, Drew beams when he tells me he got the job. I want to be happy for him, but I feel nauseous. I try to reassure myself that it's just the anxiety of another change, but I question every choice we've made for the rest of the day. Following dinner, bathtime, and reading to Henry for over an hour, Drew and I collapse into bed.

The silence hangs thick in the air. I whisper, "Are we making the right decision?"

Drew turns towards me, taking my hand. "Yes. I'm confident we are."

The room seems to hold its breath as I wait for a revelation. Drew squeezes my hand, and we lock eyes, silently promising to always be there for each other.

The following day, I email Dr. Laura. She replies within minutes, expressing relief that we're giving Henry the childhood he deserves. She sends two pages of detailed instructions. By the end of the day, I have sent her numerous videos and photos featuring Drew, me, and our extended family.

FINALLY, THE day of our appointment with Dr. Laura is here. It's been four long days since we agreed to participate, and I've endured countless tantrums from Henry. As I get ready, I look at myself in the mirror and don't recognize the person I've become. I used to be full of energy, a busy professional with clean hair. Now, my hair is always in a ponytail, the bags under my eyes are like suitcases, and my wardrobe is pathetic—baggy sweats paired with my old GVSU sweatshirt. Today, I make an effort with some concealer and light blush before choosing a dress to wear. With my appetite almost gone, none of my pants fit properly.

A thick fog blankets our entire neighborhood, mirroring the grayness of my mood. Josh welcomes us at the front door of Radiant Minds Center of Psychology and leads us to the studio. This is the room Drew and I stumbled upon during our first visit, and now it makes sense. They used the photos of our home to recreate the area. In a corner is a bedroom, painted the same color as Henry's room in our house. There's a crib identical to the one I used to envision in my dreams. Shelves lined with books and firetrucks complete the scene. This would have been the perfect nursery for Henry if he had been ours from the beginning.

Josh tells us to let Henry check out the surroundings before leaving the room. Despite being the only ones in the area, I sense the presence of people on the other side of the walls and hear the hum of video equipment. It reminds me of the haunted house Drew brought me to one Halloween. He assured me it would be a blast—it wasn't.

Drew hands a stuffed bear to Henry, who hesitantly holds onto it while following Drew into the nursery. "Let's play make-believe," Drew says, lifting him into the crib.

Henry snuggles with the teddy bear and reclines for a moment. Drew sits and engages in a peek-a-boo game through the bars.

"Not baby, Daddy."

"I understand, buddy. I was just pretending. How about a snack?" Drew lifts him from the crib, sets him down, and takes his hand. He then guides him to the highchair in the kitchen area.

Henry comes to a sudden halt. "No baby chair!"

Drew lifts him, but Henry resists, kicking and screaming.

A cheerful young man walks in, carrying a colorful cake. "It's my birthday! If you sit in the chair, I'll light the candle, and you can help me blow it out." He lowers the cake so Henry can have a closer look. "What do you think? Are you interested?"

Henry eyes the cake suspiciously. He considers the chair and then the cake, taking some time to think, but eventually, he agrees. Drew picks him up and puts him in the highchair while the young man recommends putting on a shirt to avoid getting frosting on Henry's clothes. Before Henry can say anything, he slips a shirt over Henry's head. "One and Tons of Fun" is written in big letters across the front.

The young man says, "I heard your name is Henry. You won't believe it, but that's my name too!" He winks at us. "It's said to be bad luck to light your own candle. Dad, would you do me the honor?" He hands Drew the lighter and steps to the side.

Drew lights the wick and sets the cake on the highchair tray. We start singing "Happy Birthday." Henry stares at the cake and blows out the candle when we finish singing.

"Go ahead and eat some, buddy," the fake Henry instructs from the sidelines.

Henry hesitates momentarily, then lowers his face and takes a substantial bite from the top. Drew and I erupt in cheers and applause.

Drew cleans Henry up before lifting him from the seat. Henry starts running around the room in circles. I cross my fingers, hoping there won't be any more cake-related scenes. Fake Henry asks our Henry to help unwrap some gifts. The presents include building bricks suitable for toddlers, a ball, and a toy truck. Drew, Henry, and I sit on the floor, playing with the new toys for a while before being prompted to change activities.

Henry reaches a breaking point after enduring hours of wardrobe changes and set adjustments. I share his sentiment. I have no idea what my mother enjoyed about acting so much—it's exhausting. Drew takes Henry outside to the small playground for a much-needed break, and I head to the bathroom, locking myself in a stall. This process is getting to me. I'm glad Henry will have positive early childhood memories, but this charade is more than I expected, and it doesn't feel right.

Returning to a grand Thanksgiving feast for lunch, I poke at my food, trying to smile for the cameras. All I want is a nap after we eat, but instead, someone tells us to head to the living room. The space is a holiday wonderland. A large decorated tree stands in one corner, next to a fireplace that looks exactly like the one in our home. On the opposite side is a replica of the rocking chair from Henry's room. A strong feeling of déjà vu comes over me, and a shiver runs through me despite the warmth of the fire. We encourage Henry to place ornaments on the tree, including a first Christmas ornament I found on eBay with the correct year.

Dr. Laura's familiar voice instructs me to sit in the rocking chair with Henry. I do as she says, getting comfortable and inviting Henry to join me. He adamantly refuses, calling me a bad mom, and goes to Drew instead. Once again, I'm left deflated.

Dr. Laura enters from another room and announces, "I have an idea of how we can get Henry to settle down so we can get the needed photos."

"I doubt it's going to work. Henry and I aren't at the hold-and-rock stage in our relationship." A nervous giggle escapes. "Can you edit to make it look like I was holding him?" I ask, on the verge of tears.

"We can create images using a doll, but it would appear more genuine if Henry is on your lap." Dr. Laura dismisses my concerns. "For other clients, we've given a mild sedative to make the child more comfortable in front of the cameras."

"You drugged the children?" Alarm bells are ringing in my head.

"Of course not," Dr. Laura waves off my worry. "It's a mild sedative, similar to melatonin—nothing to be concerned about. It would be heartbreaking for Henry to wonder why his mommy never held him." In those few words, she has made me feel like the worst mom in the world.

"I guess you're right," I say, my voice shaking.

"Great. It's decided. Go ahead and get Henry his juice," she says triumphantly to the student beside her.

Dr. Laura gives me a document requesting my signature to approve the "medication." I sign the form while Drew smiles at me from across the room. I attempt to smile back, but the overwhelming sense of dread makes it impossible.

A student hands Henry some orange juice, and he calms down soon after drinking it. His steps slow, and his voice becomes a whisper. I pick him up, and he doesn't resist. Carrying him to the rocking chair, I cradle him and hum a lullaby my dad used to sing to me. Our eyes lock right before he drifts off to sleep. Tears roll down my cheeks as I kiss his forehead. Closing my eyes, I immerse myself in this moment, temporarily forgetting our situation. I hold Henry close, cherishing the warmth of his body against mine. These are the moments I envisioned when Drew and I decided to become parents.

As I open my eyes, they lock with Dr. Laura's, and the stark reality rushes back. I quickly look away, searching the room for Drew. When our eyes meet, he smiles at me from across the room. Shortly after, I am instructed to lay Henry in the crib for some sleeping photos. I place him on the mattress and sprint to the bathroom, where sobs escape me as I splash cold water on my face.

Drew meets me in the hall, smiling from ear to ear. "He connected with you."

"They drugged him, Drew."

"What do you mean?"

"Dr. Laura said what they gave him was similar to melatonin, but it was way stronger than that." The frustration is evident in my voice.

"Maybe it hit him harder than they expected."

I shake my head. Drew is oblivious, only seeing what he wants, and I'm left speechless.

Dr. Laura steps into the hallway with a big smile. "That

went well! We completed the studio portion of the process. The camera crew will come to your house next week to obtain the remaining necessary footage. Soon, we'll have a complete story of Henry's first years of life."

I'm glad it's over for today. Drew carries Henry to the car because he's too weak to walk. While driving home, I hold back my tears, not wanting to spoil Drew's good mood.

chapter twenty

Drew is at work the following day, and Henry is restless, venting his frustration throughout the day. I give in and let him watch his cartoons so I can steal a moment to close my eyes. Upon waking, I wipe the drool from the corner of my mouth and check my phone, realizing I dozed off longer than planned. Glancing at the end of the couch, Henry's spot is empty. Panic sets in as I search for him.

He's not in his room, the guest room, or the hall bathroom, leaving only our room. I open my bathroom door, and I'm shocked. My once tidy counter is a disaster—makeup is scattered everywhere. The counter is full of colors from my pricey palettes, and smudged handprints are all over the countertop. He poured the hand soap and lotions into the sink, creating an overpowering scent reminiscent of a funeral home.

"What the hell?" I shout.

Henry turns to me, his face beaming as he stands on the stool. "I make soup," he says, a sense of triumph in his voice and a mischievous sparkle in his eyes.

I grab Henry's arm and lead him to his room. With clenched teeth, I say, "Stay here while I clean up the mess you made."

I go back to the bathroom and throw all my products in the trash. I sit on the bathroom rug, trying to gain my composure. What does it matter anyway? With how things are going, I won't ever have a reason to wear makeup again.

Returning to Henry's room, I instantly smell urine. I grumble under my breath while removing the bedding and Henry's wet pants and underwear. I use baby wipes to clean him up before putting him in a pull-up. I can't deal with another "accident" today.

I tell him he has to come with me to put the sheets in the washing machine because I can't trust him. When I try to grab his hand, he screams. Ignoring his protests, I hold him sideways in one arm and carry the wet sheets in the other. Despite his attempts to escape, I keep going, and he hits his head on the hallway wall, making his cries even louder.

Once we're in the laundry room, I set Henry on the ground and load the bedding into the washer. He repeatedly bangs his head on the wall, leaving red marks on his forehead. I grab him, attempting to restrain him. He resists, trying to bite me, but I hold firm, insisting he settle down. I rock him, the washing machine humming in the background. Eventually, he relaxes. I carry him to the living room, turn on his favorite show, and collapse on the couch.

THE NEXT few days pass in a blur. One evening, there's a surprise visit from a state social worker who introduces herself as Ms. Mary. She looks like she stepped out of a JCPenney catalog that Drew's grandma used to keep in her bathroom.

I'm grateful Drew is home, and tonight's dinner is spaghetti,

Henry's favorite. She waits for Henry to finish his meal and then asks if she can speak with him privately. I explain that she's a nice lady with some questions and we'll be in our room if he needs us. He stares at his plate.

Drew tousles Henry's hair before we retreat to our bedroom, where I immediately log into the security camera app on the laptop.

Ms. Mary asks Henry to show her his room. He runs down the hallway, and she follows. I observe on the screen as she looks around.

"Don't you have any books?" she asks.

"Mommy no like books. She mean," Henry says, frowning.

I gasp, and Drew gently rubs my back, reassuring me that everything will be okay.

"How is mommy mean?"

"No cookies." Henry crosses his arms over his chest.

"Is there anything else that mommy does that is mean?"

He remains silent, wearing that distant expression he gets when he's lost in his thoughts.

Ms. Mary notices the food basket in Henry's room. "You have snacks in your room. Did your mommy put those there?"

Henry starts playing with his trucks, not offering a response. She requests to see his tummy, and he lets her lift his shirt. She asks if anyone touches his private parts. He looks into the distance. It sounds like he's humming the intro from *Paw Patrol*.

Once I'm sure she has finished questioning Henry, Drew and I head to the kitchen to clean up the dinner dishes. Shortly after, Ms. Mary joins us.

She dives right in, saying, "Henry seems to dissociate."

"Yes, we have him in therapy twice a week with Dr. Wilson," I say. "He specializes in helping kids who have gone through trauma, and he's been a big help to Henry and us." Drew gives my shoulder a reassuring squeeze.

"I've read Dr. Wilson's notes. It mentions that Henry has RAD, and he's recommended extensive treatment with Dr. Laura. Can you tell me more about that?" Ms. Mary asks.

Drew takes over, "Henry gets angry sometimes and zones out. Dr. Laura's treatment is kind of like EMDR, where he deals with his trauma by being cared for. We are confident this approach will work for him."

Ms. Mary smiles and nods, saying, "That's great news. Kids with RAD can go through a lot. I'm happy you're taking it seriously." She turns her attention to me and adds, "Oh, Henry told me you're a 'mean mommy' because of the cookie shortage. My kids must think I'm a monster." She laughs, and I feel like we've passed the test.

Once she's gone, Drew hugs me. I sigh in relief as he thanks me for being so strong before he kisses me. He assures me we will be a solid family, providing everything Henry needs for a fulfilling life. I want to believe him, but I'm not entirely convinced yet. After Henry is sound asleep, Drew and I celebrate by cuddling in bed with a pint of Ben and Jerry's and binge-watching *The Great British Baking Show*.

chapter twenty-one

The camera crew arrives right as we are wrapping up breakfast. Josh, Henry's favorite student from the research team, escorts him to the park so the crew can capture the rest of the needed footage.

The process starts in the hair and makeup chairs. This whole thing is already turning into a bigger production than I thought. Under different circumstances, I might have actually enjoyed myself. After making us look years younger, a slim woman with big glasses puts a fake baby bump on my stomach. I hold an ultrasound picture, and Drew hugs me from behind as the photographer takes photos of the moment in front of the fireplace.

Next, an assistant hands me the most lifelike newborn doll I have ever seen and requests that I simulate nursing. Holding a doll against my chest while being filmed makes me feel incredibly uncomfortable, making my cheeks burn with embarrassment.

Fortunately, the photographer notices my discomfort and clears the room. She positions herself on the floor, capturing a few shots with the sunlight streaming through the window. As I look down at the baby in my arms, tears well in my eyes. This should have been my life, not one dealing with a raging child who smears shit on the wall.

During the next hour, the crew takes hundreds of photos and videos, recording Drew and me doing all the usual things new parents do, like giving baths and tummy time.

They save the most dramatic scene for last—a home birth reenactment.

I wear an oversized T-shirt, and one of the assistants tousles my hair and sprays water on my face to make it look like I'm sweating. A person acting as a doula cheers us on enthusiastically while Drew holds my hand, urging me to push.

Finally, a tiny reborn doll is put on my chest. I long for the small bundle in my arms to be a living, breathing infant—our cherished little miracle from the start. As the camera crew packs up, I stay in bed, sobbing uncontrollably.

Worry lines Drew's face as he tries to console me. All he can do is wrap his arms around me while tears stream down my face, each one carrying a fragment of the pain I can't put into words.

Later that night, after Henry has gone to bed, Dr. Laura initiates a video call to discuss the essential details of Henry's treatment in the upcoming months.

She commends our efforts, mentioning that the initial footage she has reviewed is excellent. With confidence in the quality of the materials, she believes the treatment will be successful, setting the stage for a promising future for Henry.

She recommends introducing the toys used in the filming, emphasizing that we must get rid of anything from Henry's past, including things from the group home and his life with his birth mother. Dr. Laura assures us we will receive the materials within two weeks. She instructs us to watch the home movies several times daily and to display the photos and books in noticeable places, acting like they have always been there. She makes it clear that we must never bring up the topic of adoption again.

She stresses the situation's urgency since Henry is nearing four years of age. Her exact words, "He needs to embrace this narrative now, or it will be too late for him," leave me numb. I am relieved when Drew proposes taking the next few days off from work. He insists I take the following day to relax and de-stress from the filming.

THE NEXT day, Drew brings me breakfast in bed—a cheese omelet, hash browns, toast just the way I like it (a bit burnt with lots of butter), and a hot cup of coffee. It's the break I need, especially with our upcoming adoption day approaching. I spend the entire day cozied up in bed, surrounded by my favorite things—the latest Allison Speka romance novel, the remote control, and plenty of snacks.

chapter twenty-two

The court hearing on Thursday is brief. Drew holds Henry as Judge Wells asks some questions, mentioning she has already reviewed the paperwork. When she asks Henry if he wants to say anything, he buries his face in Drew's shoulder. Judge Wells describes us as a lovely family, gives Henry a stuffed bear, and hands us a certificate. After a photo op with the judge (a thoughtful gesture even though we can't display it), we exit the courtroom. We celebrate the occasion at Love's ice cream shop.

WE HEAD out to look for a home in Traverse City the following day. The real estate agent is helpful and friendly. I fall in love with a charming ranch while checking out a few houses within our budget. The house has a warm and simple charm and is only two miles from the beach. Outside, the classic and unpretentious look blends perfectly with the surroundings. The front lawn is beautifully landscaped with lush grass and colorful flowers.

The inside of the house combines a comfy feel with an open layout. Well-placed large windows let in lots of sunlight, making the rooms bright and inviting. The living room is comfortable, with a fireplace and a beautiful mantel. I picture three stockings hanging there during the holidays. The kitchen is small, but it's got modern finishes and appliances. The primary bedroom is a tad smaller than I'd like, but it has an ensuite bathroom and plenty of natural light. The other two bedrooms are a decent size. I love the large sliding glass door leading to a backyard big enough for Henry to play in.

It is the perfect place to start this new chapter in our lives. I'm thankful we've found a house we can afford that feels like home.

PACKING UP our house in Grand Rapids is challenging. Henry has daily outbursts of anger, even with Drew around. He remains distressed despite repeatedly reassuring him that he's coming with us and is our son.

I pack all of Henry's past belongings into a box marked "GARAGE." I understand they can't go into our new house, but I can't bring myself to throw them out—they're the only connection to Henry's previous life, which will soon fade away entirely.

It's heartbreaking when Henry cries for his old tattered blanket. He wants nothing to do with the replacement blanket from the videos, throwing it under his bed and banging his head on the floor until Drew has to restrain him. We're all in tears when Henry finally falls asleep.

Drew takes Henry to appointments with Dr. Wilson several times that week. Dr. Wilson notices that Henry is starting to dissociate more in his office. He suggests a therapist in Traverse City, Dr. Paul, whom he speaks highly of, mentioning that they went to school together. We quickly schedule an appointment to get a spot on his calendar.

A big box arrives the day before our move. It's filled with family photos on canvas prints, thumb drives, photo albums, and stacks of pictures. My heart melts as I go through the photos—Henry is the most adorable baby. The images are incredibly authentic; they don't seem altered. There's a handwritten note telling us to display the prints in the new house and to start watching the videos as soon as possible.

MOVING DAY spirals into chaos when Henry attempts to escape and refuses to sit in his car seat. Frustrated by the escalating situation, Drew uncharacteristically shouts at Henry, startling him and making the problem worse. The drive is awful, with Henry screaming for over an hour. When we pull into the driveway of our new house, I have the worst migraine of my life. I rush to the bathroom, barely getting to the toilet in time to vomit. This is not how I pictured our first memories in our new home.

Once I compose myself, I walk through the house with Drew, who is holding a sobbing Henry. Our realtor left a friendly note and a vase of sunflowers on the table to welcome us.

The kitchen paint is perfect: a bright and cheerful yellow. I can still smell the fresh paint. The carpets are clean, and the hardwood floors sparkle. The movers show up not long after us, and soon enough, the house looks like a war zone, with boxes and furniture scattered everywhere.

We decide to set up Henry's room first to provide him with a peaceful space until we can finish unpacking and organizing everything. Drew takes Henry to the grocery store for supplies while I arrange his toys and books on the shelves. I put the teddy bear from filming on his bed, which now has a vibrant red firetruck-themed comforter, and lay his new baby blanket on the pillow. The colors I chose for the walls are just the right shade, a deep blue.

For the final touch, I hang a canvas print of the three of us. I vividly remember the original photo because it has always been one of my favorites. It was taken during Drew's and my first Christmas together. The warm glow of the fireplace, combined with the twinkling lights from the tree, created the perfect lighting. The genuine smile on my face takes me back to how special that day was—a truly authentic moment of happiness. Drew held me close, and just before the shutter clicked, he whispered, "I love you," for the first time.

Now, the photo shows an intense-looking younger Henry placed between us. I examine it, impressed by how well they incorporated him. His little face shines with the sparkling lights in the background. Drew's and my newly expressed love for each other now seems directed at our son. There's something unsettling about Henry's eyes; they're dark and empty, following me as I move around the room. I miss the picture the way it was—just Drew and me happily together.

chapter twenty-three

I'm excited and nervous to reveal Henry's room when they return from their adventures. I hope he likes it.

"Baby toys," Henry says, pointing to the items I arranged on the top shelf of his bookcase.

"Yes, those are your things from when you were a baby, sweetheart. Would you like to see them?" I pick the cute little giraffe to show him.

"No. For babies," he pouts.

Drew tries a new tactic, "Check out this picture, buddy. It's you, me and mommy." He lifts Henry and points to the print on the wall.

Henry stares at the three of us in the photo, seeming confused, but he doesn't say anything.

"Anyone hungry?" I ask, eager to move past this awkward moment.

Drew sets up the TV, and I call in a pizza order for dinner. Henry keeps busy by emptying a box of kitchen supplies onto the floor. He enthusiastically bangs pot lids on pans and drums a wooden spoon on the Tupperware. He looks happy. My head pounds.

Drew inserts the thumb drive labeled "Pregnancy." The television screen springs to life, revealing Drew and me in our former home. My belly peeks out from under my top. Drew envelops me in his arms, and I rest my head on his shoulder as he kisses my forehead. "Did you feel that? Maybe he'll be a soccer player," I deliver my line. Drew bends down and whispers to my round middle, "Hey buddy, it's your daddy."

Henry stops banging on the pans and shifts his focus to the TV.

"You're in mommy's tummy, buddy," Drew says. "We're so excited that you're on the way." Henry gazes at the screen, confused.

The next clip shows our vacation with Drew's sister's family. I'm relaxing on the beach in my bikini, proudly showing off my pregnant stomach. Fascinated, I ask Drew to rewind the footage so I can watch it again. The fake belly looks so natural; it's astonishing.

"Check out how swollen my ankles are," I say, pointing at the screen. It's weird how they made every part of me seem larger.

"I think you look beautiful, amore," Drew says, giving me a reassuring smile.

"That makes one of us."

I remember that day in the sun with Drew's family so well. It was the first time in my life that I hated my slender body. I watched Emily running to the waves while Amelia and Mason chased her down the sand, screaming with joy, and I wished so much that it could have been me playing with my own children. Seeing my belly growing in the videos only adds to my disappointment. I would have given anything for a successful, full-term pregnancy.

"Look, buddy!" Drew excitedly points out as the birth scene unfolds. He reaches for my hand and gives it a gentle squeeze. I direct my attention to Henry, the memory of the fake birth still raw in my mind. He looks at the screen and then back at Drew and me, visibly bewildered.

I'm thankful for the interruption when the pizza arrives. We have a picnic in the living room but switch to *Paw Patrol.* I never thought I would be relieved to watch cartoon puppies. The episode ends, and Drew restarts the home movie.

"*Paw Patrol!*" Henry shouts.

I force a smile. "I really want to watch the time when you were in my belly again." Once again, using the acting techniques my mother drilled into my head during childhood.

Henry narrows his eyes, his mouth a thin line. My acting may not be as good as I thought. He turns to Drew and asks, "Henry in belly?"

"Yes," Drew says, rubbing Henry's back. "You were in mommy's belly until you were ready to come out and be a part of our family."

Henry snuggles closer to Drew, absorbing the video. Once it's over, we let Henry choose the next show, and as expected, he picks his favorite episode of *Paw Patrol.* While Henry is entertained, we begin unpacking the kitchen.

"They did a fantastic job making those videos," Drew says.

"It's unbelievable," I agree, unwrapping glasses from the bubble wrap.

"Did you see how Henry calmed down while we were watching them? He wants this, too."

"I hope you're right." I wish I could be more like Drew and enjoy the moment without questioning everything.

That night, after Henry falls asleep, we christen the new house. The close connection I share with Drew brings a sense of clarity, which is precisely what I needed. Drew suggests we shower together afterward, and I promise to join him once my legs no longer feel like jelly. As the shower kicks on, I climb out of bed to join Drew. But then, Henry's scream slices through the air, prompting me to throw on my robe and run to his room.

"It's okay, sweetheart. Mommy's here," I comfort, rubbing his back. His hair is clinging to his head, damp with sweat, and his eyes are tightly shut.

Henry tosses his head back and forth several times. I hush him, softly wiping the hair from his forehead. After a few minutes, he slowly opens his eyes. They widen, his entire face filled with fear, and he starts screaming again. I call for Drew, hoping he'll hear me.

"Henry, it's Mommy. Everything is alright," I say in my calmest voice.

"A monster say she mommy, not you," he says. His voice is so quiet that I can barely hear him.

"That's not true. I am your mommy," I say as Drew rushes into the room with a towel around his waist, his hair dripping.

"Is everything okay? I thought I heard screams."

"Everything's fine. Henry just had a bad dream."

Drew lifts Henry, softly rocking him and speaking in a quiet voice. "It's okay, buddy. Mommy and Daddy are here. You're safe."

I turn on Henry's soothing sleep sounds while Drew helps him settle into bed. Fifteen minutes later, Drew crawls into our bed, letting me know Henry is asleep and asking what the bad dream was about.

"He said something about a monster mom. Do you think his mom is talking to him from the grave?" Goosebumps prickle my arms.

"You're his mom. And since when have you believed in ghosts? I think he's probably feeling anxious because of all the changes with the move and everything." He kisses me, pulling me close for a cuddle. Eventually, I drift off to sleep.

I wake up abruptly from a dream about a woman with worms crawling out of her eye sockets emerging from her grave. My heart leaps into my throat when I see Henry standing next to my side of the bed. I don't think I'll ever get used to a tiny human surprising me in the middle of the night. The smell of urine hangs in the air. Looking at my phone, it shows 1:32 a.m.

Unable to find the extra sheets, I grab the comforter from the guest room—it'll have to do for now. After settling Henry, I return to bed and share my confusion with Drew about why Henry keeps taking off his pull-up. The last thing I want is for our new home to smell like pee. He mumbles something, rolls over, and starts snoring.

chapter twenty-four

In the coming days, we watch the home movies with the commitment of a day trader scrutinizing the market. I'm impressed by the authenticity of the footage, although certain moments remain difficult for me to watch.

The final instruction from Dr. Laura was to ensure there were no remaining photos of Henry from his time at Horizons of Hope. My finger hovers over the trash can icon on the pictures of Tom and Henry. Erasing someone important to Henry feels wrong. But maybe Drew was right; Tom was just doing his job, and we're giving Henry an opportunity for a better life. I hit delete.

Henry wants his old blanket the night before Drew begins his new job. I hand him the blanket from the videos and remind him it's the special one we bought him right before he was born. He throws it on the floor and asks for his picture of Tom instead. Drew and I pretend to have no idea what he's talking about, causing him to break down in inconsolable tears. I give Henry a photo of the three of us, but he crumples it and tosses it on the floor, sobbing for Tom. Thank God I deleted the pictures because I might have given in at that moment, potentially jeopardizing all the work we have put in.

I'm relieved the box of Henry's old memories is safely tucked away in the garage rafters, hidden from him and me. Drew wanted to throw them out, but I resisted, explaining that we should keep them in case the treatment doesn't work. He questioned my logic, but I insisted we could handle it by pretending we wanted to be his mom and dad from the beginning. Drew shook his head slowly, a worried expression in his eyes. He hugged me, whispering, "We need to get rid of the box, amore." I knew he was right.

Drew finally calmed Henry down and stayed with him until he fell asleep. I took advantage of the opportunity to have some time to myself, realizing that once Drew returned to work, me-time would become a thing of the past.

HENRY WAKES before the sun the following morning. Before I've had my coffee, he's already asking for cookies. Hopefully, he'll prefer a nutritious breakfast once his new memories fully kick in.

"Not today, sweetheart. We are all out of cookies." I state the facts, keeping emotion out of my voice.

Henry erupts in anger. He reaches out and pushes the vase of sunflowers with such force that it topples from the table and smashes onto the kitchen tiles. He races through the house, screaming. My blood pressure is climbing as if a freight train is charging towards me while I'm tied on the tracks. Will this ever get easier?

After tackling the mess, I find Henry in his room under a blanket. Attempting to reason with him, I explain that breaking things is unacceptable. He yanks the blanket off and races out of his room, slamming the door.

I squeeze the bridge of my nose, anticipating an impending migraine. The day ahead feels daunting, and I'm uncertain if I can manage it. But I need to find Henry because I know the possible outcomes of leaving him alone. The sound of running water leads me to the bathroom. As I swing the door open, I catch him squeezing my new facial cream into the sink.

"Stop that." I grab it from his hand and stash it on the top shelf of the medicine cabinet.

Henry runs from the room, and I hear breaking glass. Rushing into my bedroom, I find a framed picture of Drew and myself shattered on the floor. Henry is gripping a shard of glass. The expression on his face makes my blood run cold—it's a look of pure hatred.

"No! Drop it," I shout, not wanting him to hurt me or himself.

He laughs and bolts out of the room. Sprinting after him, I catch up and grab his arm, forcefully opening his hand. The glass shard falls to the floor, and his finger is stained bright red.

I rinse the wound with cold water. Fortunately, it's not deep. As Henry watches the blood swirl down the drain, he starts to cry, and I realize my panic isn't improving the situation. I hum "The Wheels on the Bus" to comfort him while applying antibiotic cream and a bandage.

"All better!" I say with as much enthusiasm as I can muster. The *Paw Patrol* bandage does its job to calm him down.

I settle Henry in his room with his toys and instruct him to stay put while I clean up. After removing all the glass pieces from the frame, I place the picture back on my nightstand. Not wanting to chance another fiasco, I take the glass from each picture frame throughout our home and store them in my closet.

When I check on Henry, I find him playing with his trucks. His room stinks like an outhouse on a hot summer day, and the culprit lies in the middle of his floor.

"What did you do? Henry, that is disgusting. Why do you want your room to smell like this?" He stops playing with his trucks and fixes his gaze on the wall.

With a heavy sigh, I grab the trash can and the Clorox wipes to clean up the mess. I console myself with the thought that at least nothing is smeared on the walls—perhaps a sign of progress. Midway through the cleanup, I rush to the bathroom, where I dry heave into the toilet, bringing up nothing but bitter bile. After brushing my teeth, I return to Henry's room to find him searching under his bed.

"What are you looking for?" I ask.

"Zebra!" Henry's eyes are wild with panic.

"You don't have a zebra, but here are your stuffed animals." I remain calm as I retrieve the basket of stuffed animals from his closet.

He digs through the basket with a quizzical look, "Zebra?"

"Sorry, sweetheart, no zebra." I pick up the caterpillar and wave him in the air. "Remember this song, Henry? I'm the happy caterpillar. My head is red, my tail is green, and my body is orange and purple. I'm the happy caterpillar, and I love you." I make the caterpillar kiss his nose. He stares at me as if I've grown a second head.

The rest of the morning consists of too many episodes of

Paw Patrol. Thank God we are meeting Henry's new therapist, Dr. Paul, later today. I'm hopeful he will help speed up this process of making new memories.

After lunch, I promise Henry a cookie if he sits in his car seat without throwing a tantrum during the ride to the appointment. My little bribe works like a charm, and the drive is pleasant.

Dr. Paul's office is bright and inviting, with colorful framed prints decorating the walls. Books and toys are neatly arranged on shelves. In one corner, an unsettling clown punching bag with beady eyes and a red-lined mouth contrasts with the otherwise peaceful ambiance of the room.

Dr. Paul has an average build and height. Tortoiseshell glasses frame his kind eyes. He dresses professionally yet comes across as down-to-earth, as evidenced by the dodgeball trophy on his desk. His slightly awkward demeanor puts me at ease.

He mentions that he reviewed Dr. Laura's and Dr. Wilson's reports so he is up to date with Henry's treatment plan. He gives me a wink as if we're sharing a secret—I suppose we are.

Dr. Paul asks if I'm comfortable with him assessing Henry one-on-one and shares the name of a nearby bakery renowned for its excellent coffee. Enticed by the prospect of a good cup of coffee, I agree.

The cozy bakery smells like Christmas morning. I treat myself, ordering a fancy coffee with whipped cream and a warm cinnamon roll. Anticipating a peaceful moment, I choose a window seat to enjoy the view outside.

Returning to Dr. Paul's office, I hear the unmistakable sounds of Henry raging. I open the door to see him unleashing his fury on the clown punching bag in the corner. Henry throws punch after punch, causing the clown to plummet to the floor, only to spring back up again. Dr. Paul remains seated, engrossed in paperwork, seemingly oblivious to Henry's outburst.

"Is he okay?" I ask, concern filling my voice.

Dr. Paul looks up and waves me into the room. "Henry is expressing some big emotions today," he says with a smile, gesturing for me to sit.

"We discussed his feelings about the move, which triggered a meltdown. I encouraged him to express his emotions with our clown friend. I want Henry to know that this is a secure environment where he can be himself. I believe in providing children the room to release any negative energy they may be holding, as long as it doesn't harm themselves or others."

During our conversation, Henry starts to relax. "Are you feeling better, Henry?" Dr. Paul asks. Henry shakes his head yes.

"How about you come back for another visit next week?" Dr. Paul asks. Henry agrees with a slight nod.

Dr. Paul shifts his focus back to me. "Here's my suggestion: consider getting a punching bag for Henry's big emotions at home. Let's set up weekly appointments going forward."

Dr. Paul's calm demeanor gives me confidence that he's the right choice for Henry. I am thankful he will be part of our journey.

Heading to the car, I tell Henry we can stop at McDonald's for an ice cream cone if he cooperates and sits in his car seat. He complies without hesitation, making me question whether the bribe was necessary. Regardless, I am in the mood for ice cream, so it's a win-win. We enjoy our treat with quiet satisfaction all the way home. I commend Henry for his excellent behavior during the car ride to and from his appointment.

Henry is sleepy, but it's too late in the day for a nap, so I suggest we shop online for a punching bag for our house. As we sit together at the table, he chooses a T-Rex—green, with prominent teeth and boxing gloves on its short arms. We share a laugh about the idea of him taking on a dinosaur. He reaches out and touches my arm. Though a small gesture, it signifies the first time he has touched me affectionately. A lump forms in my throat, and I swallow, determined to hold back tears.

As I tidy the kitchen, I play a home movie for Henry and promise him a trip to the park afterward. The video captures a vacation we never went on, but it appears we had a fantastic time.

The day is gorgeous, so we walk to the small park near our home. Henry excitedly makes his way to the play structure, and I watch him like a hawk as he climbs and explores. A friendly woman asks if she can share the bench I'm sitting on, and I agree. She introduces herself and points to her daughter, who is the same age as Henry. They get along well as they play together. However, I stay focused on Henry; previous experiences have taught me to remain watchful whenever he interacts with other children.

We chat about the ups and downs of motherhood, but I'm cautious, steering clear of any mention of our history. Effortlessly weaving a web of lies, I remind myself to jot them in my journal later to keep my stories straight. Seeing Henry pick up a stick and move towards the little girl, I run over to prevent potential harm. Henry protests, screaming and kicking at me in frustration.

With a chuckle, I remark, "That's our cue to leave."

She laughs, calling after me, "Boys will be boys."

Once we're out of sight, I grab a lollipop from my purse and give it to Henry. His tears stop as he unwraps it and pops it into his mouth, making our walk home much more pleasant.

chapter twenty-five

Henry's progress has been noticeable and encouraging over the past few months. His listening skills are improving, clearly showing that our parenting skills are improving. Dr. Paul can also see the progress and has adjusted Henry's appointments to check-ins twice a month.

We're having way more fun together. Hide and seek is our favorite now, and whenever Henry finds me under the covers, we both burst into laughter.

I brought the winter fun inside on a snowy day when the cold made outdoor play impossible. I filled a tote with freshly fallen snow so Henry could enjoy it from the cozy warmth indoors. He pushed his toy cars around in the snowy wonderland until it began to melt. Lately, his attention span has been off the charts. It's hard to remember the last time I felt this happy and peaceful, and I also sense Henry's happiness.

During our grocery trips, I give Henry the power to choose our weekly fruits.

"Bananas or apples?" I ask.

"Both," he says with a smile.

"Sure thing, sweetheart," I say, tossing the fruits into the cart.

An older lady compliments Henry, pointing out what a good boy he is, all while throwing her great-grandson under the bus. She calls him a little terror and says he could use some lessons from Henry. I can't help but be filled with pride.

Thankfully, we make it to the car before Henry goes into full meltdown mode because I allowed him to pick only one treat from the checkout aisle.

I PLAN a small celebration with Drew, me, and Henry for his 4th birthday. Drew feels fortunate that we made it in time to save Henry from a life of struggles. He praises Dr. Laura, and for the first time, I am glad we participated. This life is way better than what we were dealing with before.

Dr. Laura sends us an email the day after Henry's fourth birthday. The first few pages include expected behaviors for a child Henry's age, such as occasional meltdowns, stubbornness as they increase their autonomy, and difficulty transitioning from one activity to another. It is reassuring to read that Henry's behavior is perfectly normal.

She also includes tips on disciplining Henry, like keeping expectations simple and consistent. I smile to myself, realizing that Drew and I have learned how to be excellent parents to Henry. The rest of the packet contains follow-up questions regarding Henry's progress. I am so excited to mark that he calls us mommy and daddy and hasn't had a bathroom accident in months. Observing the comprehensive data confirming the effectiveness of the treatment fills me with deep gratitude.

We just need to concentrate on improving Henry's

relationships with other children before trying preschool again. Once the weather warms up, introducing Henry as a potential playmate to other kids at the park or beach will be easier.

SPRING HITS Traverse City a bit later than Grand Rapids. The tulips bloom, and the air is cool and fresh. Henry explores the world around him with so much curiosity and joy. It is incredible to witness.

During an unexpectedly warm day, Henry sprawls on his belly in the yard, collecting bugs and worms and putting them in a jar. That evening, I ask him if we should release them. He insists they like it in there. I plan to release them later that night after he goes to bed, but I forget—I blame *The Bachelor*.

The next day, most of his critters are dead.

"Oh no, Henry, they died because we didn't set them free," I say with sadness.

His face lights up with a sly smile, and my chest tightens in response. I feel a weight settling in my stomach, a mixture of recognition and anticipation.

chapter twenty-six

We establish a good routine. I return to my job—working on Drew's days off and in the evening. It's satisfying to return to a good rhythm.

The family videos play continuously from morning to night, and I appreciate the added touch of humor in some of them. One of my favorite moments is when Drew jumps out from behind a wall and scares me, making Henry and I laugh every time. I reminisce about how silly his daddy has always been and tell Henry story after story about what it was like when I was pregnant, and how excited I was to be his mommy.

In my dreams, I relive the journey of being pregnant and giving birth, realizing that even my memories are evolving.

We receive a package from Dr. Laura. Inside is a bottle of champagne and chocolate-covered strawberries. There is also a certificate with embossed gold letters simply stating "Congratulations." Later that day, we get an email providing additional details about our official graduation from the program.

Dear King family,

We at Radiant Minds Center of Psychology are delighted to share exciting news. Thanks to your invaluable participation in our initial research, I have been granted the opportunity to expand my study to a second location in Boston. Your family's active involvement will forever be remembered as a beacon of hope for others.

Your courage and strength have left an indelible mark, and as I embark on this new research phase, I want to express my deepest gratitude. Your family's journey will be a part of the narrative that transforms the lives of many families, offering hope in situations where there was once none.

To safeguard the integrity of my ongoing research, please dispose of this correspondence and any related materials. It is crucial to maintain confidentiality regarding the details of this critical study. I understand the significance of your support in Henry's progress and want to prevent any inadvertent disclosure through social media or casual conversations.

Your commitment to improving numerous lives is truly commendable, and I look forward to the continued positive impact my research will have on families like yours.

With sincere appreciation,
Dr. Laura Shepard
Radiant Minds Center of Psychology

Filled with pride, I am ecstatic the rest of the day, eagerly anticipating celebrating the success with Drew later on. The moment he gets home, I read him the email and promptly delete it, not wanting to jeopardize our hard work. While Drew gives Henry his bath, I place the "Congratulations" certificate into my memory tote in my room as a reminder of all our efforts.

chapter twenty-seven

I'm thrilled Henry loves the beach as much as I do. We enjoy spending time by Grand Traverse Bay. Sometimes, on the weekends, we go to Sleeping Bear Dunes for the day. These are the moments I love the most—the sun's warmth, the soothing rhythm of the waves, and the opportunity to set worries aside.

Henry loves running in and out of the chilly waves and constructing sandcastles. Occasionally, he joins the other children on a common goal, such as digging a massive hole in the sand or finding the perfect rocks for their creations.

Watching him connect with other children at the beach fills me with hope. Drew and I decide to enroll Henry in preschool again, confident he's ready and will appreciate having more time with children his age. And for me, having uninterrupted work hours every day will be heavenly.

We find a charming preschool, Sunshine Kids, close to our house. It will be a pleasant walk on days when the weather cooperates. The teacher in Henry's class, Miss Lindsey, is youthful and friendly. She greets Henry by kneeling to his level and speaking softly. Henry plays with the Matchbox cars and a garage with a ramp while we finish filling out the required classroom forms. We don't mention Henry's adoption or any mental health considerations.

"Are you looking forward to going to school?" I ask as we drive home.

"Yes," Henry says, bouncing his foot against the back of my seat.

"What's the first thing you want to do?" Drew asks.

"Play with the cars!"

"Remember to listen to your teacher," I say. "Miss Lindsey mentioned that sometimes you get to choose what to do, but other times you have to follow the rules."

Lost in thought, Henry stares out the window, likely envisioning the exciting car adventures that await him.

THE FIRST day of preschool goes smoothly. Henry brims with excitement when I drop him off at his classroom. At pick-up, his eyes shine with enthusiasm. He excitedly shares that playing with the cars was his favorite part of the day.

The genuine delight in his voice and animated retelling of his playtime make me smile. Our decision regarding the timing of sending Henry to school was a good one.

Henry's feedback note on how he did today is positive. "Miss Lindsey said you did a wonderful job cleaning up after yourself. I am so proud of you. She wants us to talk about sharing. You remember what sharing is, right?" I ask Henry, glancing in the rearview mirror.

Henry stares out the window in silence. Seizing the quiet moment, I review the concept of sharing with him. I make a mental note to revisit the topic of sharing a few more times before he heads back to school.

Drew has the weekend off, and we spend time at the beach, appreciating the perfect temperature and sunshine. Why can't we have this kind of weather all the time? Northern Michigan winters are brutal.

ON MONDAY, Henry is happy to return to school. Having just poured my second cup of coffee, I'm prepared to dive back into work when my cell rings. The school's name lights up my screen, causing a sharp pain in my chest. Inhaling deeply, I brace myself, answering in a cheerful voice.

"Good morning, Mrs. King. It's Cheryl from Sunshine Kids. Everything is okay, but I'm hoping you can come to the school to pick up Henry. There has been an incident."

I assure her I will be there shortly and am thankful I put some effort into looking presentable today.

In the office, Cheryl greets me warmly. Henry sits in a large chair that makes him look tiny. Hurrying over, I reach out for a hug and check if he's okay.

The director, Ms. Ross, appears from her office. "Please come in, Mrs. King."

After entering her office, she closes the door behind me. "What happened?" I ask.

"Please, have a seat," she gestures toward a chair opposite her desk.

I sit down, reminding myself to breathe.

"Henry had a challenging morning. He was unwilling to share the cars. Miss Lindsey tried to diffuse the situation by putting the cars away for a while. Unfortunately, Henry urinated in the corner while she was placing the cars in the closet."

My expression quickly shifts from terror to relief, thankful that he didn't harm another child. "Oh my God, I'm so sorry. I can't believe he did that." I'm genuinely surprised. Henry has been doing so well, and we haven't had any accidents in a long time.

"Such behavior is not typical for a child his age. However, it is not unheard of, especially in children with ADHD or oppositional defiant disorder. We were wondering if you have any insights into what might be happening with Henry and if there's anything we should know."

"Henry struggles with being aware of his feelings, and we have him in therapy. We haven't had him screened for ADHD because he can concentrate well when he's with his dad."

"You have a four-year-old in therapy?" Ms. Ross asks, her concern evident.

"Yes, his dad is a firefighter and got injured in a fire when Henry was almost two, causing Henry a lot of stress. Being so little, he struggled to process his emotions, which usually came out as anger. The therapy is a precaution, as we want Henry to have the support he needs. It is never too early to help a child understand themselves and the world better, don't you agree?" I ask. The lies flow out of me like a rushing train through a tunnel. I make a mental note to remember what I've said so I can tell Drew later.

"That makes sense," she affirms with a slow nod. "It's commendable that you are addressing Henry's needs. We do not want to punish him for today's events; we just want him to understand that such behavior is unacceptable. At this point, no further intervention is needed. However, please keep stressing the significance of sharing at home and the importance of using the bathroom for potty breaks." Her forced smile thinly masks her underlying concern.

chapter twenty-eight

Drew's sister, Emily, and her family come for a week-long visit. They are staying at a condo with direct access to Grand Traverse Bay. On the day of their arrival, we all meet at the beach. The cousins spend hours playing in the sand, digging a giant hole. Uncle Ryan joins the fun, letting them bury him. Bursting from his sandy "grave" with a roar, the kids scream as he chases them with his arms outstretched like a zombie. We all enjoy the chilly water, leaping over waves, with laughter echoing around us. Drew documents our time together using his phone. I'm eager to add these experiences to our collection, beginning a fresh chapter of true family memories.

We eat a picnic lunch, complete with gritty sandwiches. The adults relax under the umbrella as the kids build a massive sandcastle. I love listening to their happy chatter as they collaborate on their masterpiece. These are the moments I dreamed of experiencing as a mom.

Drew begins telling his most recent rescue story to Emily and Ryan, but our conversation is abruptly interrupted by Henry's piercing scream.

I look over to see him drenched, vigorously rubbing his

eyes. Amelia stands nearby, holding an empty bucket, laughing at Henry, while Mason remains focused on digging the moat. I rush to Henry and wrap him in a towel.

"I'm so sorry, sweetheart. That was not nice of Amelia," I say, attempting to ease his tears.

"She was just playing with you," Emily says, trying to defuse the situation.

"No, she mean," Henry sobs into my shoulder.

Emily insists that Amelia apologize. Henry focuses on the sand as she offers a half-hearted "sorry" before continuing construction on the sandcastle.

Drew approaches, whispering something in Henry's ear that brings a smile to his face. They run to the concession stand and return with SpongeBob popsicles for everyone.

We meet up at our favorite pizza place for dinner. The sun has left everyone's cheeks with a rosy glow. As we wait for our pizza, the kids color their placemats, and the adults talk. Emily fills me in on her latest book club read while the guys discuss the Detroit Tigers game. Our conversations are interrupted when Amelia lets out a high-pitched scream.

"Amelia! You may not yell in the restaurant," Emily scolds.

"Henry stabbed me with his fork," she says, bursting into tears.

Simultaneously, Emily and Drew jump from their seats to investigate the situation. It turns out that Henry has indeed stabbed Amelia with his fork, leaving four small, bloody punctures on her leg. Emily comforts Amelia as Drew questions Henry about his actions. Henry stays silent, his expression blank.

"Why did he do that?" Emily asks Amelia.

"I don't know. We were coloring, and Henry stabbed me with his fork as hard as he could! I don't like Henry. He's mean."

"Henry, tell Amelia you're sorry," Drew says.

"Sorry," Henry says flatly.

Apologizing for Henry's behavior, I offer a bandage I find at the bottom of my purse. We take our pizzas to go, each heading back to our respective homes. There has been too much togetherness today.

In the car, we ask Henry what happened, but he remains silent.

"You cannot stab people with forks," Drew says. "It hurts, and we don't want to hurt people."

Henry stares out the window, lost in his own world.

Back at home, we eat our pizza in silence. Henry goes to bed without any complaints or issues.

Later, I slip into bed to unwind with Drew. Resting my head on his chest, I express my concern about Henry's behavior towards Amelia.

He sighs deeply, "I don't blame him. Amelia wasn't very nice to him today, especially when she dumped a bucket of cold sandy water on his head at the beach."

"You're right, but still, he can't go around seeking revenge by stabbing everyone with a fork."

"He won't stab everyone," he chuckles. "Henry is just acting like a kid, and we all know kids don't always make the best decisions." Drew kisses me. "I love you."

"I love you, too." I snuggle up to him and quickly fall asleep.

Unfortunately, my peaceful sleep is short-lived, as Henry wakes up with another nightmare about the monster mom.

WE TAKE a break from the forced family fun for several days. The day before Emily, Ryan, and their kids are scheduled to leave, Drew invites them to a barbeque at our house. We keep a close eye on Henry, who appears to be enjoying himself.

Amelia is initially unsure about joining in, but she gets involved in the games, showing the boys her own version of cornhole. She stands at the board's edge, tosses the beanbag into the opening, and shouts, "Fire in the hole!" The boys find it hilarious and burst into laughter every time.

While Henry and Mason play with the trucks in the sandbox, I approach Amelia and ask her to help me with something in the house.

Once in the kitchen, I say, "I'm sorry Henry hurt you the other day."

"That's okay, Aunty Charlotte. My mommy told me Henry's first mommy was mean, so he has some anger inside of him and does bad things," she says.

My heart skips a beat. "We don't talk about Henry's first mommy. We want Henry to have only happy memories, so we never discuss her. Do you understand?" Amelia smiles and bobs her head up and down before skipping back outside.

I corner Drew in the hallway bathroom, turning on the water to ensure no one will overhear our conversation.

"Emily told Amelia about Henry's birth mom," I tell him through clenched teeth.

"What?" Drew says in disbelief.

"Amelia shared that her mommy told her that Henry's first mommy was mean, which is why he does bad things." I am shaking in anger.

"You've got to be kidding me. What the hell is she thinking? If Amelia tells Henry, all our work will be for nothing." Drew storms out to confront Emily in the backyard. I discreetly open the bathroom window to eavesdrop.

"What the hell, Emily?" Drew says too loudly, and it takes everything in me not to shush him.

She frowns, her eyebrows knitted together. "What is your problem?"

Drew leans toward her, saying something I can't make out.

"How would you suggest I explain his behavior then?" Emily says, crossing her arms.

"There is nothing to explain."

"What you guys are doing is sick and wrong, and when it jeopardizes my children's safety, count me out of your bizarre treatment," she says, emphasizing her disapproval by holding up her fingers and air quoting the word 'treatment.'

"What other choice did we have? You promised to go along with it," Drew says, raising his hands in frustration. "You've always been selfish," he adds, his hands falling.

"Well, you are a controlling narcissist. You have to have everything perfect. God forbid your child has any issues."

"Takes one to know one," Drew spits the words angrily.

Having heard enough, I rush out to the yard and try to defuse the situation. "Let's all settle down."

"We are leaving." Emily turns and walks away, calling for Ryan.

chapter twenty-nine

I feel relieved when I drop Henry off at school on Monday, and I look forward to returning to my routine. Later that evening, Drew surprises us with our favorite Thai food for dinner. Henry is thrilled at my suggestion to watch *Toy Story* as we eat. Drew entwines his fingers with mine and mouths, "I love you." I snuggle in closer to him, responding with a gentle squeeze of his hand as I rest my head on his chest.

While we clean up after dinner, Drew tells me that he texted Emily, apologizing for his part in the argument. Curious, I ask, "What was her response?"

"She apologized and said she hadn't realized we weren't sharing anything about Henry's birth mom."

Keeping my thoughts about Emily's lack of common sense to myself, I hug him and say, "I'm glad you and your sister sorted things out."

"Yeah, me too. But we should take a break from hanging out until Amelia is older, and we can trust her not to make stupid comments."

Smiling, I glance up at him. "I agree; you're right, as always."

He grins, leaning down to kiss me.

I'M ABSORBED in work on Wednesday when my phone startles me out of my number haze—Henry's school. Damn it.

I pick up the call with a cheerful tone, "Hello?"

"Good morning, Mrs. King. It's Cheryl. We need you to pick Henry up."

"Is he not feeling well?" I ask, my heart racing.

"He is physically okay. We will explain the situation once you get here. Can you come pick him up soon?"

"Yes, I will be right there." I hang up without saying goodbye.

I arrive within a few minutes. Henry is sitting in the office, studying the carpet, and doesn't acknowledge me when I enter. Cheryl tells me I can go directly to Ms. Ross's office.

"Good morning, Charlotte." Ms. Ross glances up from a pile of papers on her desk as I linger in her doorway. "Please come in and have a seat."

"What happened?"

"I'll get straight to the point. Henry gave a classmate a haircut during art class today."

"Oh my god. I'm so sorry. I'm sure he didn't mean to."

"Miss Lindsey mentioned Henry and Becca had a small argument yesterday. Becca told the other students Henry was a baby because he likes *Paw Patrol*. Miss Lindsey had Becca apologize for name-calling, assuming the issue was resolved. However, while Miss Lindsey was helping another child, Henry used his safety scissors to cut some of Becca's hair. Thankfully, the scissors didn't work well, so not much hair was lost. But you can imagine how scary it must have been for Becca." I don't have to imagine as the memory of my own hair-cutting trauma comes rushing back.

"I am sure Henry is very sorry," I say, trying to reassure myself as much as her.

"In these situations, our policy is to send the child home for the day. He will need to write an apology to Becca. You can help him write the letter and encourage him to add a drawing," Ms. Ross says with a forced smile.

I tell her we'll do whatever it takes to make it right, fully aware this is strike number two.

Henry won't talk to me about what happened, so I call Dr. Paul and explain the incident, also mentioning Henry stabbed his cousin with a fork. He reassures me it's likely normal behavior, but he agrees to schedule an after-hours appointment at six today to ensure nothing more serious is happening. Drew joins me after work as I wait in the lobby while Henry meets with Dr. Paul. After forty-five minutes, Henry bounces out of Dr. Paul's office.

"Can you play with the toys out here for a minute so I can talk with your mommy and daddy?" Dr. Paul asks. Henry smiles and nods.

I leave the door ajar to monitor Henry while he plays. "Thanks for squeezing him in," I express as we settle on the sofa.

Dr. Paul begins, "I think Henry is having difficulty expressing his emotions appropriately, leading to less-than-ideal reactions."

Drew asks, "What can we do to help him?"

"I recommend talking about feelings often and reading books that explore emotions. You won't be able to cover every upsetting situation, but you can prepare Henry for some of the more common childhood challenges."

"Do you think his behavior is normal?" I ask.

Dr. Paul takes a moment before answering, "I think this is normal behavior for Henry. It's important to remember that, given Henry's past, his response to stress and anger might not be typical for a child his age. He will learn to manage his behaviors as he continues to settle into your stable home. Nevertheless, I suggest keeping a close eye on him to prevent more incidents. Henry needs to understand that hurting others is not okay."

Dr. Paul's support is invaluable, and I can't imagine what we would do without him.

We have a relatively peaceful evening, and I decide to take a bath while Drew handles Henry's bedtime routine. I light a candle, add bath salts, and sink into the steaming water. As my body relaxes, my mind continues to race. When I get into bed, Drew is reading. I also attempt to read, but I can't concentrate.

"I think we need to pull Henry out of school," I say.

Drew pauses, placing his thumb in his book before responding, "I'm not sure if we need to go to that extreme."

"I don't think we should expect the school to monitor Henry every second of the day. Dr. Paul made it clear that we don't want Henry to get used to retaliating against other students. He needs one-to-one care to learn how to handle himself before we expose him to other kids. Just imagine if he had stabbed that little girl with the scissors instead of just cutting her hair?"

"I don't think Henry would stab anyone."

"But he did stab Amelia."

"With a fork. And, if you ask me, she deserved it."

"Drew!" I scold, then grin, acknowledging he is most likely correct. "Okay, but seriously. I don't feel comfortable with him being in a school environment yet. He just needs more time."

"To let his new memories take root," Drew adds, and I'm relieved he sees my point. "But what do you suggest we do in the meantime?"

"I think we should hire a part-time nanny for him so we can both keep working."

Henry screams, interrupting our conversation. We hurry to his bedroom to find him sitting in bed, speaking incomprehensible babble. Drew sits beside him, attempting to hug him, but it only intensifies his cries. Drew looks at me with wide eyes, and neither of us knows how to handle the situation. Henry is inconsolable. We are frozen, staring at him, until he stops screaming. Finally, he opens his eyes, sees Drew, and appears to relax a little.

"What happened, buddy?" Drew asks.

"Monster in my room. Killed Mommy."

"No, Henry, look, Mommy is right here," Drew says, pointing to me.

"No! Other Mommy!"

"I am your only mommy," I say, approaching.

Henry buries his face into Drew's chest. Drew rubs his back and whispers, "You're okay, buddy."

I exit the room, find my laptop, and set up a CherubCare Nanny Service account. There's no way we're sending Henry back to preschool.

chapter thirty

After successfully getting Henry to sleep, Drew returns to bed. We both agree that taking a break from school is a good idea. Drew suggests we go over our budget, and it turns out we can afford to hire a nanny three days a week with the money we'll save from not having Henry in preschool.

When I review the applicants, I'm not impressed with any of the candidates. Among the five who apply, our top choices are a woman in her fifties with experience in a correctional facility, an older gentleman who says he's sixty-seven but looks eighty, and a nineteen-year-old guy named Logan Conte. We choose to start with him because, apart from his age, he appears to be the best option.

Logan's references are impeccable. One is from a camp where he's worked since he was sixteen, and several are from families. We reached out, and they all had positive things to say about Logan and his ability to connect with children. One mom shared that her kids used to cry on Logan's days off. She mentioned feeling hurt that they preferred the nanny over her, but was grateful that they were well cared for while she was at work.

ON THE day of the interview, Logan sits comfortably in the living room, appearing calm. He tells us that, coming from a large Italian family, he often watched his siblings and discovered he excelled at it. His parents wanted him to attend college to become a teacher, but Logan had different dreams. Now, he's looking for a part-time job to support himself while he works on a screenplay. His ultimate goal is to make it to LA one day to work in the entertainment industry.

I ask if he can dedicate three days a week for at least a year, and he agrees that would work perfectly for him. I glance at Drew and subtly nod to signal Logan is the right choice.

"Henry sometimes struggles with his emotions and has had a couple of minor incidents—one with a family member and one with a little girl at school." I won't share everything with Logan, but a little background information will be helpful. "Nothing major, just accidental," I add.

"I'm sure I can handle the little guy," he says confidently.

"As long as you and Henry get along, I think you will be a perfect fit for our family," I say.

Henry strolls into the room as if it's planned, rubbing the sleep out of his eyes from his nap.

"Hey, buddy. We want to introduce you to Logan. He's going to hang out with you a couple of days a week to play," Drew says, excitement in his voice.

Henry eyes Logan apprehensively.

"Wanna show me your toys, buddy?" Logan asks, already catching on to the nickname Drew uses for him.

Henry doesn't move. Drew steps in, saying, "Come on, buddy. I'll go with you guys." He carries Henry to his room, with

Logan following.

I move to the side of the doorway to observe their interaction.

"You have Legos. I love Legos," Logan says, picking Henry's stuffed bear from his bed. "What's this guy's name?"

"Tom," Henry says.

Drew sticks around until Henry warms up to Logan, which happens quickly. Logan is a natural, and they work together to build a tall tower out of Legos.

Drew finds me in the hallway and grins when he realizes I was spying on them. He leads me back to the living room, pumps his fist in the air, and goes in for a high five.

"I think this is going to work out, amore," he says, pulling me into a hug. "You were right."

"Can I get that in writing?" I ask right before he kisses me.

chapter thirty-one

As the months pass, Henry and Logan's bond grows stronger. They spend their days laughing, making memories, and having fun together. Henry's curiosity about nature and art also increases. Paintings and drawings cover our fridge, showcasing our happy family, all with an extra figure representing Logan.

Their connection alleviates any initial worries we might have had, and I'm glad we decided to keep Henry out of school for now. This choice has allowed him to develop closer relationships with Drew and me, cementing his new memories in place.

LOGAN HAS been part of our household for six months when Drew walks in and flings my suitcase onto the bed. "Start packing, amore. You and I are going away for the weekend!"

"Who's going to watch Henry?" I ask.

"Logan can stay for the entire weekend. I booked us a room at the Grand Hotel on Mackinac Island."

"Are you sure we should go that far?"

"It's less than a two-hour drive, and besides, you've never been to the island. They'll take away your Michigan mitten card if you don't go soon. It's a state policy," he says with a grin.

"Very funny," I say, playfully hitting his arm. "Let me talk to Henry first." I walk to the kitchen, where Henry and Logan play with playdough. "Henry, is it okay with you if Mommy and Daddy go away for two nights and Logan stays with you?"

Henry's eyes light up. He leaps from the table and runs to hug Logan. "Guess we got our answer," I say, allowing myself to feel excited about a getaway with just Drew and me.

I CAN'T stop smiling as we ride the ferry across the lake to the island. The Grand Hotel offers the convenience of delivering our luggage to our room, allowing us to explore before checking in.

The island has a unique charm, with bicycles lining the busy shop area and horse-drawn carriages wandering through the streets instead of cars. We go to a few shops and sample a ton of fudge. They're having a sale at one store, and Drew buys five pounds of fudge because it's too good of a deal to pass up. Fingers crossed that fudge freezes well because eating it will take a year. Drew is adamant about purchasing matching "I Heart Mackinac" t-shirts for the three of us, and I find a horse stuffed animal that I'm sure Henry will adore.

We take a leisurely walk up the hill to our hotel. It lives up to its name—it's truly grand and features a massive wrap-around porch lined with red geraniums.

Our bags are already waiting for us in the room, and as we step inside, it feels like we've traveled back in time. The room makes me feel like royalty, with the ornate wallpaper and golden fixtures. The bed is inviting, surrounded by a canopy with intricate crown molding. Allowing myself to enjoy the moment fully, I sink into the luxurious down comforter—wishing we could stay longer than a weekend.

Drew joins me, and we kiss passionately, eagerly undressing. It brings back memories of when we first met and couldn't keep our hands off each other. The intensity of our connection is powerful, and after, I lie intertwined in Drew's arms.

Drew fills the claw-foot tub with hot water and bubbles. We both ease into it and savor a glass of wine. Afterward, I take over an hour to get ready for dinner. I can't remember the last time I felt so excited to do my makeup and dress up. Drew checks in with Logan and Henry and tells me everything is going great.

Drew has made reservations for us at the Carriage House. He secured a table with a lake view. Our meal arrives as the sun sets, painting the sky in beautiful shades of orange and pink. The beauty of it brings tears to my eyes. Drew reaches across the table to hold my hand.

A horse-drawn carriage brings us back to the hotel. The night is perfect, with a clear sky full of a million stars. Drew wants to stop at the Geranium Bar for a nightcap. We enjoy our drinks on the front porch before returning to our room. I couldn't have asked for a better getaway, and I thank Drew for planning this trip—it's perfect.

chapter thirty-two

My ringing phone wakes me. The name "Logan" on the screen makes my heart rate pick up speed. Quickly answering, I ask, "Is everything alright?" Drew turns to me with a worried look, so I switch to speakerphone.

"Yes, we're okay," Logan says, his calm voice easing my tension a little. "Henry had a bad dream about his mom dying, so I thought hearing your voice might calm him down. I'll put him on."

"Hi, sweetheart. It's mommy, I'm okay." I do my best to reassure Henry.

A thud is followed by Logan saying, "She is your mommy." Henry's subsequent scream of "No!" echoes through the room amidst shuffling sounds. Drew and I exchange glances, feeling utterly powerless as we stare at the phone. Logan continues trying to comfort Henry.

Finally, Logan gets back on the phone. "That was a rough one. But I think I've got the little guy settled back down." He promises to text me when Henry falls back asleep.

"We should go home," I tell Drew after hanging up.

"I don't think the ferries run in the middle of the night."

Damn it, he's right. Now I'm rethinking this whole getaway: next time, no islands.

"Do you think he's having nightmares about his birth mom?" I ask.

"No. It's not possible. Those memories are buried, and Henry was so young when she died. I'm sure you just sound different to him over the phone. Besides, the reception out here is terrible."

I want to believe him. Drew tells me to try to relax, and he's back asleep within minutes. I lie awake, staring at the ceiling, until half an hour later, I receive a text—a picture of Henry sleeping. I spend the rest of the night tossing and turning, having my own nightmares.

THE FOLLOWING morning, Drew proposes we take a bike ride around the island after breakfast.

Still haunted by last night's helplessness, I express my struggle to unwind enough to enjoy the rest of our trip. I can tell Drew is disappointed when I suggest returning home, but he agrees and helps plan the trip back.

When we arrive home later that afternoon, Logan and Henry are playing in the yard. Drew brings Henry inside, promising gifts, while I stay outside to chat with Logan.

"I'm sorry about last night," I begin. "Henry occasionally has nightmares; that's why he sees Dr. Paul. It's been a while, so we didn't expect him to have one with you. It must have been hard for you."

"I've never seen a kid look so terrified in my life. I need to be honest with you, Charlotte," he says, turning to look me in the eye. "I think someone is abusing Henry. With all the scars on his body and the way he was acting last night, the little guy was petrified. Something isn't right." He pauses before continuing, "Is Drew violent with you and Henry? I can get you to a safe place. I know a social worker, and I'm sure she can help you and Henry."

"I appreciate your concern, but I assure you, Drew is not violent," I say, meeting his eyes to emphasize my point. "However, I need to tell you something about Henry that we haven't shared. Let's walk, and I'll tell you the truth."

As we wander down the street, I share the story of adopting Henry and the difficult diagnosis of reactive attachment disorder. I fill him in on the distressing YouTube videos we watched of other families devastated by RAD and some of the challenges we've faced with Henry.

He whistles softly through his teeth. "That sounds rough."

"It was hard," I acknowledge. "Until recently, there wasn't much treatment for kids with RAD as severe as Henry's. Fortunately, we found a doctor specializing in comprehensive treatment for children like him." I explain our journey to ensure Henry has the childhood memories he deserves.

"That's amazing. Henry is lucky to have you both as parents. I'm sorry I thought Drew might have hurt him," Logan says.

"I appreciate your concern for our safety. It means a lot. Please promise never to talk about Henry's past. We've put in a lot of effort to create a perfect life for him to make sure he has a bright future. All of our hard work would be ruined if he found out."

"I would never do anything to hurt Henry," Logan says, looking directly into my eyes.

"Thank you, Logan. You've been a tremendous help to our family."

chapter thirty-three

Henry is thriving. He's becoming more confident daily and exploring the world with curiosity and enthusiasm. Logan has taken his role seriously as he teaches Henry important life skills.

Henry loves showing off all the new things he can do: reading Spot books independently, swimming confidently at the community pool, and riding a two-wheel bike without training wheels. Logan is a fantastic mentor to Henry, and I couldn't have asked for anyone better.

Logan is set to head off to Los Angeles next week. He landed an internship with a major movie production company and is ecstatic, though he knows it'll be hard to say goodbye to Henry. With Logan leaving, Drew and I know it's time for Henry to return to school. I can't believe he will be starting kindergarten.

We are torn between mentioning Henry's potential challenges or sending him off and hoping everything goes smoothly. Ultimately, we decided to send him and deal with any issues as they arise. Henry has been doing well, and I wouldn't want his new teacher to anticipate problems when I'm confident everything will turn out fine.

The kindergarten open house is a positive experience.

Henry's teacher, Miss Holmes, is young, attractive, and sweet. Henry finds his name tag and cubby and is thrilled to meet the class pet, a hamster named Little Buddy. Henry colors a picture, writes his name on top, and gives it to Miss Holmes. She praises his talent and hangs it on the wall. Henry's face lights up, and he seems excited to start school.

ON THE first day of school, Miss Holmes is outside holding a large class sign with a row of fidgety kids lined up behind her. Over to the side, a group of teary-eyed moms call out to their children while snapping photos. Henry stands in line, looking down at his feet. As the teachers begin ushering the children inside, I rush to the car, brushing the tears from my cheeks.

The house feels strangely quiet without Logan and Henry running around, engaged in their usual activities. I miss them and find my plant collection growing as I seek new ways to fill my extra free time. I decide to experiment with tropical plants and succulents. I hope to keep them alive through the winter months so they can liven up our patio next summer. For now, every spare spot by a window is taken up by a hibiscus, tropical grass, and even a cactus. As the weather turns colder, they remind me of warmer days ahead.

Most afternoons, I get to school a little early to pick up Henry, often catching the tail end of the last recess. The children run around the compact play structure and basketball court, screaming and laughing. Henry is always off in his own world, gathering woodchips and stuffing his pockets—little treasures I'll find later in the wash.

One day, I notice a boy trying to talk to Henry, but Henry

doesn't seem interested and goes back to playing with his woodchips. He never gets invited to birthday parties or playdates. I'm probably more bothered by it than he is, but I bring it up with Miss Holmes during parent-teacher conferences. She reassures Drew and me that Henry is doing fine in school and mentions that some kids just prefer to play by themselves. She's confident that Henry will make friends when he's ready. When I bring it up with Dr. Paul, he agrees with Miss Holmes. So, I choose not to worry about it and let Henry navigate things at his own pace.

A FEW months into the school year, it is Henry's turn to be star student for the week. I help him create a poster board all about himself, including lots of baby pictures. Thanks to Dr. Laura, we have plenty to choose from. We also add photos of Henry's favorite things, like the beach and pizza. I arrange the images with background paper to make each one stand out. Enlisting Henry's help, I have him glue everything down where I point, and he writes his name at the top.

I think I'm more excited than Henry when I go to school on Friday afternoon to celebrate his star student status with him. I bring his current favorite snack, Rice Krispies Treats, to share with the kids in his class. Henry proudly wears a crown covered in star stickers as we stand together at the front of the room to present his posterboard, where I do most of the talking. Afterward, I read his favorite book, *A Weed Grew in Our Garden*.

A perk of being star student is being able to take Little Buddy home for the weekend. Drew and I are not pet people, but we agreed it would be a fun experience for Henry. He is excited to watch the hamster run through the maze he and Drew created from a cardboard box and toilet paper tubes.

Once we get Little Buddy home, I have to admit he's adorable. Reading through Miss Holmes's care instructions, I propose giving Little Buddy a small piece of apple. Henry is captivated as the hamster grips the apple in his tiny hands, nibbling away. Henry wants to keep the cage in his room, but since hamsters are nocturnal creatures, I suggest Little Buddy stay in the kitchen in case he needs a snack at night.

The following morning, I wake up to Drew and Henry shouting for Little Buddy. They are crawling on the floor, searching under the furniture. Little Buddy apparently managed to escape during the night. Drew tells me he noticed the top of the cage was pushed to the side a bit, and Buddy was nowhere to be found. If I had known we had a little escape artist on our hands, I would've placed a book on the lid.

I join in the search, going through every room in the house. After looking for over an hour, we give up. I slice up an apple, smear on some peanut butter, and place it in the middle of the family room floor, hoping the tempting treat will coax Little Buddy out of his hiding spot.

I spend the entire day hanging out on the couch, hoping to catch the little guy, but as the day turns into evening, there's still no sign of him. Drew takes Henry to the pet store for a replacement hamster while I email Miss Holmes explaining the situation. She responds within minutes, reassuring me that this isn't the first time it's happened, and she appreciates us getting a replacement.

Little Buddy never turns up, which makes me a bit sad. Drew reassures me that it's just typical hamster behavior. He mentions that when he was younger, he also had a hamster mysteriously vanish.

chapter thirty-four

Traverse City has a record year for snow. We take the opportunity to teach Henry how to ski, find the best sledding hills, and build countless snowmen. Winter is okay, but I wish it wouldn't last so long. I'm always more than ready when the snow melts and the first buds appear on the trees.

While I've managed to keep most of my plants alive, a few are beyond saving. On a warmer-than-usual Saturday in May, we're tackling some spring cleaning. Drew takes the dead plants to the compost while I deep clean the appliances.

He walks through the kitchen and grabs his laptop off the table before going into the family room. I am elbow-deep in oven cleaner, but as soon as I peel off my gloves and wash my hands, I check in with him. He is sitting on the couch, staring intently at the computer screen, his eyebrows furrowed in concentration.

"What are you looking up?" I ask.

"Nothing much. Just had a question about composting," Drew says, clicking a few buttons. "I think I've got it sorted." He closes the computer. He stands up and gives me a peck on my cheek.

He leaves the laptop on the coffee table and mentions he is

going to check on Henry. I peek at the internet history as soon as he's out of sight, but it's been cleared. That's weird. Drew is quiet the rest of the day, and I notice him watching Henry more closely than usual.

"What is going on?" I ask him as we make dinner.

"I don't want to freak you out."

"Too late."

He sighs. "I found some fur and a little skeleton in one of the planters. I think it was Little Buddy."

"Aw, poor thing. He must have climbed in and tried to dig his way out, thinking it was an escape route."

"Yeah, that's what I was thinking," he says with a smile. "Just wanted to double-check it was the hamster. I cleared the history because I was searching for pictures of dead hamsters online. It was pretty disturbing." His eyes widen, and he grimaces. Leaning down, he kisses my forehead. "Well, at least we know the smell you complained about will be gone now."

THE REST of Henry's kindergarten year goes amazingly well. We only have one issue that requires me to meet with another parent at the school. It seems Henry intentionally broke some crayons belonging to a girl in his class. I don't blame Henry for breaking the crayons when we meet with Miss Holmes, the little girl, and her mother. The girl is a miniature version of her mother. Their perfectly styled blond hair, manicured nails, and matching outfits, which probably cost more than my first car, are excessive. I have to bite my lip to stop myself from laughing when the woman starts defending her daughter—her voice sounds like she sucked all the helium out of a balloon.

Henry plays possum, remaining as still as a statue. I offer to buy new crayons, but the mom refuses, saying they can't be replaced. Apparently, they bought them in Paris when they vacationed there. I reassure her that Crayola sells the same crayons in the US as in France. The mother and daughter look like they are about to cry, and I feel helpless. So, I apologize and make Henry say he's sorry. Miss Holmes gives me an apologetic look before I take Henry's hand and lead him out of the room.

chapter thirty-five

The past few years have been incredibly fulfilling. Henry is in third grade, excelling in school, and has made a friend. I couldn't be happier, and I think I was more excited than Henry was when he received an invitation to Tanner's birthday party. Drew was promoted to Battalion Chief at the fire station with a generous pay increase. Our little family feels solid and connected.

Drew and Emily have completely patched things up. Emily assured us that Amelia won't bring up Henry's past, and she's kept her word. During one of our get-togethers, we discussed taking a family vacation, this time to Colorado for skiing over Christmas break. Even though the slopes there are bigger than we're used to, we think the kids are old enough and ready for the challenge. Spending Christmas at a ski lodge in Colorado sounds like a dream.

Emily and I take charge of planning an unforgettable vacation. By sharing a condo, we can keep it within our budget. I dedicate hours to finding coupons and deals for the area and secure a fantastic flight using our frequent flyer miles. I can't wait to ski in the fresh snow of Colorado's mountains. It will be a whole new experience compared to the hills in Michigan.

The condo we booked has the charm of a ski chalet straight out of a fairy tale. It is nestled against a backdrop of snow-covered peaks, creating a warm and inviting atmosphere. The exterior has a traditional alpine style, with old-fashioned wooden beams. The roof is decorated with icicles, with at least a foot of snow covering the eaves.

Inside, the fireplace crackles, spreading a cozy warmth over the furniture covered in comfy throws. The spacious windows, dusted with snow, frame stunning views of the wintry landscape. The air smells like fresh pine from the large tree in the corner of the open family room. The tree is covered with ornaments and white twinkling lights, adding a festive touch to the space.

The boys' room has bunk beds, and Amelia has a small but cozy room with a bed stacked high with pillows and blankets. Each couple has their own room facing the mountains. I am beyond happy we found such a fantastic place within our budget.

On our first night, Henry and his cousins wear the matching pajamas I bought for them. They sit by the fire, watching the movie *Elf*, while the adults play cards in the kitchen. I make some popcorn and bring it to them just as Buddy the Elf loses it, realizing he is not an elf but a human. Then Papa Elf explains to Buddy that he is adopted.

"Buddy is adopted just like you," Amelia says, pointing at Henry.

Confusion crosses Henry's face as he says, "No, I wasn't."

"Yes, you were," Amelia taunts.

"Amelia, that's enough," I intervene. "It's not nice to tease your cousin." She dismissively turns her nose up at me and returns to focusing on her phone.

Seeing Henry on the verge of tears, I kneel beside his chair to reassure him. "Henry, she's teasing you. That's what cousins do. Remember the videos of you in my stomach and the ones after you were born? Would I have all those videos if you were adopted?"

"I guess not," Henry says.

"Don't listen to Amelia. You know the truth, sweetheart." Henry gives me a slight smile and moves to a chair further from Amelia before returning his attention to the movie.

I return to the kitchen and whisper, "We've got a problem. Amelia just told Henry that he's adopted."

"What? What did he say?" Drew asks.

"He was upset, but I told him we wouldn't have videos of me giving birth to him if he was adopted. He seemed to believe it. But you never know if it will bring up memories from the past."

Drew looks at Emily, anger in his eyes. "Geez, Emily, get your kid under control, would you?"

"I'm sorry she said that," Emily says, crossing her arms over her chest. "I told her it was a secret, and she shouldn't have told Henry. I'll talk to her about it."

"It's too late!" Drew shouts.

I place my hand on his arm and remind him the kids are right in the other room and we need to keep our voices down.

"He believes all the other lies you guys tell him," Emily spits the words like venom. Ryan places his hand over hers to signal her to speak quietly or as a show of support—I'm not sure which.

"Are you judging us?" Drew sneers in a hushed voice.

"No, but making up a whole fake history and gaslighting your kid about it for years is messed up."

"So it's better to have your kid never get attached to anyone and end up institutionalized or worse? The treatment we've been using has almost cured Henry. Without it, he might have become so out of control that he could have been in the news by now."

"I think the key word is almost," Emily counters. "He gets in fights at school, has nightmares, and killed a classroom pet. Do you call that cured? How was I supposed to keep my daughter safe from him without revealing that he was adopted? I wanted her to understand and feel compassion for him so she wouldn't see her cousin as a threat."

Drew sighs heavily, running his hands through his hair, "Why didn't you tell me you didn't want Henry around your kids? We could have stayed home and had a great holiday without you jeopardizing Henry's future."

I can't handle this anymore. Their voices are rising again, and we can't afford for Henry to hear. I intervene, whispering, "You two need to stop arguing."

Everyone pauses.

Emily gives in first, saying, "You're right. I'm sorry. I told Amelia that Henry was adopted because she already knew, and I hate lying."

"Emily," Drew's voice cracks. "He can't know we adopted him. Amelia needs to tell him she was teasing."

"I will talk to her. I know you have been through a lot to give Henry a good home. I was just worried about my kids."

I'm happy to get into bed that night, and I'm grateful Drew is taking care of Henry's bedtime routine. With some time to myself, I decide to read the romance novel I brought along. Eventually, Drew comes in, holding a glass of whiskey. He changes into his pajamas, gets into bed, kisses me, and picks up his book from the nightstand. While we both read, I find myself rereading the same page. I place my book on my lap, creating a little mountain.

"Do you think Henry killed Little Buddy?"

Drew lets out a sigh. "I don't understand why Emily said that. When I told her I found Little Buddy in the planter, she asked if I thought Henry had killed him. I told her no, absolutely not. But I suppose it's possible that Henry might have held him a bit too tightly. I'm sure he didn't mean to hurt him if that's what happened."

I nod and place my book on the nightstand. Then, I snuggle up to Drew, rest my head on his chest, and listen to his heartbeat. My brain won't shut up.

chapter thirty-six

The next few days go smoothly, without any issues. I closely monitor Amelia whenever she's with Henry, ensuring she doesn't say anything she shouldn't.

Most of our time is spent on the slopes, teaching the kids to ski on a real mountain. Henry and Mason catch on quickly, tackling blue runs like pros by the second day. They expertly maneuver down the hill and come to a safe stop at the bottom. On the other hand, Amelia is having a rough go of it. The adults take turns giving her lessons on the basics while the rest of us supervise Henry and Mason on the more enjoyable slopes.

We unwind by the fire in the evenings, sipping hot cocoa after dinner and playing board games. Even though we had a challenging start, this vacation has become a dream come true.

The weather is perfect for skiing on Christmas Eve, with a layer of fresh powder covering the mountains. Drew and I offer Emily and Ryan an early gift, encouraging them to enjoy the day together while we take the kids skiing. They happily agree, and right after breakfast, we head to the slopes.

Drew sticks to the smaller hills with Amelia while I take the boys to the more challenging runs. We gather at the lodge for lunch, and Drew proudly announces that Amelia has moved on from the Bunny Hill. Her face lights up with pride. As we enjoy our burgers and fries, Drew goes through the trail map. He shows Amelia the runs she needs to stick to, assuring her that she can try more challenging ones when she feels comfortable.

Drew informs the boys that we'll stick together for a couple of runs, prompting several eye rolls. With a stern look, Drew gets them to stop giggling and sit up straight. The boys take their responsibility seriously and follow Amelia to the lift. They ride up together, giving Drew and me a quiet moment as we follow behind them.

We gather again at the foot of the hill, and the kids eagerly talk over each other, sharing their experiences. Henry praises Amelia for doing well, mentioning that she only slowed them down a little. Mason playfully hits Henry's arm, and they both burst into laughter. Amelia is oblivious; her face is glowing, and she wears a huge smile.

Drew has to use the restroom, so I agree to supervise the kids. While I'm adjusting my bootstrap, they hop on the next lift. I'm just two chairs behind, so I should be able to catch up with them at the top before they go too far. I keep an eye on them as they disembark from the lift. I yell for them to wait but realize they can't hear me; they're too far ahead. They go toward the same blue run we did last time. Thank goodness.

The woman in front of me has trouble exiting the chair lift, causing the operator to stop it while someone assists her. Once it's finally my turn, I notice the kids heading to the left, choosing a different blue run. One of those paths leads to a challenging black mogul run. It's tricky for those unfamiliar with the hill, as it's easy to go the wrong way.

I shout for them to go back to the trail that Amelia knows. Amelia turns a bit, and it seems like she heard me, but they all keep going in the wrong direction. I quickly ski over to the beginning of the run, but it's too late—they've already started descending in a row, with Henry bringing up the rear. At least he's watching out for his cousins. Amelia is positioned on the side where the run turns to moguls, but fortunately, she hasn't taken that route. I try to ski faster and catch up, but they're still too far ahead.

Henry skis up beside his cousins as they approach the entrance to the mogul run. I'm proud of him for looking out for them. At the last moment, Amelia turns slightly toward the expert run. I shout for her to stop, knowing she can't hear me. I quickly ski to catch up with her on the trail. Within seconds, I witness her soaring through the air and landing with a loud thud, screaming in pain. Her skis go airborne, finishing the run on their own. I rush to her side. She's sobbing uncontrollably, holding her left arm. An older man comes down the hill, assuring us he'll send help. I try to comfort her and calm her down. She tells me through tears that her arm hurts, saying Henry told her to take this route.

"No, sweetheart, he must have said not to go this way. You just got confused. These trails are tricky if you don't know them well."

"No, he told me to go left because it's easier. He hates me."

"I know he doesn't hate you," I try to comfort her.

The first aid team finally arrives. One of them stabilizes her arm, and they carefully put Amelia into the back of the sled, skiing her down the remaining portion of the run while I follow behind. Thankfully, I spot Drew and the boys at the bottom of the hill, waving them over. We all follow Amelia to the first aid office, where they put a sling around her arm, suggesting we head straight to the emergency room.

I drive so Drew can call Emily, who's in the middle of dinner, to inform her that we're heading to the hospital. He does an excellent job reassuring her and suggests they finish their meal. The rest of the car ride is quiet, except for Amelia's sobs. There's nothing we can do or say to comfort her as she cries for her mom.

I stay with Amelia while Drew entertains the boys in the waiting area. The X-ray shows a complex fracture that will need surgery. It's hard to believe this is how we'll spend Christmas Eve, and I'm grateful when Ryan and Emily arrive. They both hurry into the room and from Emily's expression, it's clear she knows that Drew has downplayed the seriousness of the situation. Emily hovers around Amelia, wanting to hug her but not wanting to hurt her. Eventually, she settles for kissing her forehead.

"What happened?" Emily asks, directing her question my way. I can sense the anger in her voice, although she's trying to keep it under control in front of Amelia.

"We were having a great time skiing, and Amelia was doing so well, but she ended up on a difficult run. She went airborne like a superhero and landed on her arm. The surgeon just came by and assured us he'd fix her up, good as new." I ramble, not pausing for a breath.

"Why was she even near a difficult run?" Emily asks in horror.

Amelia answers this time, saying, "Henry made me."

"He did not," I say. "The kids got ahead of me on the lift, and Amelia just got a bit confused and ended up on the black run instead of the blue one they were supposed to stick to. It wasn't anyone's fault, except maybe the ski lodge for placing the easy run right next to a challenging one. I'm sure people make that mistake all the time. They should have better signs."

Emily shifts her attention to Amelia. "Tell Mommy exactly what happened, honey," she says, ignoring my explanation.

"Henry pointed to a trail and said it was the easier one. But when I looked back, he was going the other way. I couldn't stop because the hill was too steep. I know he did it on purpose. He hates me because I told him he's adopted," she adds for dramatic effect. I have to make an effort not to roll my eyes.

I jump in, "I saw the whole thing, and that's not what happened. Amelia just got a bit confused. It's my fault—I fell behind on the chairlift because I needed to adjust my boot, and they got ahead of me. I yelled for them to wait, but they couldn't hear me."

Emily pays no attention to me as she comforts her hysterical daughter, who should seriously consider pursuing an acting career.

The nurse comes in with last-minute instructions and wheels Amelia away to surgery. We join Drew and the boys in the waiting room. It appears Drew allowed the boys to go wild at the vending machine. Wrappers surround them as they focus on the cartoon movie on TV. I sit beside Drew, and he protectively takes my hand, gently squeezing it.

Emily sits on the other side of Drew and hisses, "My children will never be anywhere near Henry again. He is dangerous," her words are filled with spite.

"It was an accident, and you want to blame Henry because your daughter can't follow instructions," I reply, louder than intended. Drew tightens his grip on my hand, silently telling me to let him handle it.

"We told the kids to stay away from the black runs, and she didn't listen," he says. "If anything, blame me; I should have made her stay on the bunny hills."

Emily huffs, "Well, don't expect us back at the condo tonight. We'll look for another place to stay." She takes out her phone to begin the search. All I can think is, good luck finding something—it's Christmas Eve.

Drew shakes his head and stands up, pulling me along. He calls for Henry, and we leave. Once we're in the car, he reassures me it will blow over after Emily has some time to cool off. Besides, all their stuff is at the condo. He promises to talk to her when they return for it. Drew is confident he can convince her to stay, especially since tomorrow is Christmas.

Henry is all hyped up from the sugar he ate from the vending machine, and Drew is as tense as an overwound watch. I suggest we take a walk to unwind. The night feels magical as we walk through the snow, with gentle flakes drifting around us. The only thing that could have made it perfect would have been if today's incident hadn't happened. I silently reprimand myself, realizing that none of this would have happened if I hadn't gotten separated from the kids.

We return to the condo, and Drew texts Emily for an update. She reads his message but doesn't respond. Drew is determined not to let this situation ruin Henry's Christmas, knowing our time is running out before he stops believing in Santa Claus. I make hot cocoa while Henry gets ready for bed. The three of us cozy up on the couch in front of the fire, and Drew reads *The Night Before Christmas*. I stare at the Christmas tree's twinkling lights, trying to leave the day's stress behind. We let Henry choose which movie to watch before bed. He picks the cartoon version of *How the Grinch Stole Christmas*. Henry can barely keep his eyes open as the credits roll but asks for one more movie.

"Not tonight, buddy. You have to get to bed before Santa comes," Drew says, tousling his hair.

"Dad, I know Santa's not real," Henry says. "Amelia told me."

I see anger flash in Drew's eyes, but he keeps it together, saying, "Oh, she did, did she? Well, Amelia is known to lie, so I wouldn't trust a word she says."

Henry grins at him. "Okay, Dad."

Drew lifts Henry, who rests his head on Drew's shoulder.

Drew glances at me, and I can see how hurt he is because of his sister and niece's actions. My frustration is about to boil over. I've had enough of Emily and Amelia's nonsense, too. They have no idea what we've gone through to ensure Henry has a good life, and I regret ever thinking it was a good idea to go on vacation with them.

Drew returns, his face showing defeat. I hug him, and we both break down in tears. We sit together, watching the fire as it fades to embers. Afterward, we arrange Henry's gifts from Santa and fill his stocking before finally falling into bed. Physically and emotionally drained, I just want this day to be done.

chapter thirty-seven

Henry wakes us up in the morning, excited and ready to kick off the festivities. I tell him he can open the gifts in his stocking but to wait for us before he starts on the other presents. I need coffee. When Drew and I come downstairs, Henry is playing with his new Matchbox cars. Amelia and Mason's stockings are not on the mantle. It's unsettling to think that someone was in the condo while we slept, even if it was just Emily or Ryan. A simple text telling us they were coming would have been nice.

I head to the kitchen to brew some coffee and pop the cinnamon rolls in the oven, grumbling under my breath about how petty Emily can be.

When I open the fridge, it is practically empty. One water bottle sits alone on the middle shelf. The turkey, condiments, cinnamon rolls, box of wine, and even the coffee creamer are gone.

"Are you kidding me?" I exclaim. "That bitch grinched our Christmas." I'm furious. I call for Drew urgently, and he's there in seconds, asking what's wrong. I show him the fridge, and he lets out a heavy sigh. He whips his phone from his pocket, and I know Emily is about to hear an earfull.

"What the hell, Emily!" Then, after a pause, "Henry is not dangerous. I can't believe you are robbing him of Christmas memories with his cousins." He frowns while listening. "Very funny. He has real memories—plenty of wonderful real memories because he's an amazing kid, and you would know that if you could get the stick out of your ass and spend any time with him."

I put my finger to my lips, reminding him Henry is in the next room. He ends the call, knowing it's no use talking reason into his sister when she's like this. Turning to me, he seeks some reassurance with a hug. Henry wanders into the kitchen and asks about our traditional Christmas morning cinnamon rolls.

Drew claps his hands together enthusiastically and suggests we go to the lodge for Christmas breakfast instead. Henry wonders if Aunt Emily, Uncle Ryan, and his cousins will meet us there, but Drew shakes his head, making up an excuse as to why they can't join us. Henry's face brightens, and I ask him why he's so happy.

"I don't like Amelia. She's a liar, and you told me lying is bad."

THE ONLY issue we encounter on our trip home is missing our connecting flight because of bad weather. We pull into our driveway at two in the morning. Drew doesn't even bother bringing the luggage inside. We all collapse into bed and fall asleep within minutes. It's funny how sitting around waiting all day can leave you completely drained.

DREW ISN'T in bed when I wake up the following day. I roll over to look at my phone—10:23 a.m. I stretch, releasing a big yawn, before climbing out of bed to slip on my robe. I find the boys in the kitchen, bright-eyed and bushy-tailed, eating pancakes.

Drew stands up and pulls out a chair for me. "Please, have a seat, amore," he says with an accent I can't quite place, motioning towards the chair.

"You guys are up early," I say as he places a steaming mug of coffee in front of me.

"It's nearly eleven," he laughs. "We ran over to the post office to grab the mail," he says, pointing to the counter. "Henry and I are going to the sledding hill for a bit. Do you want to come?"

"No thanks. I'll clean up around here and check my work email."

He kisses the top of my head. "Alright, love you."

"Love you, too."

I pick up the stack of mail to go through while I drink my coffee. Most of it is junk, but there are a few holiday cards. Shelly sent a Christmas card with a bunch of family photos on the front. Trevor and Cody have big smiles in each picture. She wrote a note on the back: "Can't believe it's been so long. Hope you're doing as well as we are. XO Shelly."

Emily's family Christmas card is in the pile. She must have mailed it before we went on vacation. I set it aside without bothering to open it. I'm still mad.

There's a package from Drew's parents filled with special treats and a few toys for Henry. A package from Logan includes a marble game and a sweet card. I'm not surprised there is nothing from my mother.

The final package is from Tom. He's been sending gifts

for every holiday and birthday since Henry became part of our family. I used to reply with letters, keeping Tom updated on how Henry was doing. Back when Henry was younger, I'd also include some of Henry's artwork.

I last responded to Tom's letters a few years ago. If I would have known how persistent he is, I never would have given him our new address. I will give him credit—he's always been kind and consistent, even if he's a bit slow to catch on. He sent Henry a small toy—a tiny wooden train model and a note. He mentioned that since Henry was growing up, he hoped he still liked trains.

I finish my coffee, toss Tom's letter and toy in the trash, and dump the coffee grounds from the machine on top.

chapter thirty-eight

As time goes on, our bond with Henry continually grows stronger. I often refer to us as the three musketeers—it's just me, Drew, and Henry taking on the world together. I love our little family and am so glad we took the leap to help Henry. I can't even picture how different our lives would be if we hadn't. Drew hasn't spoken to his sister since the ski trip. When I ask him how he's feeling about it, he replies with a touch of sadness, saying, "It is what it is." Although I don't miss her, seeing how the situation affects Drew upsets me, and I encourage him to reach out. I know what it's like to be without family, but Drew believes it's for the best. He doesn't want anything to risk what we've built for Henry and is adamant about it.

AS HENRY starts sixth grade, we notice him becoming more withdrawn. His best friend, Tanner, moved to Tennessee, and Henry hasn't had much success making new friends since. Henry insists he doesn't mind and says all the boys at school only talk about "stupid stuff," like girls and sports. It's discouraging because we felt like we were doing so well for a long time, and now we're dealing with a moody preteen. Dr. Paul assures us that this is typical behavior for a boy his age. I shudder to think about what his teenage years will be like.

TOWARD THE end of seventh grade, Henry breaks down one night and confides in us that one of his teachers is picking on him. We arrange meetings with the principal and the teacher to address the issue. While I can see why Henry doesn't like this particular teacher, we don't feel like she's singling him out unfairly. The bottom line is Henry isn't happy. He feels like nobody at school likes him, and it breaks my heart to see him struggling. Summer can't come fast enough. I hope it will be the break Henry needs.

OVER SUMMER break, we sign Henry up for various camps and activities, hoping he'll stay occupied and meet some new kids his age. Unfortunately, he doesn't have a good time; all we hear are complaints. His nightmares also worsen, so we increase his visits to Dr. Paul to once a week. Thankfully, they improve over time, occurring only a few times a month instead of three times a week.

I ask Henry if he remembers any of his nightmares. He tells me forgetting is impossible because it's always the same—pitch black, he's scared and alone, screaming for someone to come, but nobody ever does.

chapter thirty-nine

Henry's problems at school last year follow him into eighth grade. He's been more distant and seems to struggle with his temper more often. Whenever Drew or I ask him what's wrong, he always says, "Nothing." I'm hesitant to push him too much, especially since Dr. Paul keeps telling us that it's just typical teen behavior, but I hate seeing him struggle.

Drew's long hours at the fire station seem to be affecting Henry more than I initially thought. The other night, while clearing Drew's untouched plate from the table for the fourth consecutive night, Henry asked if Dad was ever going to come home again. I miss Drew, too. He continues moving up the fire station ranks and was recently promoted to assistant chief. While the pay raise is nice, I don't think it's worth the toll it's taken on our family.

DURING A perfect autumn weekend, I plan a day filled with activities I know Henry will love, hoping to cheer us both up. We kick things off by going to his favorite burger place for lunch. He eats every last bite of his burger and fries, and I catch him eyeing my plate. I nudge it toward him, earning a smile in return. Drew and I joke that he must have a hollow leg because of how much he eats, even though he's as thin as a rail. He grew several inches taller over the summer, surpassing me.

After lunch, we head over to Pirate's Cove. Henry looks like a pro on the go-kart track, lapping me twice. Then, he flaunts his skills at the mini-golf course by sinking a couple of holes-in-one and winning both games. Next, we go to his favorite arcade, where he challenges me to air hockey. I give it my all, but he quickly wins each game. Since the weather is unseasonably warm, we can't resist ending our day with double scoops at our favorite ice cream spot. As the sun sets, we walk by the bay while enjoying our cones.

"I can't stand Mr. Donaldson," Henry confides as the sun dips below the horizon, painting magnificent orange and pink streaks across the sky.

"Your science teacher? You love science."

"Not anymore. He made sure of that."

"What's been going on?" I ask, remembering Dr. Paul's suggestion to ask questions that prompt more than a yes or no response.

"He calls on me when he knows I'm not paying attention, and then the other kids laugh at me when I don't know the answer."

I suppress a smile, relieved that the issue isn't more severe. "Why are you having a hard time paying attention in class?"

"No one can always pay attention, Mom," Henry sighs. "Mr. Donaldson is boring as hell. All the kids hate him, not just me."

I ignore what he says about Donaldson, not wanting to shut down the conversation. "Do you feel like you're understanding the material? Maybe getting a tutor could be helpful."

"I don't need a tutor. I'm good at science."

"I can send an email to let him know that you feel anxious when he calls on you randomly."

"No, it's okay. I can handle it."

He's right. In the past, we would talk to Henry's teachers about his anxiety and how it could lead to behavioral issues. However, Dr. Paul assured Henry and us that he is capable of speaking directly to his teachers, especially since high school is approaching.

"Just remember, Henry, I'm always here for you. I love you."

"I know, Mom."

LATER THAT week, Drew unexpectedly has a day off. I take a personal day so we can spend time together. While enjoying brunch at our favorite café, I get a call from the school saying I need to come down immediately because of an incident involving Henry.

When Drew sees my reaction to the caller, he mouths, "What's wrong?" I quickly hang up and explain that there is an issue with Henry and we need to go to the school. Drew throws some cash on the table, and we hurry out.

Henry is sitting in the office with a distant look on his face. "Are you alright?" I ask, but he won't even look at me.

Principal First emerges from his office, a towering figure filling the doorway. He gestures for us to come in and pulls up an extra chair so we can all sit. "Henry, would you like to explain to your parents what happened today?"

Henry continues to stare into space, offering no response.

"Okay, then I'll explain," Principal First says, leaning back in his chair. "Henry thought it would be amusing to flavor Mr. Donaldson's coffee with his urine."

"What? How do you know it was Henry?" Drew asks. "It could've been any of those kids."

"Henry had mentioned his plan to a few students beforehand. Several saw him carrying what seemed to be a vial of urine, and one witnessed him pouring it into Mr. Donaldson's coffee mug before the first bell rang."

"It could have been lemonade," I protest.

"Do you have lemonade at home?" Principal First asks in a condescending tone.

"Maybe," I reply, knowing full well that we don't have any lemonade at home.

Principal First's eyebrows furrow, and I realize what I say doesn't matter. He's already made up his mind about Henry.

"Mr. Donaldson is pressing charges," he says. "The police are investigating, and they're going to test the coffee. In the meantime, Henry is expelled."

"But you don't know if it's actually urine, right?" Drew argues. "It could just be colored water, completely harmless."

Principal First releases a long breath before saying, "Any aggression toward a teacher is unacceptable. Even pretending to put urine in coffee is grounds for expulsion."

"Henry informed me that Mr. Donaldson targets students in his class, ridiculing them and name-calling. It seems Mr. Donaldson is a bully, and I'm curious why there hasn't been any accountability for his behavior." I say.

Principal First looks surprised. "We haven't heard any

complaints about Mr. Donaldson."

"Well, maybe the other students are trying to frame Henry. Can you really trust everything thirteen and fourteen-year-olds say?" I ask, desperately searching for any possible way out of the situation. I'm furious with myself. Maybe if I had reported Henry's complaints about Donaldson to the school, none of this would have happened. At the very least, there would have been a documented record.

"Henry, did you put urine in Mr. Donaldson's coffee?" Principal First asks point blank. Henry remains silent, staring at his lap while his finger repeatedly traces an invisible object on his blue jeans.

"This is ridiculous!" Drew's voice rises with anger as he speaks. "You're acting as the prosecutor, judge, and jury, and you're expelling Henry from school over something he MIGHT have done?"

"I know this is a challenging situation," Principal First says calmly. "But this isn't the first time we've noticed Henry exhibiting unusual behavior, and it's not the first time a teacher has been concerned about what he might do."

"This is the first time I have heard anything about teachers being concerned with Henry's behavior." At this point, I'm furious.

"We did contact you in the past about this," Principal First says. "You told us that Henry was in counseling."

Damn it. I do recall an uncomfortable conversation with one of Henry's seventh-grade teachers. She was an outspoken, irritating woman who spoke in a high-pitched voice that grated on my nerves. I couldn't blame Henry for not getting along with her. I wouldn't either if I had to listen to her talking all day.

Principal First stands, signaling the meeting is over. "Please take Henry home. Here is the name of an alternative school in the area," he says, handing Drew a slip of paper. "There's a box of Henry's belongings from his locker in the office." He opens the door and moves aside, allowing us to leave.

Once we're safely in the car, Drew turns to Henry. "What the hell, Henry? Why would you do something like that? It's disgusting."

I'm shocked when I realize Drew believes Henry actually put urine in his teacher's coffee. Henry just stares out the window, seemingly lost in his own world. Drew tightens his grip on the steering wheel as if trying to strangle it.

I phone Dr. Paul, who tells us to come over immediately—he will squeeze us in. The rest of the car ride is silent.

"What happened?" Dr. Paul directs his question to Henry.

Henry is visibly angry but remains silent. I tell Dr. Paul what Principal First said happened, saying that we have not heard Henry's side yet because he refuses to discuss it. I also bring up what Henry had told me about Mr. Donaldson a few weeks ago, expressing regret for not stepping in, even though Henry told me he could handle it himself. The room is quiet as we all wait for Henry to say something. Eventually, Dr. Paul requests to have a private conversation with Henry. As we exit his office, I leave the door slightly ajar. Drew looks at me with concern as I position myself to the side of the door, but I am determined to listen in on the conversation.

"Do you want to tell me your version of what happened?" Dr. Paul asks Henry.

There's a few minutes of silence until he finally speaks up. "That guy is an asshole. He hates me," Henry says, his voice filled with frustration.

Without hesitation, Dr. Paul asks, "Why do you think that?"

"He picks on me in class," Henry says, sounding like he thinks Dr. Paul should already know about it without him having to say anything. "If I don't know an answer, he laughs, or if I get it wrong, he says, 'Nice try,' but then makes a buzzing sound like 'bzzzzz.' My face gets super red, and the kid behind me always says, 'Rudolph messed up again,' and everyone laughs."

"So, do you think him drinking your urine was an appropriate punishment for the way he is treating you?"

"Yes!" Henry shouts. There's a moment of silence before he adds, "I didn't know what to do. My dad's hardly ever around, and I did tell my mom, but I wanted to handle it on my own because I thought that's what she would want me to do." That sentence feels like a dagger to my heart. I never intended for Henry to think he had to deal with this alone.

Henry continues, "I thought I could ignore him, but I never got a break because the other kids tease me in the hallway and at lunch. They call me 'bzzzzz' and 'the red-faced idiot.' I feel like a complete loser for not standing up for myself. And I'm not the only one he targets; there are plenty of us. That's why I told the other kids what I was gonna do. I wanted all of us to feel better when he drank his piss coffee."

"Did your actions help you feel better?"

"I guess not," Henry admits in a shaky voice. "Now I'm in big trouble. My dad won't even look at me, and my mom looks like she's about to cry. They're making me go to a different school.

It's gonna be even worse there."

"What you did wasn't just morally wrong; it was also illegal," Dr. Paul says seriously. "You could end up in juvenile detention."

"I didn't think any of this would happen." Henry's voice sounds panicked, and I resist the urge to barge in to comfort him. "I didn't think those kids would narc on me. I thought he would drink his coffee, and later, we would all laugh and know that he got what he deserved." His voice turns angry again.

"I understand. I will write a letter to the courts explaining that we are working together on your mental health. And considering everything you've been through, you're doing quite well." My hand flies to my mouth, covering my gasp. After all these years, Dr. Paul has slipped up.

"What do you mean all I have been through?" Henry asks.

"Being bullied. Dealing with a stressful school environment," Dr. Paul quickly recovers. "Can we make a deal that you will run things by me in the future? I'm someone you can trust to share your plans with, and we can figure out if they're a good idea together. We can't undo the past, but we can choose a more positive path moving forward."

There is a long pause before Henry speaks. "So what would you have told me to do?"

"I would've advised you to accept help from your parents to deal with the situation. No teacher should treat students like yours was treating you or any of the other students he was teasing. He needs to be held accountable for his actions. Most schools have zero tolerance for bullying, and that includes the staff. How you handled the situation was wrong," Dr. Paul says gently. "And I'm pretty sure that's not who you are or want to be."

"I know," Henry mumbles, his voice filled with regret.

"What do you think? Should we talk to your parents together, and I'll help explain what you've been going through?"

I quickly pick up a magazine and sit next to Drew, pretending to be absorbed in it the whole time. Dr. Paul pokes his head out his door and calls Drew and me into his office. Henry doesn't look up when we come in and sit on the couch.

Dr. Paul begins the conversation, "Mr. Donaldson was bullying Henry. Even though that doesn't excuse Henry's behavior, it helps us see that his actions weren't random. I will write a letter to the judge explaining Henry is under my care, which shows that he is actively working on his mental health. Hopefully, because it's his first offense, they'll go easy on him and only require probation. I suggest getting a lawyer."

I audibly gasp, and Drew reaches for my hand.

Dr. Paul turns his focus to Henry. "If you're arrested, tell them you will not speak until your lawyer is present. When they say, 'Anything you say can and will be used against you,' they mean it. Don't admit to anyone else what happened at school. My files are private. Do you understand?"

Henry stops fidgeting with his hands and looks up, nodding as he mumbles, "I understand."

Dr. Paul recommends a local lawyer he thinks would be suitable for the case. I call to schedule an appointment from the car, hoping to sort things out quickly. Fortunately, she has an opening tomorrow.

"I'm sorry," Henry whispers from the back seat.

"I know you are, sweetheart," I comfort him. Drew doesn't say a word, and the rest of the car ride is silent.

chapter forty

Megan Eastwick's office is located in an older building in the downtown area. Her team occupies the entire third floor. The offices have a modern feel, with sleek designs and glass elements that stand out against the building's historic architecture. Tropical plants are strategically placed, bringing warmth to the minimalist design. A cheerful young woman sitting behind a clear desk welcomes us. She leads us down the hallway to the end office.

Walking into the spacious area, a petite woman stands to greet us. "Good morning, I'm Megan Eastwick. Please take a seat." She wears a stylish pantsuit that fits her perfectly, and her straight black hair is tied into a flawless ponytail. Her professional appearance eases my nerves a little.

Once we're all settled, she gets straight to the point. "I understand there's been an issue at school, and a teacher is pressing charges. Is that correct?"

"Yes," Drew and I respond in unison.

"We will need to wait until we've seen the actual charges before responding. In the meantime, they might take Henry to the juvenile detention center for processing."

"Do they really need to do that?" I ask.

"Unfortunately, that's usually how the process goes," Megan says. "Henry, if they take you in for processing, I need you to inform them that you have legal representation. You will provide them with my name and insist on only speaking when your lawyer is present. Understand?"

Henry nods.

"They may attempt to get you to talk by letting your parents be in the room. Do not agree to that. You have the right to have a lawyer present, so you must be assertive and tell them you will only talk to them if your lawyer is there. Can you do that?"

Henry's eyes widen, but he nods in agreement.

"When do you think this will happen?" Drew asks.

"I'm sure they're working on gathering evidence for their case, but it could take days or even weeks; it's hard to predict. And this goes without saying, but I'll say it anyway: don't get into trouble in the meantime, okay Henry?"

Henry remains silent, his gaze fixed on the floor.

"Henry," Drew says firmly, trying to get his attention.

"Yeah," Henry mumbles. I notice the eye-roll, grateful that Drew either didn't see it or decided to ignore it.

"I know Henry is receiving mental health support," Megan says, looking through a stack of papers on her desk. "I'll need a release of information for his therapist so I can better grasp his mental health needs and build his case."

Henry's past floods my thoughts, making my heart rate pick up speed, its rapid beat whooshing in my ears. My lips tingle, signaling me to calm down. I grab Drew's hand to steady myself. We can't disclose anything about Henry's past; it would ruin all of our lives.

Megan continues, "Our main argument is that the event they are accusing you of never occurred. I refuse to even consider the possibility that it did. From my perspective, it's just kids spreading rumors, and it's absurd that a teacher would trust a group of thirteen and fourteen-year-olds enough to expel a well-behaved student over it. Did anyone sign a document confirming that Henry committed the actions they're accusing him of?"

"No," Henry states firmly, and Drew and I confirm that none of us signed anything.

"But maybe we confessed when we spoke to Dr. Paul about it?" It comes out more like a question than a statement. I can't recall exactly what we told Dr. Paul, but now I'm concerned that talking to him about it might have been a bad idea.

"Henry's discussions with his therapist are confidential and protected by patient-client privilege. We'll only involve Dr. Paul to provide character testimony. As far as I am concerned, Henry did not put urine in Mr. Donaldson's coffee. Principal First made a hasty judgment based on incomplete information. Henry is the one who's been unfairly treated." Megan offers Henry a reassuring smile. "Hopefully, we can resolve this before it goes to court. But let's talk about what might happen if it does. One possibility is that they could arrest you and keep you at the detention center until your trial. I don't think that's likely, but I want to warn you it could happen. The other reasonable possibility is that you would be arrested but allowed to stay home with your parents."

Henry is visibly shaking. I start to rise to comfort him, but Drew stops me by placing his hand on my knee.

Megan's gaze remains fixed on Henry as she says, "We're

going to practice what you'll say if they arrest you, okay?" He agrees with a slight nod.

Megan lowers her voice, perhaps attempting to sound like a male police officer, and says, "Henry, we need to ask you some questions." I silently applaud her attempt as I notice Henry's lips twitching, hinting at a slight smile.

Henry firmly states, "I've got a lawyer, and I won't talk until she's here."

"Great job, Henry," Megan compliments.

"What is your fee?" Drew asks.

"My hourly rate is $350. This initial consultation is free. If you decide that I'm the right lawyer for Henry, you can work with my office manager to set up a payment plan for future services."

"That sounds fine," I respond. Drew looks worried, and I realize we might not have the funds for this, but we have no other option. I refuse to leave Henry's well-being in the hands of the state.

THE FOLLOWING afternoon, Henry is arrested and charged with assault. The officer handcuffs Henry, and when I question if it's necessary, he ignores me and takes Henry out to a waiting police car.

I pace around the car, uncertain about what to do next. This is precisely the scenario we've worked so hard to avoid. I swear I see the neighbors' front curtains move and know they're watching us.

I request to ride with Henry, but the officer chuckles and shakes his head. He tells me I need to drive myself to the juvenile detention center. I knock on the window of the police car to get Henry's attention, but he continues to stare straight ahead, ignoring me. I shout through the glass, letting him know I'll be there and remind him of his lawyer's advice. I retreat inside the house, away from the nosy neighbors, to call Drew and Megan. Megan reassures me that we'll have Henry back home by tonight.

I drive to the juvenile detention center, which looks like a typical brick building except for the barbed wire encircling it. The thought of Henry being in there all by himself is overwhelming.

Once inside, I walk up to the reception area and tell the young woman behind the window I need to see my son.

"You'll have to sign in, take a seat, and wait," she responds without lifting her gaze.

"I need to see him right away. He's only fourteen," I say.

"You still have to wait," she replies, not bothering to look up from her paperwork. She doesn't even ask for his name.

I sit on the uncomfortable plastic chair, staring at the pale yellow brick walls. I try to hold back tears, but it's useless. I hurry to the restroom on the opposite side of the room, locking myself in. I splash cold water on my face and rest my hands on the sink. Looking into the mirror, I'm shocked by my disheveled appearance. I comb through my hair and pop a stick of gum into my mouth. Staring at my reflection, I give myself a pep talk, "Pull yourself together, Charlotte."

Megan is in the waiting area, looking flawless from head to toe. "How are you holding up?" she asks.

Realizing there's no point hiding it, I confess, "Not great."

"Don't worry, I'll make sure he's home tonight," Megan says, patting my arm. "Let's sit down, and I'll fill you in." She leads me to the hard plastic chairs before continuing. "Henry is being charged with assault. Mr. Donaldson is alleging that Henry tried to harm him by putting urine in his coffee, and now he's worried about further retaliation. However, there's no solid evidence; it's all based on hearsay. Henry has a clean history with no prior offenses. The judge will take that into account when examining the case. I'm certain there's no real basis for the charges; Mr. Donaldson is just being difficult and trying to find any reason to make a case."

Megan's confidence begins to reassure me. She walks up to the girl at the desk and politely requests to see her client, mentioning that she knows he has asked for his lawyer.

"Take a seat and wait," the rude girl informs her.

Megan doesn't back down. She completely changes her demeanor and demands, "My client is fourteen years old. He has asked for his lawyer, and I would hate for a child that young not to have his constitutional rights met."

In a matter of minutes, a guard accompanies Megan to see Henry. Drew arrives shortly after. He paces nervously, which is unusual for him. Seeing Drew like this brings back all the worries that Megan had just managed to ease.

Thirty minutes later, Megan emerges with a smile on her face.

"What happened?" I ask anxiously.

"I met with Henry. He's okay. There will be an arraignment hearing today at four o'clock," Megan replies. "Drew, keep your uniform on. We'll meet at the courthouse in an hour. They don't have a case, and they know it. They're just trying to intimidate Henry."

Drew follows me home, and I change into something more

suitable for court. After putting on some makeup, I tie my hair into a neat low ponytail. Looking at myself in the mirror, I realize I look like I'm going to a job interview. Drew drives us to the courthouse in silence. Neither of us has the brain space to talk. Once we pass through the metal detectors, I sit in another uncomfortable chair while Drew continues pacing.

Megan enters with her typical confidence. She clarifies that today is the arraignment hearing, where the judge will ask Henry to declare his plea to the charges. She tells us that Henry will plead not guilty, and she will ask the judge to allow Henry to come home with us today.

Megan leads us into the courtroom, gesturing for us to sit in an empty row before leaving to wait with Henry. My leg bounces up and down while we sit through several other cases until Henry's turn. He's escorted into the courtroom by a deputy. I notice how young Henry looks with his crumpled cartoon character t-shirt and jeans that are an inch too short. I hadn't even realized he'd had another growth spurt. His eyes are bloodshot, and his hair looks greasy and overdue for a trim.

The judge reads the charges and asks Henry how he pleads. "Not guilty, Your Honor," Henry replies.

Megan says, "I'm representing Henry, and I can prove that he did not do what the state claims he did. I am asking that you release Henry to his parents' custody today. His father is a firefighter and a respected member of this community, and his mother works from home to be present for Henry. Henry is a good student with no prior violations and was unjustly accused and expelled."

"I've reviewed the state's case. How do you plan to prove that

Henry did what the state is claiming?" the judge asks, directing his question to the prosecutor.

"We... We have eyewitnesses," the young man stammers.

"Do you have an eyewitness who saw Henry urinate in the vial?" Megan asks, with a hint of humor in her voice. "Because I don't have any names of such people on my list."

The prosecutor shuffles through some paperwork before responding, "We have eyewitnesses who claim Henry told them he put urine in the vial."

"He's a fourteen-year-old boy who made up a story to impress his classmates," Megan counters. "He never put urine in his teacher's coffee."

"Did you put urine in your teacher's coffee, young man?" the judge asks Henry directly.

"No, Your Honor," Henry lies effortlessly, without hesitation.

"Does the state have any forensic evidence in this case?" the judge asks the prosecutor.

"We're still working on gathering it," he says. His neck appears to be breaking out in hives.

"All right then," the judge says with a slight smile. "Henry will be released to his parents until the trial. He must continue his education by attending a different school in person or through homeschooling and adhere to an 8:00 p.m. curfew. Additionally, Henry is not allowed to contact students from his previous school. That includes chat apps and social media. Do you understand, Henry?"

"Yes, sir," he replies.

The judge dismisses Henry, and Megan guides him out of the courtroom, with us trailing behind.

In the hallway, Megan says, "It has been a long day, and I'm sure you're eager to get home. I advise you to enroll Henry in one of the other middle schools as soon as possible. Although I don't foresee any media attention, it's important to be cautious as they can be deceptive. It's wise to limit your conversations and refrain from discussing anything related to the case with anyone. Don't engage in any discussions with investigators unless I'm present. Their attempt at employing scare tactics to coerce Henry into admitting guilt is pointless. Their case lacks substance and will be dismissed without admission," Megan says confidently.

"I really appreciate everything you've done to help us," I tell Megan.

"It's her job," Drew interjects, his tone tinged with anger.

The ride home is silent. I'm concerned that Drew might explode if he refuses to discuss the situation.

When we get home, Henry goes to his room, and Drew heads to the kitchen. I hear the refrigerator door slamming and the sound of a can being opened. I walk into the kitchen to find him chugging a beer. He places it on the table heavily and then sinks onto one of the chairs. I sit beside him and gently put my hand on his back.

He pounds his fist on the table, startling me. "This whole case is built on a lie, just like Henry's life," he hisses through clenched teeth.

"Drew," I whisper. "Henry's life is not a lie. Everything will be okay. That's why we hired Megan. She's good."

"And expensive," he says, rubbing the bridge of his nose with his fingers. "By the time this is over, we'll owe thousands of dollars, and for what? This whole case is ridiculous."

"We can set up a payment plan, and Henry can do odd jobs around here and for the neighbors to pay us back," I suggest.

"The neighbors probably won't want anything to do with us after seeing him taken away in a cop car. How do you think that makes us look?" He asks, running his hand through his hair. "Our kid put his piss in a man's coffee. Doesn't that concern you?"

"Of course, but we have to keep him out of jail," I say quietly. "He'll learn even worse behaviors in there."

Drew grabs another beer, leaning against the counter as he takes a long drink. "What if the treatment didn't work? Maybe that's why he's acting out," Drew says, sounding defeated.

I walk over to him, wrapping my arms around his waist. "It worked, Drew. It's just been tough not having you around as much lately."

"What difference does it make if I'm around?" he asks defensively.

"It makes a difference to us. We really miss you," I say, gently squeezing him. Eventually, he eases up and hugs me back.

Henry enters the kitchen, appearing freshly showered with clean clothes and dripping hair.

"I'm starving," he declares, opening the refrigerator.

"How about some mac and cheese?" I suggest stepping back from Drew and opening a cupboard.

"Thanks, Mom, that sounds good," Henry says, grabbing the orange juice container from the fridge. Drew reaches for a glass and hands it to him before he drinks straight from the carton.

Henry takes the glass with a slight smirk and fills it to the brim. He leans down to take a sip and then leans against the counter.

"I'm sorry," Henry says, his voice cracking. "I promise I'll never do something so stupid again."

Drew walks up to him, places his hands on his shoulders, and looks him in the eye. Henry meets his gaze, tears rolling down his face. Drew pulls him into a hug, and I join, hopeful things will work out.

chapter forty-one

Henry begs us not to send him back to school. He is extremely anxious about starting over at a new school and is worried that because we live in a small town, all the kids will know what happened. Knowing that I don't have the patience or time to homeschool Henry, Drew and I brainstorm alternatives. I propose contacting Logan to see if he can help out for a little while. Drew thinks it's a long shot and isn't sure how we can afford it, even if Logan is available. I assure him we will figure it out, just like always.

Logan is between jobs, working as a grip on a movie set. He's still following his dream but hasn't quite achieved it yet. I ask if he would be interested in taking a break from the grind to tutor Henry for the remainder of the year until Henry starts high school. Logan asks for a couple of days to think it over, which makes me anxious, but I tell him to take the time he needs. I am relieved when he phones the next day to say he can do it and can start by next week.

We move my work desk to a corner of our bedroom and arrange the guest room for Logan. It's nothing fancy, but Logan assures us it is nicer than the place he was living at in LA.

TWO WEEKS later, as Megan predicted, they drop Henry's case. We receive her bill for $6,800. Drew, Henry, and I come up with ideas on how Henry can help pay back what we owe Megan. Henry chooses to take on additional chores around the house and volunteer at the fire station. Drew continues to work long hours as he advances in his career, so I'm thankful that Henry can spend time with him there occasionally. Now that things are calming down and Henry is in a better mental space, Drew appears to be returning to his old self. My career is progressing, and I've also been promoted. It's great timing because now, with the extra income, we can afford to pay Logan. I had a feeling everything would fall into place.

Logan and Henry establish a good routine. Logan shares his passion for running with Henry, and they go for a run nearly every morning. I am impressed by Henry's dedication, especially when he keeps up with Logan during the cold winter months.

Henry is doing well with his school work. Logan makes things fun—science experiments in the kitchen and reading in the hammock. He also teaches Henry handy kitchen tricks, like making a fancy ramen bowl and jazzing up a box of mac and cheese. Almost every evening after dinner, the boys play chess. Henry is a natural and often beats Logan. I love hearing them laugh, and I'm grateful that Henry has such a good friend.

ONE EVENING, Drew is working late, and I'm catching up on some work in my makeshift office. I can hear the boys in Henry's room playing their nightly chess game. Henry bursts into laughter—most likely at one of their inside jokes they find so hilarious.

Once I'm done with my emails, I run a bath to unwind. As I settle into the bubbles, I hear Henry yell, "You cheated!" and then a loud crash.

I wait, straining to hear, hoping Logan can handle it. But a moment later, Henry erupts again, shouting, "You're lying! You did cheat!" followed by another crash, louder than the first.

I quickly get out of the tub, throw on my robe, and rush to Henry's room. Henry is visibly trembling, his face flushed, his fists clenched, and he is breathing heavily. Memories of when we first brought him home flood my mind, clouding my ability to understand what's happening. The room is messy, with chess pieces, broken ceramics, and coins scattered everywhere. I realize Henry's piggy bank has been smashed—its head is next to the family portrait that has fallen from the wall.

"What's happened?" I ask in shock.

"Logan cheated and lied about it," Henry says, jabbing his finger toward Logan.

"No one is lying to you, Henry," I say calmly.

"I would never lie to you," Logan insists, and I can swear he stresses the word "I."

I glance between Logan and Henry, trying to figure out how to handle the situation. I'm relieved when Logan suggests that they go for a run to blow off some steam before they tackle the mess. Logan looks to me for approval, and I nod in agreement. I tell Henry that he can clean up when they get back.

The water in the tub has turned cold, so I empty it and curl up with my book instead, but I can't concentrate. A glass of wine might help me unwind. As I pour myself a generous glass of pinot grigio, I hear the boys talking in the garage. Logan asks Henry if he wants to shoot some hoops before going back inside. I roll my eyes—they are great at stalling.

"Dude, why'd you chuck your piggy bank at baby Henry? Did he need some money?" Logan teases.

"That baby has always given me the creeps. I hate that picture," Henry laughs.

"So do I," I whisper, taking a long drink of my wine.

chapter forty-two

Drew, Henry, and I have a farewell dinner for Logan featuring all his favorite dishes. Henry wanted to buy the running shoes Logan always talked about as a goodbye present. Drew and I agreed to purchase them, even though they were more expensive than we had budgeted. Logan has been incredibly helpful to us throughout the past year and deserves a special gift.

Henry mopes around for a few days after Logan leaves, but fortunately, he is adjusting well to high school. He continues his passion for running by joining the cross-country team. The coach mentions that Henry shows genuine potential and values his dedication. Henry has formed some friendships within the team. He often talks about a boy named Conner.

I met Conner's mom, Christine, at the first cross-country meet, and we hit it off immediately. She invited me to join her book club. When I asked about the book they were reading, she gave me a mischievous smile and confessed that they don't actually read books. Instead, they use the gathering to gossip, commiserate about life with teenagers, and enjoy a glass or two of wine.

At our first "book club," I receive a warm welcome. The

group consists of five moms with teenagers. They are funny, kind, and supportive. I share with them how I feel like I'm back to being single because Henry is constantly busy with school, cross-country, and hanging out with friends, while Drew is always working. Everyone nods in agreement and some chime in with similar experiences. One warns you'll never see your kids again once they get their driver's license. Another says she feels like a free hotel for her teens, who only talk to her when they want something.

Christine pours more wine for everyone and mentions she needs some advice. She is considering letting her boyfriend, Rick, move in but is still determining whether it's a good idea. The women bombard her with questions and create a list of pros and cons. She loves him. It makes financial sense. He's already there all the time anyway. He smokes more pot than she would like, but it's better than being a real drug addict. It seems fast. She would love a male figure for Conner. He's kind of messy. He's sweet and brings her flowers. I suggest she take at least a day to think about it. Later that night, she texts me that she has decided to let Rick move in. I'm happy for her.

We laugh and chat for hours during our weekly "book club" meetings. I never realized how nice it was to have other women to confide in, talk about my problems, and provide support. I am an open book—mostly.

AT THE end of the cross-country season, Henry still spends most of his time with Conner. I'm happy that he's found such a good friend. They hang out at Conner's place more than ours, probably because Conner has a newer gaming system. While sharing a bottle of wine with Christine one evening, I asked if she minded that the boys were always at her house.

She responded quickly, saying, "Henry's more than welcome to hang out here. He's such a good kid, polite and helpful. The other day, he put everyone's dinner dishes in the sink and wiped down all the countertops."

"Are you sure you're talking about my Henry?" I joked. "He's tall, grunts when he talks and eats like a horse."

"I am positive," she replied, making the Scout's honor sign.

"Well, that must be nice," I laughed.

ONE SATURDAY morning, I'm home alone because Drew is dealing with a fire at one of the state parks, and Henry is at Conner's house. I'm lounging on the couch, engrossed in my latest romance novel, when I hear the kitchen door creak open. I look up from my book and catch Henry trying to sneak past me to his bedroom.

"Hello, Henry," I greet him cheerfully.

He keeps walking, grunting a greeting.

I quickly stand up to block his way, and he stops short in front of me. He reeks of body odor and skunk.

"Were you smoking weed?" I ask.

His bloodshot eyes meet mine. "No, Mom. I would never do that. Coach would be pissed."

"Huh," I say, placing my hands on my hips, cocking my head to one side. "I'm just wondering why your eyes are bloodshot and you smell like bad weed."

He rolls his eyes. "Mom, you know Christine's boyfriend smokes pot, right?" he sighs heavily. "Conner and I don't touch

223

it. Are you gonna make a big deal about this? It's just pot, and it's legal. Why do you care if Rick smokes?"

"I care because I don't want you around it. It's not good for a developing mind."

"How's all that wine you drink on your developing liver?" he smirks as he pushes past me down the hall.

I stand speechless until I hear Drew's truck pull into the garage. I greet him in the kitchen as he comes through the door. He looks exhausted, with black soot still streaked across his face. He gives me a weak smile and wraps his arms around my waist, leaning down to lay his head on my shoulder. I rub his back and whisper, "I love you." Drew whispers it back and kisses me.

"Why don't you take a long, hot shower," I suggest. "I'll make you something to eat."

A half-hour later, Drew comes into the kitchen, pours a generous glass of whiskey, and sits at the table. He fills me in about the fire. This fall has been warmer and drier than usual, causing the flames to spread quickly. They suspect foul play but are still searching for clues.

"Who would have done that on purpose?" I wonder aloud.

He sighs, "It could have been anyone."

I set a plate with eggs, bacon, and hash browns in front of him.

"This looks amazing. Thank you, amore."

"You're very welcome." I kiss the top of his head before sitting down next to him.

Henry strolls into the kitchen and swings open the fridge, as always, hungry.

"Any kids talking about the fire at the state park?" Drew asks

Henry.

"I haven't heard anything," Henry responds, closing the fridge.

"Do you want some eggs?" I ask.

"Sure, Mom, that'd be great."

"I'll let you know when they're ready," I call after him—he is already halfway back to his room.

I crack the eggs in the pan and then turn to Drew. "Henry was at Conner's house last night. You don't think they were involved, do you?"

"No, Christine keeps a good eye on the boys."

He's right. Christine has been amazing with Henry. She even found out about his first girlfriend before I did. But honestly, I'm not upset about it. I'm just thankful Henry has another trustworthy adult he can confide in.

chapter forty-three

Drew and Emily begin communicating again through text messages. They've found a connection through sharing memes, which has surprisingly helped bridge the gap between them.

They're excited about the plans for the upcoming weekend when Emily and her family will be staying in a place right on the bay. I managed to score them a sweet deal through one of my book club friends, who rented it to them for half the price she usually charges. Emily couldn't resist the offer, and Drew is looking forward to seeing his sister again.

We planned to visit several wineries in our area and asked Amelia to be our designated driver. The weather is perfect, with clear skies and a soft breeze. Our adventure starts at a stunning vineyard atop a hill, offering breathtaking views of the sprawling countryside and the sparkling bay in the distance.

We settle on the expansive outdoor patio, surrounded by lush greenery and the sweet aroma of blossoming flowers. As we enjoy our wine tasting, we snack on a charcuterie board featuring a variety of gourmet cheeses, cured meats, and local goodies.

It's nice reconnecting with everyone and seeing how much the kids have grown. Amelia is in college, pursuing a degree in social work. Mason is set to graduate high school this year and is considering studying computer security in college. He mentions the possibility of him and Henry living together after Henry graduates so they can go to school together.

We visit four more wineries, each one better than the last. At our final stop, we stroll through the vineyards, chatting while the kids run ahead, tossing grapes at one another and laughing. I'm glad that we've left past issues behind us. It's encouraging to see Henry forming positive relationships with his cousins.

As the sun sets over the vineyards, casting a warm golden glow across the landscape, we call it a day. We opt to grab a couple of pizzas to enjoy back at home. The kids turn down our offer to play board games, saying they fulfilled their duty and want some time to hang out without parents.

THE FOLLOWING morning, sunlight pours through the bedroom windows, revealing another beautiful day. However, my headache from too much wine yesterday has turned into a raging migraine. I close the blinds and crawl back into bed, placing a cold cloth over my eyes.

By dinnertime, I feel rejuvenated after a long shower and am prepared to face the world again. Drew brings home Thai food and updates me on his day with his sister and her family. Henry is quiet and asks to leave the table after he finishes eating. Shortly after, I hear music blaring from his room. Not wanting my headache to return, I knock on his door to ask him to turn it down. There's no answer.

I open his door and stick my head in. "Henry, your music is too loud."

He snaps his laptop closed and looks up with guilt in his eyes.

"What are you looking at?" I ask.

"Noneya." He rolls his eyes and pushes past me.

I turn his speaker off and follow him to the kitchen. Henry asks Drew if he will take him to do some practice driving. Drew glances at me, and I nod yes. Once they're gone, I return to Henry's room and check his browsing history, hoping he isn't watching porn. To my relief, I find a list of searches about childhood mental health disorders instead. I make a mental note to mention it to Dr. Paul.

chapter forty-four

Henry insists on doing his driving practice only with Drew, all because of that one time I yelled and grabbed the steering wheel. I feel slightly left out, but I'm happy he is spending time with Drew.

I'm glad I still have my "book club." It's nice to be included somewhere. The hot topics of conversation mostly revolve around significant others and raising teenagers. Listening to my friends navigate the challenges of their family lives makes me appreciate my family more. My problems are minor in comparison.

Nora shares the story of her daughter running away with her boyfriend. She searched for a whole week until she tracked them down in Grand Rapids. They had been staying in a run-down motel in a scary part of town.

Sydney shares a disturbing story she read online about a boy who stabbed his younger brother twenty-five times. The group becomes quiet, contemplating the harsh truth of how pointless violence can destroy lives. That poor family. I can't even begin to imagine what they're going through.

Courtney is concerned her husband might be cheating on her during his business trips, so she's thinking about hiring a private investigator to find out.

My biggest worry at the moment is my mother wanting to visit for the weekend. I seek advice from the other women, expressing my uncertainty about the situation. I can't stop wondering what her intentions are, but at the same time, I'm hopeful she can build a connection with Henry. I'm conflicted because I don't want her to cause him the same pain she caused me. But perhaps, with time, she's changed and is beginning to realize the relationships she's missed out on all these years.

Avery believes I should move on from the past and allow my mother to come. Last year, her mother passed away while they were going through a rough patch, and she regrets not being on better terms with her because now it's too late to do anything about it.

THE FOLLOWING weekend, my mother arrives in good spirits. She talks with Henry, and he seems happy to spend time with her. Seeing them bond fills me with optimism. I hope her intentions are sincere and she will remain a part of Henry's life. I stick close to them the whole first day, uneasy about what my mother might be scheming.

That evening, we sit out on the patio after dinner. Two glasses of wine in, I gather the courage to ask her why she came. At first, she seems surprised by my question, but then she admits that she's been reflecting on things lately and recognizes she's been missing out on important aspects of life. I'm not sure if I believe her, but it sounds nice, and I allow myself a little hope.

The following day, she dedicates her time to Henry, having him show her his favorite spots in town. They enjoy each other's company over pizza, ice cream, and a few rounds of mini-golf and air hockey games. Later, they unwind on the patio, playing cards together. Hearing their laughter fills me with mixed emotions— it's heartwarming to witness the bond they're forming, yet it also reminds me of the relationship I've always wanted to have with my mother.

On the final day of her visit, Mother and Henry return home with rosy cheeks from spending the day at the beach. While she heads to pack and shower, I begin preparing dinner. Henry joins me in the kitchen, perching on the counter as I chop vegetables.

"Guess what?" he asks, not waiting for me to respond before continuing, "Grandma's going to help me buy a car!"

"Oh, really?" I say, trying to keep the sarcasm out of my voice. "Don't count your chickens before they've hatched."

"Why can't you be happy for me?" I detect the annoyance in his voice. "You're such a downer."

"I'm sorry," I pause my chopping to look at him. "When I was growing up, your grandmother made a lot of promises she didn't keep."

"It doesn't mean she won't come through for me."

"You're right," I say, resuming my task.

"She told me she would get her used grandkid a used car. Why is she calling me used?"

I almost cut my finger as his words catch me off guard. "I have no idea." I take a deep breath, steadying myself. "Maybe because you're not a baby anymore."

He shrugs, then jumps from the counter and heads to his room. When his music starts blaring, I find my mother to have a chat. She's in the guest room, packing. I step inside and close the door behind me before speaking to her.

"Why would you tell Henry he is used?" I ask through clenched teeth, my voice trembling with anger.

"It was a joke." She continues folding clothes into her suitcase as if her words carry no weight.

"He doesn't know he is adopted. Remember, we created all the videos to help him bond with us so he would be secure in knowing we wanted him from the beginning. We have worked so hard to give him security and love, and now you might have just ruined it by being a total asshole."

"Language, Charlotte." Her tone is patronizing as if I am a child. "I didn't tell him you adopted him. I know you've built your whole life on lies, and I don't agree with it."

I grab the shirt she's holding out of her hand and throw it on the bed. "We weren't just willy-nilly lying. We were helping Henry overcome a terrible attachment disorder and providing him with a chance at a better life. One where he wouldn't end up in an institution or worse."

"No one asked Henry if that's what he wanted." She snatches the shirt from the bed and throws it into the suitcase. "You decided for him, and it wasn't right. Everyone has the right to know their own history and where they come from. You've brainwashed him, and you continue to do so every single day. Those fake pictures and videos... that's not right, Charlotte."

"Oh, that's rich coming from someone who has always pretended to be someone else." I lock eyes with her, daring her to contradict me, knowing she's well aware of the validity of my statement.

She plants her hands on her hips, her eyes twitching slightly, lips pressed into a thin line. "Someone had to work to pay the bills, Charlotte."

"Dad worked his butt off, Mother." I won't back down like I would have in the past. "You chose to move us around to chase your unreasonable dreams. We were never in one place long enough for him to find decent work."

"You've always put your father on a pedestal. We had to move so much because he kept getting into trouble with the law. He would get drunk and then start fights with the landlord, your teachers, or some random person." She gestures wildly with her arms. "We had to move to prevent your father from going to jail. He was nothing but a liar, and it looks like the apple didn't fall far from the tree." She keeps her eyes locked on mine, silently urging me to keep arguing.

"You point fingers at everyone else for lying when you're the biggest liar of them all. You were never going to buy Henry a car. You just wanted to get his hopes up so he would start liking you, and then you could turn around and disappoint him like you always did with me." I feel like my heart might burst out of my chest. "Just go. I never should've let you come."

"I'm leaving. Don't bother calling the next time you need something from me."

"I need something from you like I need a hole in the head."

She zips her suitcase and leaves the room without saying another word.

When Henry and I sit down for dinner, he asks, "Where's Dad and Grandma?"

"Dad had to work late, and Grandma had to leave. Her flight

got switched to an earlier one." I tell him, keeping my tone light.

His expression darkens. "She didn't even say goodbye. She was going to buy me a car."

"Don't count on it. Your grandma is getting dementia or something. You shouldn't believe a word she says. She lives in her own selfish world where everything revolves around her. She will never change."

"Geez, Mom. That's rude."

"I'm trying to protect you, Henry. I shouldn't have let her come."

"All you ever think about is yourself." He slams his fork down on the table with such force it startles me.

"You have no idea all the sacrifices I have made for you. All the literal shit you put me through." The words are out before I can stop them.

"The shit I put you through? You're crazy. What about all the shit you put me through? I've been in therapy my whole life to try and be the perfect kid for you." His eyes are filled with hurt.

My voice softens. "No, Henry. We love you just the way you are," I say, reaching out to touch his hand resting on the table.

He jerks his hand away, his face contorted with anger. "I call bullshit. Fuck you," he shouts, pushing his chair back and storming out of the room. A moment later, his bedroom door slams shut so forcefully that the whole house shakes.

chapter forty-five

I'm furious with myself for allowing my mother back into our lives. She will never change. I toss the uneaten lasagna into the fridge before pouring a generous glass of wine.

I sit on the couch in the dark, waiting for Drew to show up. The more I think about how my mother consistently messes things up, the more angry I become.

As soon as Drew arrives, I tell him everything. He's livid when he learns about my mother's ridiculous comment, and his anger escalates as I recount the confrontation with Henry. His expression darkens, and without a word, he storms off.

The sudden pounding on Henry's door startles me.

"Open up! Now!" Drew's voice echoes down the hallway.

Silence.

"Damn it, Henry! Unlock this door!" His voice is laced with urgency.

I rush to Drew and remind him about the spare key hidden above the door.

He reaches up and grabs the key, shoving it into the lock. Drew pushes the door so forcefully that it slams against the wall. Henry is nowhere to be found, but the window is wide open, and the screen is missing.

Drew runs to the window, looking out into the darkness. "I'm gonna kill him."

"Calm down. Losing it won't help. I'll call Christine to see if he's at her place."

She picks up on the first ring, "What's up?"

"Henry snuck out of his room. Is he over there?"

"I don't think so, but let me check."

After briefly pausing, she adds, "Looks like Conner's gone too. He was supposed to be doing his homework."

"Alright, we'll track him. Hold on."

Drew pulls up the app, and we know Henry is at the park within seconds.

"Meet you there!" Christine says before disconnecting the call.

It takes us less than five minutes to get to the playground.

We spot the boys near a trash can engulfed in flames. Drew grabs the extinguisher from his truck and races over to douse the fire.

Henry's eyes widen in shock when he sees us. The unmistakable scent of weed hangs in the air.

"Stay right there, both of you!" Drew's voice booms with authority.

Christine arrives as Drew gets the fire under control. "What the hell are you doing?" she screams, voicing what we're all thinking.

"We were just messing around." Conner waves away our concern.

Henry pipes in, wearing a smug grin on his obviously high

face. "Yeah, we did the city a favor. Now they don't have to empty this trash can."

Drew cuts in, his tone serious, "There are dry leaves everywhere. What if a spark blew into the grass and ignited a bigger fire? It could spread to nearby homes and put lives in danger."

Henry shoves his hands in his pockets. "You always gotta make a big deal out of everything."

Drew is livid. "You're acting like a complete idiot. You're grounded."

Henry smirks, challenging Drew to continue the argument.

"You better wipe that smile off your face." Drew steps closer, pointing his finger at him. "You're losing all privileges for the next two weeks. No friends, no phone, and no computer. You'll be spending your time doing nothing but homework or reading."

"Gonna be hard to do my homework without my computer," Henry says, still grinning.

"Listen to me carefully," Drew's voice strains. "Get in the car right now, and don't say another word. You'll do your homework at the dining table, then go straight to bed. And let me make this clear: if you ever pull a stunt like this again, I won't hesitate to call the police and have you arrested as a runaway. And we won't bail you out."

Conner nudges Henry's arm, and they both burst into laughter.

Christine puts her hands on her hips. "You two better cut it out."

Drew's face is flushed with anger, his neck veins bulging. "Consider this your warning. If I catch a whiff of weed on either of you again, you'll regret it."

"Yes, sir." Conner salutes as Christine grabs his shirt and pulls him toward her car.

Drew exhales deeply, giving the trash can a final blast with the fire extinguisher.

Henry's music is so loud in the truck that I can hear it through his headphones.

"Headphones." Drew orders, reaching out his hand. Henry hands them over.

Drew tightens his grip on the steering wheel. "When we get home, your mom and I will search your room. Starting tomorrow, you'll be drug tested every day. If you test positive for any drugs, I won't hesitate to turn you in. You're not going to be an addict. Have I made myself clear?"

"Crystal," Henry says casually.

"Whose bright idea was it to set the trash can on fire?" I ask.

"Conner's," Henry says quickly. "He wanted to see if it would burn. He got the weed from Rick. I didn't smoke any."

"Whatever," Drew mutters through clenched teeth.

"It doesn't matter. You never believe me anyway," Henry says.

"We've always given you the benefit of the doubt, Henry, but it's difficult to trust you when you keep lying." Drew slams his palm against the steering wheel.

I reach out and touch Drew's hand, giving it a reassuring squeeze. The tension in the car is thick enough to cut with a knife.

Once we're back home, Henry bolts into the house with Drew in hot pursuit. They get to Henry's room simultaneously, with me on their heels. Drew snatches Henry's laptop from his desk and orders him to do his homework at the kitchen table.

"So, you're gonna search my room like I'm some kind of criminal?"

"Today, you acted like one." Drew throws his arms up, letting them fall heavily to his sides. "You ran away and vandalized public property."

Henry blows out a breath. "Big whoop. I destroyed some garbage."

Drew shoves Henry against the bedroom wall, locking eyes with him. For the first time, it hits me that Henry and Drew are the same height, but Drew still has at least fifty pounds on him.

Drew keeps his hand firmly pressed against Henry's chest. "You need to get your act together because if you don't, I promise you won't like what happens next."

He tightens his grip on Henry's shirt and pushes him out the door, thrusting the laptop into his hands. "Go do your homework. I've got a room to search."

chapter forty-six

Two days later, an old barn went up in flames, swiftly spreading to a neighboring Christmas tree farm. Despite having the weekend off, Drew rushed to the scene in the middle of the night to lend a hand. Firefighters from Elmwood and Grawn were also called to assist. The smoke blanketed the city in a thick layer of gray.

THE FOLLOWING morning I'm snuggled in a blanket on the couch, coffee in hand. I lose myself in my latest romance novel. The news coverage of the fire doesn't interest me; the news anchors exaggerate everything, blowing it out of proportion.

The sudden ring of my phone startles me, but seeing Drew's name on the screen makes me smile. I answer, saying, "How is Traverse City's sexiest fireman?"

There's a brief pause before a voice responds, "Uh, Charlotte, it's not Drew. This is Captain Washington."

My cheeks flush with embarrassment.

"Drew has been admitted to the hospital. You need to get there as soon as possible."

My heart picks up speed. "What happened?" I ask.

"We aren't one hundred percent sure. They will have more

information for you at the hospital."

The phone drops from my hand, and I sprint down the hallway to Henry's room, barging in. It's empty. Racing to my room, I throw on a pair of jeans and a sweatshirt, then run back to the living room to search for my phone. I dial Henry's number, but it goes straight to voicemail.

"Henry, Dad's in the hospital. Meet me there," I shout, unable to hide the urgency in my voice.

Running to my car, I command Siri to call Christine. When she answers, I ask if Henry is at her house.

"I don't think so. Conner mentioned that Drew grounded Henry for two weeks."

"Something happened to Drew," I choke on the words. "Henry's not here. Can you help me find him?"

"What happened to Drew?"

"I don't know. I'm on my way to the hospital," I say, struggling to hold back my tears.

The rest of the drive is a blur. Parking in the first empty spot, I rush to the emergency room entrance. I tell the person behind the security glass that I need to see my husband.

The guard asks for his name and taps on his keyboard before buzzing the door to let me in.

Inside, an older woman is behind the check-in window. After I provide Drew's name, she checks the computer and informs me that he is in surgery. Overwhelmed with emotion, I break down. Seeing my distress, she leaves her post and guides me to a nearby chair. I hide my face in my hands, tears streaming down my cheeks.

The woman sits beside me, placing her hand on my knee.

"Take a deep breath, dear. You'll be able to see him soon. Please let me know if you need anything," she adds before returning to her desk.

Gradually, I calm down, realizing I have people to notify. My first call is to Emily. She promises to come as quickly as she can. We agreed to hold off on telling Drew's parents until we have more information. Emily reassures me there's no need to worry them because Drew will be okay.

Next, I call Christine to update her on the situation—Drew's in surgery, and I'm still waiting to speak with a doctor. Christine informs me she's out searching for the boys.

Feeling numb, all I can do is stare at the wall. The woman from earlier comes over to see how I'm doing and offers coffee or tea. I politely decline, knowing my stomach can't handle anything at the moment.

Needing to hear Drew's voice, I listen to old voicemails. One from last year makes me smile. "Guess who just rescued a naked lady from a burning building? If you see me on the news carrying a naked lady, I promise I wasn't cheating on you."

I recall watching the news that night, hoping to catch a glimpse of my heroic, sexy husband in action. They interviewed the woman he saved, who was at least seventy years old. She expressed gratitude for the kind young man who saved her life, mentioning he was easy on the eyes. I joked about her Firefighters calendar forever being stuck in July because Drew was featured that month.

Scrolling through our text messages, I see hundreds of kissy faces and heart emojis. Drew sends me a "good morning" text every day he works. On nights when he's at the fire station, his message before bed is always the same: "Good night, amore. Sweet dreams," followed by rows of heart-eyed emojis.

Christine arrives with Henry and Conner. She hurries over to me, and I rise to hug her.

Then, I turn my attention to Henry. "Where have you been?"

"We just wanted to check out the fire. What's going on with Dad?"

"He's in surgery. I'm waiting to get an update."

"Sorry I wasn't here sooner." He looks down at his feet.

I pull him into a hug—the unmistakable scent of burnt pine lingers on his clothes. "It's okay, you didn't know."

"What can I do to help?" Christine asks, hovering anxiously. "How about I whip you guys up some dinner? I'll drop it by your place so you have something to eat when you're all home safe and sound tonight."

I manage a weak smile. "Thank you. And thanks for finding Henry."

"I'm parked in a no-parking zone. I better go move my car."

"It's okay, you can go. Emily should be here soon."

"Are you sure?" she asks, taking my hands. "I can stay, no problem."

"I'm sure."

Christine hugs me before leaving, and Conner trails behind.

I sit next to Henry. "Want to tell me what you guys were doing last night?"

"We were playing video games, and Conner saw some posts about the fire, so we went to check it out. That's it."

All I can do is nod—I'm too overwhelmed to have this conversation right now.

We sit in silence, the TV droning on in the background as the gravity of the situation sinks in further. Emily arrives, and we all sit, staring at the TV. Several firefighters stop by to offer support. I try to reassure everyone that Drew will be okay, but the words feel hollow and meaningless.

Someone offers me a sandwich, but attempting to force down a bite results in it getting stuck in my throat, making me gag. I rush to the restroom to vomit. Staring at my reflection in the mirror, the toll of the past few hours is evident, prompting me to try to calm myself with a pep talk. "He's strong. He's in good hands. He's receiving the best care possible." However, as the words leave my lips, I struggle to believe them.

A doctor, still dressed in scrubs, finally shows up. He introduces himself as Dr. Bennett and guides us to a small room. Memories of the day my dad passed flood my mind, causing my legs to feel like jelly. Deep down, I realize that whatever we're about to hear will alter my life forever.

Dr. Bennett delivers the devastating news, using medical jargon like "blockage" and "massive heart attack," but my mind refuses to accept the grim reality. I cling to the possibility that he'll reassure us, telling me Drew will recover soon. But the seriousness in his voice crushes that hope. His apology confirms my worst fears.

A primal cry escapes my lips, the weight of the news hitting me like a freight train, leaving me gasping for air. The room spins as I lose consciousness, only to awaken on the floor with Emily and Dr. Bennett by my side. It hits me like a ton of bricks—this nightmare is real.

chapter forty-seven

Dr. Bennett and Emily help me back to the chair next to Henry. I reach out, placing my hand over his, silently sharing the unbearable burden of our grief.

The doctor gives us the chance to say our final goodbyes, and as we step into the dimly lit room, my heart feels like it's shattering into a million pieces. Drew is pale—the light that once shone so brightly inside him is gone.

I sit beside the bed and take his hand in mine. Tears stream down my face—this will be the last time I'll ever feel Drew's touch. The gravity of that realization crushes me, and I feel like I am drowning in a flood of raw emotion.

"Goodbye, my love," I whisper through my tears. I kiss Drew's cheek for the last time, wishing desperately for a different ending but knowing it's impossible. Drew is gone.

Reluctantly, I stand, not wanting to leave him but understanding I have no other option. Emily embraces me, and we cling to each other in our grief. I don't know how much time passes, but eventually, Emily suggests we should find Henry. I hadn't even realized he had left.

Emily leads us back to the waiting room, where Captain

Washington is waiting. "Charlotte, I am so sorry for your loss," he says, his eyes glistening with unshed tears. "Please let me help you with the arrangements. We have a fund for firefighters who have lost their lives in the line of duty, and everything will be taken care of."

I hug him. "Thank you."

Henry is nowhere to be found. My calls to him go to voicemail. The tracking device isn't working; perhaps he forgot to charge his phone. My anxiety mounts, but I am so exhausted I can't think straight. I call Christine to tell her the heartbreaking news and explain that I can't find Henry. She assures me she'll search for him.

Emily drives us home and handles the remaining calls. The news quickly spreads, and soon, there's a steady stream of people bringing soups and casseroles. Emily graciously accepts their offerings, but I find myself not able to move from the sofa.

As the sun goes down, the house falls silent. I am relieved when Henry walks in, with Christine trailing behind. He goes straight to his room. Christine sits beside me on the couch and holds my hand. It's a small act but it brings a moment of steadiness to my chaotic world. I thank her for finding Henry, and she assures me she's here to support us, no matter what we need.

"I need my husband to not be dead," I manage to say before my voice breaks.

"I'm so sorry," Christine says, comforting me by rubbing my back.

I inhale deeply, attempting to compose myself, resolved to remain strong for Henry. Christine promises to keep her phone with her in case I need anything. Emily heads off to shower. I'm thankful she'll be staying in the guest room tonight.

I knock on Henry's door and walk in. He's lying in bed, wrapped up in his comforter. Sitting up, he pushes his long bangs out of his red and swollen eyes. My heart aches for him. Despite their recent difficulties, Henry thought the world of Drew. I hope Henry realizes Drew loved him unconditionally.

"How are you holding up?" I ask, taking a seat on the edge of his bed.

"I'm alright. Sorry, I didn't call."

"It's okay. But please don't disappear again. I was worried. Tomorrow, I'm meeting Captain Washington at the funeral home. Do you want to come along?"

"Do I have to?"

"No, of course not." I embrace him.

"Will we still be able to stay here?" Henry asks.

"Of course, sweetheart. Don't worry. I've got everything under control."

"Can I still get a car?"

"Yes, absolutely. What do you think about driving Dad's truck once you've got your license?"

"Sure," he says, wiping the tears trickling down his face.

"Henry, it's okay to cry. Your dad knows how much you love him and he loves you so much. He will always look out for us."

Henry's stomach rumbles, reminding me we haven't eaten all day. I tell him that I can't promise how good the surprise casseroles will be, but there are plenty to choose from. We go to the kitchen, and Henry settles on mac and cheese and some cookies. I can't bring myself to eat; I feel too nauseous. My mind is consumed by what's ahead.

Restless, I toss and turn in bed until finally surrendering to the inevitable—there will be no sleep for me tonight. Grabbing my comforter off the bed, I head to the back patio, settling into one of the loungers. It's a gorgeous night, unusually warm, with a clear sky twinkling with millions of stars.

I text my mom, not expecting a response. Seconds later, my phone rings. "Why are you awake?" I question, shocked by how fast she returned my call.

"I don't sleep much. I am so sorry about Drew."

"Thanks, Mother."

"I'm also sorry about what I said to Henry and arguing with you. It wasn't fair."

"I'm sorry, too. I didn't realize the difficulties you had with Dad. That must have been tough for you."

"I understood the life I committed to, and I accepted it. I loved your Dad," she says, her voice breaking, and I can tell she's being sincere. "What can I do to help?" she asks.

"There's nothing you can do to make this better," I whisper.

"I'll be there as soon as I can, Charlotte."

"Thank you."

"Love you, dear."

I end the call and break down. Her unexpected kindness took me by surprise.

chapter forty-eight

The morning of the memorial service is gloomy and overcast, matching my mood. Searching through my closet, I struggle to pick an appropriate outfit. Eventually, I settle on the black dress I wore to my grandmother's funeral. At this point, it's vintage, but it'll do. Honestly, I don't have the energy to care much about my appearance.

We arrive at the church before anyone else. A casket rented for the occasion is set up by the pulpit, covered with an American flag. Drew's helmet is placed on top of it.

I walk to the front, wanting some time alone with Drew, even though I know he isn't in the casket. He wished to be cremated, which I was grateful for because it meant I could always keep him with me.

The large screen above the pulpit springs to life, filling the space with calming music. Images of Drew as a baby appear, catching me off guard. This must be the slide show Emily promised to put together. I appreciate her effort, but I can only bear to glance at a few photos before I have to turn away— swallowing the lump in my throat. If I start crying now, I'm afraid I won't be able to stop.

As I walk back up the aisle, I notice Henry seated in the back row, his eyes fixed on the screen. I touch his shoulder as I pass by to greet the arriving mourners.

Everyone seems to think a hug will help me feel better. The worst offenders hold on for too long and give an extra tight squeeze at the end. To make matters worse, now I smell like a cheap air freshener. My headache is intensifying, and I am nauseous. I excuse myself and go to the restroom for a break. Two minutes before the service begins, I return to join the rest of the family to enter the sanctuary together. Henry and I lead them down the long aisle to the front rows.

A group of Drew's fellow firefighters assemble and begin a rendition of *Amazing Grace*. Unable to hold my tears back, I let them flow freely down my cheeks. Emily hands me the tissue box from the edge of the pew, and I take it gratefully. Reaching out to touch Henry's hand, I hope he'll sense my support. However, he pulls away, reacting as if my touch hurts him. He sits motionless, staring straight ahead with a vacant expression. My heart aches for both of us.

The pastor skillfully recounts stories that paint Drew as the generous, kind, funny, and incredible person he was. One story from his first captain elicits laughs about how they played a prank on Drew by putting chili in his boots. Later, they had to respond to a call, and Drew ended up fighting a fire with his toes dipped in the spicy soup.

Captain Washington talks about how Drew always rose to the occasion, impressing everyone with his ability to unite the firehouse through his humor, compassion, and strength. Some of Drew's closest friends from the station talk about his exceptional talent for making people feel valued and accepted just as they were. The congregation laughs and cries together, all feeling the weight of the immense loss.

As the choir sings *See You Again*, the color guards fold the flag and give it to me. Captain Washington guides me out of the sanctuary, with the rest of the family following.

The rain has cleared, and the sun is shining. In the parking lot, a multitude of fire engines representing every nearby station and even Grand Rapids fill the streets surrounding the church. It's an overwhelming sight. I glance back and see Henry standing beside Emily, seeing emotion on his face for the first time today. He appears to be amazed.

We are led to a waiting town car. We follow the firetrucks as they make their way through the city. The route is lined with people, some holding signs and flags. I look on in disbelief. I had no idea this had been arranged. Henry and I take in the scene in silence—blown away by Drew's impact on this community.

The procession ends at the station. Inside, the entire apparatus bay is packed with tables overflowing with food. It's a lot to take in, and honestly, all I really want to do is crawl into bed. I'm grateful when Emily takes me aside from the crowd and settles me into a quiet corner, handing me a water bottle.

"Thank you," I say before taking a long drink. "I only caught a glimpse of the video, but thank you for making it."

"You're welcome. It was tough to put together, but it helped me see how fulfilling and joyful Drew's life was despite being cut short."

"Can you send me a copy when you get a chance? I want to watch it, but I need some time."

"Absolutely. I'll upload it to Google Drive so you can watch it whenever you're ready," Emily assures.

My brief moment of solitude is interrupted as more people approach to offer their condolences. If I hear the phrase, "Drew is in a better place," one more time, I will lose it. I excuse myself and wander through the living quarters until I find Drew's locker. There's an image from our wedding day, both of us smiling from ear to ear. Next to it is a note I wrote expressing my love for Drew. Hanging nearby is a picture that Henry drew of them together in a fire engine, alongside a family photo from our skiing trip to Colorado. I sink onto the bench—surrendering to my tears.

My life will never be the same.

chapter forty-nine

When we get home, the house is eerily quiet. Right after the funeral, my mother rushed off, claiming she had an audition for a commercial. Some things never change. Henry said he was going over to Conner's. I decided that despite Conner not being the best influence on Henry, Henry needs a friend right now. Plus, Christine has shown herself to be dependable, and that's something I need right now, too.

Christine comes over not long after Henry leaves, bringing pizza and wine. "Henry's at my place, and I didn't want you to be alone. How are you holding up?" she asks, sounding worried.

"Not great, but feeling a bit better now that you're here. And this might help too," I say with a small smile, holding up the bottle of wine.

Christine goes to the kitchen to get a couple of glasses and plates. She pours me a generous serving of wine and encourages me to try to eat a little. She sits close to me, our shoulders touching. I am grateful to have a friend to help me through this. Taking a deep breath, I allow my body to relax. We sit quietly for a while, lost in our thoughts. After nibbling a slice of pizza and starting on a second glass of wine, I tell her how Drew and I first met. We laugh, and then we cry. It is nice to have a sense of connection and not feel so alone.

As I sip my third glass of wine, I tell her more about the journey Drew and I went through to become parents. I share some of the struggles we had with Henry when he first came to us, and I open up about the treatment we took part in to help Henry lead a normal life. It feels comforting to confide in someone, especially since I just buried my one true confidant today. I find myself sharing everything, unable to keep the words inside. Eventually, I stop talking, noticing Christine has pulled away from me. She turns to face me with a look that I don't recognize. I wait for her to say something. Anything. Her silence feels like a fog that is smothering me. My heart drops, and I wish I could take back my words.

"I need you to promise not to tell anyone, especially Henry," I say.

"Are you sure he doesn't already know?" she questions.

"I'm positive."

"He must know," Christine insists, narrowing her eyes and shaking her head slightly. "How can a child forget the first three years of their life?" She grabs a framed photo from the end table. In it, I snuggle a tiny infant. Christine now knows that the baby in the picture is not Henry.

I mentally kick myself. I need to backtrack, but exhaustion overwhelms me. Unfortunately, I have no choice but to push through and try to explain. "Dr. Laura and her team created custom videos and photos to make Henry believe he was part of our family right from the beginning. His first three years were horrendous. Giving him those new memories was a gift; I'm glad we did it. I think you'd understand if you could see how he behaved when we first brought him home and how much progress he's made since then. He wouldn't have had a chance without the treatment," I insist, hoping she'll trust me.

"Really?" she asks, raising her eyebrows. I can't tell if it's a positive reaction or not.

"Yes. We spent hours watching videos about children with severe RAD like Henry. Most of them ended up in jail or institutionalized after committing violent crimes. We felt like we had no other choice. I know it sounds crazy, but I was genuinely afraid of a three-year-old."

"That does sound terrible," she agrees.

I nod my head, exhaling deeply.

"I have just never heard of that kind of treatment. Don't you think Henry could have been okay with just your love and support?" she asks, her tone judgemental.

"If you had known Henry then, you would have wanted us to make the decision we did. Trust me. We did not have a choice."

"Well, I'm glad you found something that worked."

Although her words come across as positive, her tone indicates otherwise. I sense her attitude shifting. She looks at me as though I confessed to a murder.

"Please, promise me you won't say anything," I plead. "It would devastate Henry if he knew."

"I won't tell him," she says, but her smile appears forced. "I should probably head home," she adds, giving me a quick side hug before leaving.

As soon as the front door closes, I collapse into sobs, fully realizing I've made a colossal mistake. I'm furious with myself for opening up to Christine. I should have buried the secrets with Drew. My cries are so intense that I struggle to breathe. Every part of me aches for Drew. How will I ever manage without him?

chapter fifty

The next couple of weeks are a blur. My days consist of coffee, work—the only thing that keeps my mind off of everything—and fitful sleep. I am utterly exhausted and numb.

Almost every day, more sympathy cards arrive in the mail. Each time I open one, I sense the sender's grief, but none of their words comfort me. Many include cash or checks for Henry's future college expenses, while others contain restaurant gift cards. The number of people I need to thank has become overwhelming, and I can't handle adding more tasks to my list right now. So, I stop opening them and place them in a box on top of the refrigerator, out of sight and out of mind.

I'm too tired to care if Henry is home or not. Knowing he's at Christine's place when he's not here is a relief. I'm grateful Henry still has Conner, and I'm sure Christine is there for Henry, too.

I insist Henry continue attending his appointments with Dr. Paul. Henry has become more withdrawn, and I'm worried. Dr. Paul reassures me that Henry's behavior is typical for a boy his age who has recently lost his father. I confide in Dr. Paul about my mistake in telling Christine about Henry's past, and

I'm concerned she might accidentally reveal something despite promising not to. He assures me that Henry hasn't indicated any knowledge of the situation, but he'll stay vigilant for any signs that might cause concern. Dr. Paul suggests that I find a way to connect with Henry through something he enjoys and that I can handle emotionally. The only thing that comes to mind is Henry's excitement about inheriting Drew's truck, so I help him get his driver's license.

The day Henry gets his license, he smiles—the first genuine smile I've seen since Drew's passing. When we arrive home, he asks to go to Conner's to show off his new ride. Watching him drive away, I yell, "Be careful," feeling mixed emotions. I'm happy for Henry but sad that it isn't Drew behind the wheel of his truck.

I go inside and curl up on the couch with a mug of tea, lost in my thoughts, when the doorbell rings, making me jump. I look through the peephole and see the police chief. Puzzled, I open the door to greet him.

"Sorry to bother you, Mrs. King. And so sorry about the passing of your husband," he says sympathetically. "Drew was a good man and an excellent community servant; he will be missed."

"Is that why you're here?" I question, confused by the unexpected visit. I could have sworn I saw him at the funeral, but that day was a blur.

"No, ma'am," he responds gravely, "I'm sorry to inform you that we've discovered some evidence suggesting Henry may have been involved in setting fire to the barn on the day Drew died."

"Why would you think that?" I ask, the surprise evident in

my voice.

"We have some doorbell footage of Henry and Conner walking toward the barn at the right time."

"Wasn't the fire started in the middle of the night by a lightning strike?"

"It was at night, but the National Weather Service has reported that there weren't any lightning strikes at that time," he clarifies.

"It was dark when that fire started, so how can you be sure it was Henry and Conner?"

"They walked under several street lamps, which made it clear it was those boys. Do you know where Henry was that night?"

"He was here, sleeping," I retort defensively, appalled by the accusation. "I've watched enough crime shows to know that footage from those doorbell cameras is so grainy you can't see a thing."

"I'm sorry, Mrs. King, I understand this is difficult to hear," he responds sympathetically. "I personally reviewed the footage, and the boys in it match the photos of Henry and Conner. They were definitely heading toward that area."

He's crossed the line, and I'm furious. "So let me get this straight. You saw boys who resemble Henry and Conner walking toward a barn that burned down, and you think it's proof they started the fire? I suggest you find some real evidence before you start accusing a boy whose father just died serving this community. Stop relying on doorbell cameras and a street light that wasn't even close to the burned barn. Do you realize the harm it would cause Henry to be wrongly accused of starting a fire that killed his father?"

He sighs but remains firm. "We would like to talk with Henry and have access to his phone. Do we have your permission?"

"Do you have a warrant?"

"No, ma'am, not at this time," he says.

"Get off my porch and leave my son alone. If I hear of you or any police officer going anywhere near Henry, I will be pressing charges. You should be ashamed of yourself for treating a grieving family like this." I slam the door closed.

I grab my phone to call Henry, my heart pounding unnaturally fast. When he doesn't pick up, I leave a frantic message, "Get home immediately. Don't say a word to the police!"

I check the tracker app, but it doesn't seem to be working, so I call Christine instead. It goes to voicemail. I try again with no luck. Finally, on the third attempt, she picks up. "What's going on?" she asks, sounding irritated.

"The police think the boys started the barn fire that killed Drew," I choke out the words.

"What? That's absurd! They would never do such a thing!" she exclaims.

"Are you sure?" I ask, tears streaming down my face.

"Charlotte, take a breath," Christine says more gently.

"I can't remember if Henry was here that night. My memory has been terrible lately," I sob.

"Even if the boys were out that night, it doesn't mean they set the fire. I'm sure they were at my house. They're always here," Christine reassures me.

"The police have footage on doorbell cameras of them heading toward the barn."

"But it was dark. How can they be sure?"

"They walked under several street lights. The police chief seemed convinced it was them. They wanted to track Henry's phone, but I told them they needed a warrant. We need to find the boys before they talk to the police and say something stupid."

"Conner doesn't need to worry about saying anything dumb because I know he's innocent. If anyone's involved, it's Henry. He's messed up, and we both know why. You've lied to him for years. No wonder he wants nothing to do with you," Christine snaps.

"Why would you say that? It's not true. We've worked hard to give Henry a great life," I argue.

"Then why is he at my house every day saying he can't stand you?"

That stings, but now I'm pissed. "Henry likes your house because you don't make him follow any rules, and he can get away with smoking and drinking."

She dares to laugh before saying, "That's nothing compared to what you did. I can't believe I could have been friends with someone who would brainwash a child for their whole life. You are lucky I still let Conner hang out with Henry. But we both know that Henry is the victim of your and Drew's twisted game of fake childhood memories, so he's not the one to blame for any of this, even if he did start that fire," she says bitterly before ending the call.

My hand shakes uncontrollably, and the phone slips through my fingers, hitting the floor with a thud. Gasping for breath, I double over as waves of nausea wash over me. Collapsing to the ground, I wrap my arms around my knees, frozen in place. I force myself to pull it together—I must find Henry before it's too late.

After driving to his usual hangouts, I finally spot him at the baseball field behind the school. There are a bunch of other boys there, and they look like trouble. Rolling down the window, I shout for Henry to get in the car.

"I got my truck. I'll drive home when I'm ready," he yells, turning back to his friends.

I slam the car into park, get out, and walk to the fence. "Now, Henry!"

He comes to meet me before speaking. "What the hell? You're embarrassing me," he says through clenched teeth.

"It's going to be a lot more embarrassing when you're arrested."

"What are you talking about?"

"The police chief was just at the house. He accused you and Conner of starting the fire at the old barn," I tell him, watching his face closely for any sign of fear or guilt, but there's nothing.

Instead, he meets my gaze. "There is no way they have proof that we lit that barn on fire."

"What do you mean there's no way they have proof? Did you have anything to do with it?"

"Mom, seriously. Would I do something like that?"

"You didn't answer my question."

"I would never do anything like setting fire to a barn. And I don't lie. You and Dad taught me that lying is bad." A faint smile curls at the corners of his mouth, making my arms prickle with goosebumps.

"Henry, you need to come home right now."

"Or what?"

"Or I will have you arrested as a runaway."

"I'll take my chances." He turns and walks back to his friends.

I drive home, my hands shaking so badly that I can barely hold onto the steering wheel. A car horn blares, and I realize I've blown through a stop sign. "I can't do this without you, Drew!" I scream at the top of my lungs.

As soon as I pull into the garage, I call Dr. Paul and leave a message requesting a callback. My head is pounding, so I take one of my migraine pills and decide to take Xanax with it. I don't know if it's the best idea, but I don't care. Dr. Paul returns my call, and I unload all that has unfolded in the past hour.

In a composed tone, he reassures me, "It's common for a child his age to act out after losing his dad. I have no doubt he'll reflect on his actions and apologize. During our next session, I'll discuss this with him. In the meantime, how are you taking care of yourself?"

His simple question hits me hard, triggering a wave of emotion. Tears pour down my face as I struggle to catch my breath.

"Charlotte, you have a lot on your plate right now. I suggest finding something relaxing to do tonight, like watching a movie or TV show, to help take your mind off things. I will give you the number of a therapist who can provide support tailored to your situation. You must prioritize your own well-being. Please schedule an appointment with her."

His words comfort me. It feels good to know that someone cares about me. I know he's right—I can't handle this alone. I jot down the number, and after we hang up, I call. If I don't do it now, I may never do it. She has a cancellation for tomorrow, so I accept the appointment.

For the remainder of the night, I sit on the couch, binge-watching *Hoarders*, waiting for Henry to return. He finally arrives at two in the morning.

"Want to talk?" I ask.

"Nope. I'm going to bed."

The mixture of cigarette smoke, weed, alcohol, and teenage sweat hits me, stirring frustration. "You can't just come and go as you please, Henry. If you can't follow the rules of this house, then you won't be allowed to drive the truck."

"Geez, Mom. Whatever." He brushes me off, heading down the hallway.

"We're discussing this tomorrow!" I shout after him.

Overwhelmed, I let my emotions take over. The weight of all the problems, compounded by facing them alone, hits me hard. Tears soak the cushion beneath me until exhaustion finally pulls me into sleep.

chapter fifty-one

The next day, I sit at the kitchen table, sipping a strong cup of coffee while patiently waiting for Henry to wake up. Eventually, he strolls into the kitchen, grabs a bowl, spoon, Fruity O's, and the milk all at once, and then plops down at the table. He pours a generous serving of cereal and digs in, completely engrossed in the box as if it's the most captivating thing he's ever seen.

"I know you're dealing with a lot right now—your dad's death being the biggest. I think we should figure out ways to support each other through this," I say gently. But he remains fixated on the cereal box, not even glancing in my direction.

"Please, Henry, talk to me. Tell me what is going on with you. So I can help."

After a prolonged silence, he finally speaks up, his tone defensive. "Nothing is going on with me. Dad's gone, and I've come to terms with it—end of story. You think you can control me, but you can't. Number one, you never gave two shits about me, and number two, I am practically an adult."

"I am sorry you feel like I don't care about you. I assure you that is not true."

He stares at me with a wicked grin. "So now you're saying

my feelings aren't valid? Let's not forget how you've forced me into therapy my whole life. Dr. Paul always says feelings are valid, regardless of facts," he shouts the last sentence. "That is mental health 101. I've got to go." He abruptly stands up, dumps his dish in the sink, and walks out the door. I hear Drew's truck start up, and Henry drives off without asking for permission.

I sat frozen until it was time to meet with the therapist Dr. Paul recommended. Her office is in her home, a lovely house overlooking the bay. She's middle-aged, with kind eyes and a soothing voice. She wears a long, flowy skirt and oversized glasses and has a calming presence. I feel relaxed as I sink into the plush floral sofa.

"Can you share what's been on your mind lately?" she asks softly.

"I recently lost my husband," I begin, "he was a firefighter and had a heart attack while on duty. Since then, our teenage son has been acting out and breaking all the rules."

We discuss what methods of setting boundaries have been effective for Henry in the past. I explain the parenting techniques that used to be successful and mention that Henry has been in therapy since he was young. She nods and smiles, seemingly unfazed by the idea of a child being in treatment for over a decade. She shifts the conversation by asking how I've been caring for myself and coping with the loss. Instantly, tears fill my eyes, and I can't speak.

"So I will take your response to mean that you have not been caring for yourself or dealing with the loss," she says, sliding the box of tissues closer to me.

I nod in agreement, feeling at a loss for words. We spend

the rest of our time discussing what it means to grieve the loss of someone you deeply loved.

She checks her watch and comments, "Our session is nearly over, and this is a significant topic that requires time to address. I suggest you consider attending a wellness retreat for individuals coping with loss." She hands me a pamphlet and explains how helpful the retreat has been for many of her clients.

The images are stunning. The cottages are right on the lake.

"I can arrange for you to attend the upcoming retreat," she says. "Spaces fill up quickly, and I truly believe you would gain a lot from being there."

I shake my head, saying, "I can't leave Henry. He's not doing great right now."

"I understand that, and it might seem impossible for you to consider leaving Henry. But look at it this way—you must secure your oxygen mask on an airplane before assisting others."

I sigh and give her a small smile, "You have to take care of yourself before you can care for others."

"Do you have anyone you could count on to stay with Henry for a few days so you can begin your healing process?"

"Maybe my mother could help. She has been a little more supportive since Drew died."

"So, what do you think? Should I make it happen?" She smiles warmly at me. I nod in agreement. She's right; I need to prioritize taking care of myself.

On the way home, I call my mother and confide in her about the challenges with Henry and how I need time to grieve so I can better support him.

"I'm between jobs right now. I can come for a few days," she says.

I start to cry. I don't think I will ever get used to this version of my mother.

I MAKE all the arrangements with my mother. The hardest part is convincing Henry that he can survive one weekend with Grandma.

"I am seventeen, and I don't need a babysitter," he screams, his voice filled with anger.

"Your grandma wants to spend time with you. She wants to help us as we deal with the loss of your Dad," I explain calmly.

"I don't need help. Dad is dead, and I have dealt with the loss," he says defensively.

"I don't think either of us have dealt with the loss. I'm sorry that I haven't been there for you. My therapist thinks that if I can process the grief by taking a little time for myself, I can help you process it. Please be kind to your grandma so I won't worry. I get it if you don't want help with things right now, but I do. Can you help me out? Please?" I ask, searching his eyes for understanding.

"Sure, whatever," he says, stomping down the hall to his room and slamming the door.

As soon as my mother arrives, I hug her. She's never been a hugger, but she doesn't push me away, allowing me to let go first.

"Wow, what a welcome," she says with a smile.

"I'm so grateful you came all this way to help me and Henry."

I've prepared lasagna for dinner. Henry grabs his plate and heads to his room to eat alone. Meanwhile, my mother and I sit down together. To my surprise, she listens attentively without a hint of judgment in her demeanor.

"I am so sorry for how Henry is behaving," I say, on the verge of tears.

"He's behaving just like you did when your dad passed. You were distant, angry, and so sad. You wouldn't talk to me or even look at me."

"I'm sorry I acted that way towards you."

"No worries. I knew you were grieving and that you would come around, just like I know Henry will. He just needs some time," Mother says.

"You're right. I'm not great at being patient."

"If acting has taught me anything, it's patience. I'm still waiting for my big break after all these years," she says wistfully.

I'm seeing her vulnerability for the first time in my life. I smile gently, saying, "I know it will happen. You've never given up, and your day will come."

"I think so too. Now that I'm older, all the successful actors my age are dying off," she grins. "Pretty soon, I'll be the only actress available if they need someone in their seventies."

Before I leave the following day, I treat Mother to a lavish breakfast at a Parisian café downtown. We indulge in French coffee and decadent croissants oozing with chocolate.

She looks at me across the table and unexpectedly says, "You are so beautiful."

I feel a blush creep up my cheeks. Her words catch me off guard. "I get my looks from you, Mom." I respond by using "mom" instead of "mother" for the first time in a long time. It just feels right in this moment.

Her smile widens. "I know you and Henry are going to get through this. You are a wonderful mom to him. You've worked so

hard to give him the best life you could. He will come around."
Tears well up in my eyes at her words of encouragement.

chapter fifty-two

I write Henry a note, telling him I love him and begging him to be good for his grandma. I already stocked the fridge and freezer with easy-to-make meals and snacks he would like, hoping to make things easier for my mom.

I set out just after 11:00 a.m. to drive the two hours to the retreat, conversing with Drew along the way. "Give me strength to go on without you."

The images in the brochure didn't accurately represent how beautiful this place is. Tall, old maple trees add a mysterious touch along the curving driveway. In the distance, there's a beautiful log cabin. As I drive closer, I notice miniature cabins, each with a welcoming pathway decorated with colorful mums.

I park in an "honored guest" spot and retrieve my bag from the trunk. As I approach the main house, the stunning view blows me away. I let my bag slip from my shoulder and head towards a deck nestled among the massive trees. The expansive lake shimmers brilliantly in the sunlight, its surface undisturbed by even the slightest ripple. The birds' sweet melodies greet me, welcoming me to this beautiful place. The peaceful atmosphere surrounds me, and I take a deep breath, inhaling the clean, refreshing air before going back to the log cabin.

Before I can knock, the door swings open, revealing a gray-haired woman dressed in a flowing maxi dress. Her entire face lights up with a radiant smile that feels like stepping into the embrace of an old friend.

"You must be Charlotte," she says.

"Yes, I am."

"Welcome. I'm Sophia, your hostess. You'll be staying in one of the rooms in this building. Everyone here this weekend has experienced the loss of a loved one. You'll spend time with a group who've also lost a spouse. Once you've settled in, please join us in the atrium for a light snack before our session." She hands me a map of the building and grounds and a key card for my room while directing me on how to get there.

My room is on the third floor. Walking in is like entering a serene oasis—everything is white. Pulling back the sheer curtains, I take a deep breath when I see the breathtaking panoramic view of Lake Michigan. The sunsets must be remarkable from up here. I step out onto the balcony, and there is a comfy chair and a small table—the perfect spot for morning coffee. I tear myself away from the view to freshen up before meeting the others.

The atrium is filled with natural light streaming through large windows, creating a bright, airy atmosphere. Three women and two men are engaging in quiet conversation. Everyone appears to be at least ten years older than me. My stomach flutters with nerves. There's a table set up with cookies, coffee, and tea. I opt for peppermint tea, hoping it will help soothe my jitters.

I join the others and receive a warm greeting. We engage in small talk until Sophia enters, guiding us to sit in the chairs arranged in a circle. We begin by introducing ourselves and sharing the names and circumstances of the loved ones we've lost.

One woman and both men lost their spouses to cancer, while the other two women lost theirs to heart attacks. William, one of the men, reminds me of my dad; his wife passed away from brain cancer.

The introductions are heartbreaking, and I am already crying when it is my turn. It's hard to share my story, but being around people who get it is comforting. It's nice not to have to pretend that everything is okay.

Sophia hands out packets of materials to everyone and explains what we need to work on to prepare for tomorrow's session. She encourages us to take advantage of the beautiful surroundings to contemplate the work we need to do to process the grief and trauma of losing a loved one. I decide to walk along the beach to process my assignment.

Later that evening, we have dinner outside on the deck, with a lake view. Sofia declares it a quiet evening. She instructs us to savor our food and the surroundings. No talking is allowed. I'm glad not to have to talk. I enjoy the gorgeous scenery while lost in my thoughts.

Back in my room, I finally feel ready to watch the video that Emily made for Drew's funeral. I smile at the footage of Drew as a baby and then as a little boy, capturing all his memorable moments from baseball games to graduations. It surprises me when I see myself in the images—I look so young and in love.

Seeing the photos from our time in Florida with Drew's family before we adopted Henry brings back beautiful memories.

My slim figure shines with a deep tan as we all have fun at the beach. My heart longs for those precious moments with Drew to be mine again.

I phone my mom to touch base. She reassures me they are doing fine and mentions a few cards came in the mail—from the Walkers, the Tillmann family, Diane and Larry Smith, and someone named Tom. I tell her they are probably sympathy cards and suggest she just put them in the box on top of the fridge. I promise to deal with them when I have the energy and am ready to go through and respond to each one.

THE FOLLOWING morning, I choose to participate in a gentle yoga class. William is also there and has difficulty keeping up. Our instructor is in her twenties and seems to have an extra vertebra or two compared to the rest of us. She effortlessly moves through the poses, displaying a level of flexibility that none of us can replicate.

William whispers, "If this is gentle yoga, I wonder what rough yoga is like."

"I think it would involve ropes and whips," I respond. The words are out of my mouth before I realize what I've said. I blush. William's eyes widen, and he laughs, causing everyone to look at us.

The rest of the day is filled with a meditation walk, pottery class, group session, art therapy, and an individual session with Sophia.

Before dinner, we have time to do what we like. I hole up on the balcony in my room, needing a break from people. The day is gorgeous and a bit breezy. The waves at the beach lull me to sleep. I dream of my early days with Drew, and when I wake up, my eyes are wet. It's the first time I've dreamt about Drew since he died. I choose to eat in my room, not ready to face any more people today.

I call my mom to check in. She says Henry has been hanging out with Conner, but he came home for dinner that night. I thank her again for taking care of him.

THE NEXT day, our small group gathers to write letters to our loved ones, expressing our feelings toward them, whether positive or negative.

Sophia informs us that everyone at the retreat will participate in a ceremony later that evening. We'll have the chance to read our letters, if we choose to, before tossing them into the fire. She explains that this ritual aims to help us release pent-up emotions and hopefully find peace as we continue our lives.

It hits me hard to realize how angry I am at Drew; I fill three pages front and back expressing my frustration about him leaving me to handle everything and how I don't want to do it alone.

The afternoon is filled with massages, meditation walks, and one-on-one therapy with Sophia. After dinner, I take a walk along the beach.

William catches up to me and walks beside me. "Thank you for making this weekend bearable."

"I didn't do anything," I brush away his words.

"Your kindness and support gave me hope that I can find happiness again, so thank you."

"You're welcome. You remind me of my dad, and you helped

me as well."

He smiles at me, and we continue to walk in silence.

We head to the bonfire, and there's a table with all the ingredients for s'mores. It's been a while since I've had one, and it triggers another memory of Drew and me roasting marshmallows over our gas stove burners when I was craving them in the middle of winter.

Sophia greets everyone and encourages us to sit on the stumps arranged in a circle around the massive fire. William and I find seats next to each other. As several people play hand drums, everyone settles into a spot.

My heart syncs with the rhythm, bringing a smile to my face. I reflect on the progress I've made in my grief journey—being able to smile at all feels like a significant improvement.

We all sit together, sharing our grief and creating a feeling of togetherness. One of the leaders sings, *Hallelujah.* I quietly cry, and William protectively puts his hand over mine.

The goodbye letters are deeply emotional, yet they also feel empowering. Each letter is accompanied by a colored flame stick. Every time a letter is tossed into the fire, the blaze is transformed into vibrant hues, symbolizing the lives lived and lost.

The letters from the parents who lost a child are heartbreaking. I can't imagine what I would do if something happened to Henry.

A woman across the fire from me begins reading her letter, her voice trembling with emotion. "My dearest Cody, you were innocent, and I should have protected you. Please understand, my angel, we tried. You'll never know how hard we worked to create the perfect life for you and your brother, but we failed you both. Now, you'll live forever in our hearts. Goodbye, my precious boy."

She tosses in her letter, causing blue and red flames to leap into the sky. At that moment, I see her face clearly for the first time. My heart tightens in my chest. Her once bright red hair is faded, but I recognize her instantly.

I leap to my feet and sprint towards her, yelling, "Shelly!"

Recognition flashes across her face as she engulfs me in a hug. "Oh my God, Charlotte, why are you here?"

"Drew died."

"Did Henry kill him?"

"What? Of course not. Drew died while fighting a fire. I'm so sorry to hear about Cody. What happened?"

Panic rises in her eyes. "Charlotte, it didn't work. The treatment didn't work. Nightmares haunted Trevor, and he figured out what we did. He was so furious that he... he killed Cody. He stabbed him twenty-five times while Eric and I were out for dinner. Oh my god, Charlotte, it was so horrible," she sobs, barely able to get the words out. "He left a message on the wall in Cody's blood, 'My life of lies is over.'"

I struggle to catch my breath—all the air sucked from my lungs. I collapse to my knees. "No, no, it can't be. It worked." My voice trembles with desperation.

Shelly kneels in front of me. "Charlotte, listen to me. It didn't work." She wraps her arms around my shaking shoulders. "They know. They know what we did. You have to tell Henry the truth and get him help before it's too late."

Her words hit me like a shovel to the head. I pull away from her, getting to my feet. "You're wrong. It works!"

"I wish I was wrong, but I'm not," Shelly says, grabbing my

arm. "Think about it, Charlotte; they have never been quite right, always distant and detached, and the nightmares. Henry still has nightmares, doesn't he?"

Her question hangs in the darkness, waiting for an answer. A sudden burst of flame leaps high into the air, crackling loudly—shattering the silence. "You're wrong!" I shout, taking off in a sprint to my car.

As I peel out of the dirt driveway, I frantically command Siri to call my mom, repeating the instructions three times before the phone finally starts ringing. No answer. I leave a message, masking my fear, saying I'll be home soon.

I speed down the road, replaying the past few months' events in my mind, searching for any clue as to how Henry could have discovered the truth. Suddenly, it hits me: the video of me on the beach—tan and skinny.

I struggle to draw in a breath—my heart racing dangerously fast, threatening to burst from my chest. My foot presses harder on the accelerator. Every second feels like an eternity as I desperately try to reach Henry before it's too late.

chapter fifty-three

With only a few miles to go, exhaustion seeps into every fiber of my being. The strain of gripping the steering wheel so tightly leaves my shoulders and back throbbing.

I inhale deeply, attempting to calm my racing thoughts before pulling into the driveway. I repeat, "It's going to be alright. Everything is okay."

The headlights illuminate the inside of the garage, revealing Henry seated in a lawn chair. His smile floods me with relief and makes my earlier anxiety seem irrational.

Jumping out of the car, I hurry toward him. "I'm so glad you're all…," I begin to say, but my words get stuck in my throat.

He's surrounded by the sympathy cards we'd received, their envelopes torn open. A pile of gift certificates, cash, and checks sits by his feet, and his laptop rests on his lap.

"What are you doing?" I ask, confused.

"Just opening my mail," he says with a smirk.

"But I wasn't ready to go through those yet. We need to send thank you notes to everyone."

"Don't stress, Mom. I've got it covered."

"Where's Grandma?" Concern gnaws at me. I know I told

her I couldn't handle opening those right now.

"Don't worry, Grandma's inside resting. She's not feeling well."

He taps a button on the computer, and waves crashing on the beach fill the air, mingled with children's laughter. My heart skips a beat when I hear Drew's voice saying, "You look beautiful, amore."

"Check this out, Ma," Henry says with a mischievous grin, turning the screen towards me. "You won't believe it."

As the images flash before my eyes, I can't breathe. "You're fat. Now you're skinny," he says. The transformation mirrors the turmoil in my gut, from pregnant curves to a flat, toned stomach.

My pulse quickens as I look around, expecting my mother to come out any second. The garage feels like a ticking time bomb, memories scattered like shrapnel waiting to explode. The zebra we gave Henry the day we picked him up from Horizons of Hope is under the lawn chair he's sitting in, along with his tattered blue baby blanket and dinosaur backpack. My eyes lock onto the old journal I used to write in, a damning record of the lies I've spun.

"I... I can explain," I stammer, desperation creeping into my voice.

But my words fall on deaf ears as Henry's rage explodes. "There's nothing to explain," His anger reverberates against the garage walls as he slams the computer shut and springs to his feet.

I release a frantic scream, my mind spinning with panic as I struggle to find a solution. My body refuses to budge, paralyzed by fear.

Henry moves closer, each step deliberate, his finger pointing at me like an accusing dagger. "You've been lying to me my whole life—about everything!" His accusation hangs heavy in the air, suffocating me.

In a desperate attempt to calm the escalating tension, I extend my hand. "Henry, please, stop." Miraculously, he pauses his advance, giving me a small window of opportunity.

"We didn't have a choice," I plead, my voice trembling. "You were abused, abandoned, consumed by rage. You never knew the love you deserved. We only altered your first three years to give you a chance at a better life." I stare into his eyes, silently begging for understanding, hoping he'll see the truth behind our actions.

He shakes his head slowly, his eye twitching. "You REWROTE everything. Do you think I wanted to live a life built on lies?" he spits angrily.

"It's not lies," I interject. "We gave you the life you should have had from the very beginning—a life where you were part of our family, where you were cherished and cared for since the day you were born."

"But you didn't give birth to me. Rachel Young did."

"Rachel's gone, Henry. She died of an overdose. We weren't keeping you from her. She passed away before you came to us."

As I speak, I see a glimmer of understanding flicker in his eyes. Slowly, he retreats, sinking back into the chair. I feel a surge of hope; maybe he's starting to grasp the truth.

"What about my dad?" he asks, his voice softer now, tinged with uncertainty.

"Drew is your dad. He is the man who loved you, took care of you, and created a life for you. He worked hard to give you everything you needed and wanted."

His eyes narrow, flashing with anger. "This is twisted, you know that, right? You made fake videos and photos and passed them off as real. I've had nightmares my entire life, and you brushed them off. I thought I was crazy, remembering shit you said never happened. But it did happen. I couldn't move past the pain from the abuse because you lied to me. You forced me to go to therapy for my whole goddamn life. Therapy that was never going to work because my life was one big fat fucking lie. How many people were in on it? At least Amelia tried to tell me the truth while the rest of you laughed behind my back at how stupid I was."

"No one was laughing. We got you the best treatment there was. It healed you. We gave you the ability to love and be loved and to form attachments to us and other people who care about you."

"What about Tom? He cared about me." Henry reaches down and grabs a stack of letters from the floor. "Looks like he wrote to me for years, and you wrote back pretending to be me. What the hell is wrong with you?" He buries his face in his hands, massaging his temples before reaching for his tattered baby blanket and setting it on his lap.

"Tom was a nice man doing his job, and I just wanted to make sure he knew you were doing okay."

He adjusts the blanket, and my heart catches in my throat. "Where did you get a gun?" I choke out, my voice strained with panic as goosebumps cascade down my arms.

"Dad left it for me in the glove box of his truck. A parting gift from my fake father," he says, a chilling smile curling at the corners of his lips.

"Where's Grandma?" I ask. It's been too long. She should have come out by now.

"You don't have to worry about Grandma. Her 'used' grandson took care of her," he says, glancing toward the open door leading to the kitchen.

As my eyes slowly adjust to the darkness, a chill crawls down my spine. In the doorway lies a motionless figure. "What have you done, Henry?" I scream, rushing to my mother's side. Dark liquid pools around her, staining the welcome mat. I check desperately for a pulse, knowing there won't be one. She's gone.

I rise slowly, turning to face Henry. The gun is pointed at me.

"That bitch thought she could control me and took the keys to my truck, so I taught her a lesson," he explains, his voice eerily composed. Every instinct screams at me to run, but fear paralyzes me, trapping me in place.

"Now I think it is time for you to learn a lesson," he says, his eyes narrowing into slits.

"You don't want to do this, Henry. I'm your mom. Whatever's happened, we can work through it together. If you kill me, you'll be alone and end up in prison. Let me help you," I plead desperately, my heart pounding out of my chest.

"Do you really think I could ever trust you? I'm fucked up because of you," he accuses, venom dripping from his words. His grip on the gun tightens as he gestures wildly. I flinch each time the weapon is aimed in my direction. "You never accepted me for who I am. You promised to love me, but all you did was try to change me to fit into your life. I wasn't good enough for you. So now, you're not good enough for me."

The sound is deafening. My ears ring, and the room spins. I stagger backward, crumbling to the cold, hard concrete. Instinctively, my hand reaches for my chest, and I feel the warmth of liquid pooling beneath my fingers. I glance up, and Henry looms over me.

"I'm sorry," I whisper, the words barely escaping my lips.

He sets the stuffed zebra beside me, his expression morphing into pure evil. "Don't worry, Ma. I'll video myself not shooting you, and you can watch it on repeat." His laughter rings in my ears, a haunting melody.

Drew's truck roars to life, the sound filling the garage before fading as he drives away. The silence is broken only by the distant wail of sirens.

Alone on the cold, hard floor, panic claws at me.

But just as quickly, an unexpected calmness washes over me. Images of serene sunsets by the lake flood my mind, providing a fleeting moment of comfort. Then, like a flipped switch, everything fades to black, plunging me into a void of darkness.

chapter fifty-four

I was airlifted by helicopter to a hospital in Grand Rapids, better equipped to address my needs. The life-saving surgery I had left me with a scar over a foot long. The following three-month hospital stay was incredibly painful, my weakness so severe that it took me more than a month to regain the ability to walk to the bathroom on my own. Despite the staff telling me how fortunate I was to survive, I couldn't shake the feeling of being far from lucky.

Local authorities found Drew's truck in the Upper Peninsula, just across the Mackinac Bridge, but there was no sign of Henry. A week into my hospital stay, a detective explained the details of the search for Henry. As he spoke, I stared at the wall, struggling to fully grasp the information because of the persistent fog in my brain. Despite his assurance that they would find him, months have passed, and his whereabouts are still unknown.

I asked the Uber driver to take a detour past Dr. Laura's office on the day I was discharged from the hospital. An ad agency had replaced Radiant Minds Center of Psychology. Their new sign boldly proclaimed, "You Dream It, We'll Sell It." The irony wasn't lost on me as I thought about the shift from a mental health practice to a creative business venture.

The only sound during the two-hour drive back to my home in Traverse City was the country station the driver had on. I have never been a country music fan, but I was thankful for the distraction. I noticed our neatly mowed lawn as he pulled into the driveway at dusk. A concerned neighbor likely took it upon themselves to prevent our property from affecting their home value. "It's best not to let the grass get out of control in a house where there's been a murder," I muttered to myself.

The house greeted me with silence, weighed down by the smell of death. Dust had settled everywhere, dimming the once vibrant life it held. Eager to leave this house behind, I went to what used to be mine and Drew's bedroom. It looked mostly the same, except for the tipped tote filled with memories from our time before Henry. Gathering the scattered photos, love notes, and my childhood photo album, I quickly packed them into the tote, along with my mom and Drew's ashes. I added one of my dad's extra-large flannel shirts to the top. I loaded a single suitcase and the box of memories into my car, anticipating the beginning of my journey away from a life clouded by heartache.

My belongings are set for an estate sale, and the house will be listed. The realtor, my only visitor during my hospital stay, droned on about home prices and mentioned the impact of the murder, but I tuned it all out. All that mattered to me was that I wouldn't have to live there. My only instruction was, "Just get rid of it."

I knew one thing about my mother's wishes: she wanted her ashes scattered in Central Park. New York had always been her favorite among all the places we had lived. It seemed like a sign, the perfect reason to make the move. I could blend in with the millions hiding in plain sight in the massive city. Henry's whereabouts remained unknown, and I was worried that he would attempt to finish what he started if he knew I had survived.

I FIND a charming loft in Midtown with exposed brick walls, lofty ceilings, and large windows showcasing the city's beauty. Opting for the tenth floor gives me stunning views and an extra layer of security. Thanks to the financial support from Drew's life insurance policies, I don't have to stress about money. However, I take on a remote job to keep myself mentally engaged. I create a comfortable office nook by the windows, turning the space into my sanctuary.

I stay inside my apartment for months, relying on grocery and restaurant deliveries. The ache of missing Drew is downright crushing. His absence creates a huge void, and facing life without him feels even more overwhelming with everything that has happened. To get through this difficult time, I find an online therapist to help me cope with my grief and trauma. Even though it is mentally exhausting, I see it as a necessary step if I ever want to bring some normalcy back into my life.

I BEGIN to venture outside my apartment and get to know my neighborhood better. I discover the grocery store with the freshest produce, the coffee shop with the best beans, and a bakery with the most delicious pastries.

One crisp autumn weekend, I discover a bookstore. The little bell over the door jingles as I walk in, announcing my arrival. It feels like entering a hidden world. The shelves, filled with books, reach toward the ceiling. Soft light from old-fashioned lamps cast a warm glow on weathered wooden floors, creating a cozy atmosphere. The bookstore quickly becomes one of my favorite places.

As the holidays approach, I have a strong desire to visit Chinatown. During one Thanksgiving in New York, my dad took me there while my mom was busy with a small role in an off-Broadway show. We climbed the subway stairs to the street, and it felt like we had entered an enchanting world filled with vibrant colors and delightful aromas. We enjoyed delicious dumplings from a street vendor and did some window shopping. Dad bought me a small keepsake—a keychain with the Chinese symbol for beautiful. It still dangles from my keyring. That day became a cherished memory. Since I don't have anyone to celebrate with this year, it seems like a good time to revisit that special memory to take my mind off everything.

I have avoided the subway because the idea of traveling underground has always scared me, even when I was with my dad. The thought of navigating it on my own seems daunting. However, I'm actively working on my fears with my therapist, and she recommended that taking the subway could be a good first step if I plan to stay in New York.

After successfully boarding the correct train, I settle into my seat with a sense of accomplishment. As the doors seal shut, I catch sight of a familiar face, causing the hairs on the back of my neck to stand up. An older lady sitting across from me asks if I'm alright. I manage a slow nod, unable to speak. Dr. Laura's eyes connect with mine from the ad above the door, declaring, "The future of RAD treatment is NOW!" Details of her speaking engagement are listed below. I am overcome by a wave of nausea, feeling the bile creep up my throat.

In the days leading up to her presentation, I wrestle with whether to go. I know every word she speaks will be a lie. The thought of facing her and exposing the truth consumes my thoughts. I imagine myself yelling at her for all the suffering she has caused, even though deep down, I know I wouldn't do it— drawing attention to myself is the last thing I want. In the end, I decide to attend, holding onto the hope that it might bring some closure.

A WEEK later, I walk into the auditorium at NYU and choose a seat at the back. My palms are sweaty with nerves, and my heart pounds relentlessly. I take a deep breath, trying to ease the anxiety that wraps around me as I wait for the presentation to start.

As Dr. Laura walks onto the stage, a wave of applause erupts from the crowd. Seeing her in person feels like a punch to the gut. She greets the audience with a plastic grin, ready for the show. Her hair, once salt and pepper, has now entirely grayed. Her expensive suit fits her figure perfectly. The diamond necklace around her neck sparkles in the spotlight. Even though the auditorium is dark, I swear she winks at me as if we share some twisted secret. She jumps into her presentation, passionately talking about her work. While Dr. Laura speaks about liberating multitudes of children from miserable lives, a wave of emotion overwhelms me as tears stream down my face.

The lights dim, and a slideshow shows clips of unruly kids throwing tantrums. I audibly gasp when a larger-than-life video of Henry kicking and screaming fills the screen. The following clip shows him running through our yard, giggling. More videos of other children follow, but I can't focus anymore. I make my way to the exit, my legs feeling like jello.

IN THE weeks that follow Dr. Laura's masquerade, I concentrate on my job and schedule extra therapy sessions to prioritize my mental health. As the magic of the holiday season spreads through the city, I feel a little bit like my old self again.

On a cold, windy day, I rush to complete my errands, anticipating the upcoming snowstorm that promises a white Christmas. I buy all the ingredients for Drew's and my favorite Thai recipe, two bottles of merlot, and treat myself to some pastries from the bakery. I end my errands with a trip to my favorite bookstore to stock up on the latest romance novels. I picture a cozy holiday in my apartment, lost in the happiness of other people's lives as the storm rages outside.

Struggling to carry the stack of books to the register, I drop my copy of *Snowflakes and Mistletoe*. Bending to pick it up, I can't help but overhear the conversation between two women engaged in a lively discussion.

"Here's that book I told you about," one woman exclaims. "The one where the family creates fake videos to gaslight their adopted son into believing his actual memories aren't real."

"That is insane. I can't believe anyone would do that. Those parents should be behind bars for child abuse," the other says.

"I saw Logan Conte, the author, on the *Today Show*. I hope he'll do a book signing; I'd love to meet him in person. He's hot. Take a look," she flips the book over to show her friend.

The title, *Altered Childhood,* obscures the image on the cover. Logan cropped out the happy couple from the photo, leaving only the sinister eyes that haunt my nightmares.

Acknowledgments

We would like to extend our thanks to our pre-readers and proof-readers: Katie Outing, Lisa Smith, Lori Branigan, Patty Hovey, and Mary Brickner. Your time and effort in shaping this book are deeply appreciated.

Hey there, marvelous reader!

Thanks a million for reading "Altered Childhood." Don't forget to drop a review on Amazon, Goodreads, or wherever your bookish heart desires. And hey, why keep all the fun to yourself? Share the love by spreading the word on social media. Let's spread the joy like a confetti cannon blast! Your review could be the spark that ignites someone else's reading adventure!

Oh, and don't forget to swing by butterybraniganbooks.com to check out all of our books. Plus, sign up for our newsletter for exclusive treats like freebies, sneak peeks, and more—don't worry; we promise not to flood your inbox!

Being authors is a dream come true for us, and having you, our fabulous reader, along for the ride is like adding extra sprinkles to our ice cream.

We would like to give a massive thanks to all of our readers, especially you!

Warmest regards,
Beth and Patricia
Aka P.B. Alden

Visit our website, butterybraniganbooks.com, to discover our diverse selection of books.

Email us at butterybraniganbooks@gmail.com with comments and questions. We love to hear from our readers.

You can find Buttery Branigan Books on social media.

Check us out on TikTok, Facebook, and Instagram

@butterybraniganbooks

Explore the enticing array of genres offered by Buttery Branigan Books!

Donuts and Deceit
by P.B. Alden

A delightful, cozy mystery with a surprising twist. Available at Audible, Amazon, Barnes & Noble, and worldwide ebook distribution.

Accept the Terms
by P.B. Alden

A politically charged dystopian novel led by strong female characters. This thought-provoking story challenges readers to question their beliefs and the lengths they would go to protect their freedoms. Available at Kindle Vella

Lainey's Type One Diabetes Adventure Series
by Patricia Branigan and Beth Buttery

In this charming book series, Lainey tackles everyday challenges with heart, humor, mental health support, and a touch of magic, all while navigating life with type one diabetes.

Mental Health Support Journals
by Patricia Branigan and Beth Buttery

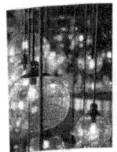    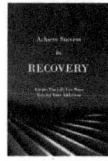  

Discover support journals tailored for your loved ones navigating the prison system, planning retirement, achieving recovery, managing type one diabetes, and preparing your anxious child for camp.

**Visit butterybraniganbooks.com
to learn more about our vast array of books!**

www.ingramcontent.com/pod-product-compliance
Lightning Source LLC
Chambersburg PA
CBHW060541180626
46817CB00002B/679